Praise for A *Murder of Crows*

"This second book in the Junction Chronicles is every bit as good as the first. . . . *A Murder of Crows* is a slick and readable thriller with great characters . . . and lots of action."

—*The Globe and Mail*

"*A Murder of Crows* is . . . told with the urgent and active voice of a storyteller who has staked his own territory. It's a must-read."

—*The Hamilton Spectator*

Praise for *The Placebo Effect*

"This novel heats up and never stops."

—*The Globe and Mail*

"The success of his epic *Shanghai*, which was published in 2008, demonstrated that Rotenberg could break away from convention without loosening his hold on the imagination of his readers. Rotenberg blends the best of [his previous] books in his latest effort, *The Placebo Effect*."

—*National Post*

"*The Placebo Effect* . . . is a thoughtful, challenging novel masquerading as a . . . thriller."

—*Quill & Quire*

"A moody speculative-fiction thriller."

—*Winnipeg Free Press*

Praise for *Shanghai*

"*Shanghai* is heart pounding and brutal. It puts you right into the thick of the city, its people, its passions."

—*Jurgen Gothe, NUVO magazine*

"Rotenberg's Shanghai . . . is a place full of effective, unexpected entertainment."

—*Publishers Weekly*

"*Shanghai* is jam-packed with story and adventure."

—*Maclean's*

Praise for the Zhong Fong series

"Rotenberg has a real talent for characterization and place, taking readers right into the urban heart of Shanghai, with its eighteen million people and conflicts between tradition and modernization."

—*The Globe and Mail*

"Rotenberg's take on the street life, bureaucracy, and sheer mass of Shanghai cleverly captures a wonderful, baffling city."

—*Toronto Star*

"This delightful series . . . gets better with each new novel."

—*The Chronicle Herald, Halifax*

"A fascinating journey into a remarkable culture."

—*Ottawa Citizen*

"Readers will be clamouring for more Rotenberg."

—*Booklist*

ALSO BY DAVID ROTENBERG

The Junction Chronicles

The Placebo Effect (Book One)

A Murder of Crows (Book Two)

Historical Fiction

Shanghai, the Ivory Compact

The Zhong Fong Detective Series

The Shanghai Murders: A Mystery of Love and Ivory

The Lake Ching Murders: A Mystery of Fire and Ice

Hua Shan Hospital Murders

The Hamlet Murders

The Golden Mountain Murders

THE GLASS HOUSE,

or

When the

Moon's too Thin

for Stories

Third Book of the Junction Chronicles

DAVID ROTENBERG

A Touchstone Book

PUBLISHED BY SIMON & SCHUSTER

New York   London   Toronto   Sydney   New Delhi

Touchstone
A Division of Simon & Schuster, Inc.
1230 Avenue of the Americas
New York, NY 10020

This Touchstone edition November 2014

TOUCHSTONE and colophon are registered trademarks of Simon & Schuster, Inc.

For information about special discounts for bulk purchases, please contact Simon & Schuster Special Sales at 1-800-268-3216 or CustomerService@simonandschuster.ca.

Cover design: Roberto de Vicq de Cumptich
Cover image: Shutterstock

Manufactured in the United States of America

10 9 8 7 6 5 4 3 2 1

ISBN 978-1-4767-1722-7
ISBN 978-1-4767-4732-3 (ebook)

For Susan, Joey and Beth

There was a time when meadow, grove, and stream,
The earth, and every common sight,
To me did seem
Apparelled in celestial light,
The glory and the freshness of a dream.

WILLIAM WORDSWORTH, "ODE, INTIMATIONS OF IMMORTALITY
FROM RECOLLECTIONS OF EARLY CHILDHOOD" (1806)

Was it a vision, or a waking dream?
Fled is that music:—do I wake or sleep?

JOHN KEATS, "ODE TO A NIGHTINGALE" (1820)

Reality is wrong. Dreams are for real.

TUPAK SHAKUR

IN A DREAM

SETH IS SURFING OFF THE COAST OF VANCOUVER ISLAND—NO, dreaming of surfing. He feels himself smiling. It's his dream of peace. He senses himself rocking to the rhythm of the waves beneath his board, feeling the earth's heartbeat as his own and hoping it will soon lead him to the clearing and from there to the great glass house.

Then in his dreaming world he senses the darkness approaching.

The sliding.

He forces himself to be calm. He floats, waits for the change.

It comes.

A knife slitting through canvas.

The pleasing sloshing of the waves beneath his board is drowned out by a high-pitched electronic hum mingled with a slur of muffled voices; his thick wet suit is no more; he lies naked on a cold slab of metal—and the gentle light of a Pacific sunset is obliterated by an intense single beam directed at his eyes.

He goes to rise but finds his torso bound to the slab, his hands laced together in front of him as if in prayer.

He yanks at the restraints.

They tighten.

He cranes his head to see past the light to the figures in the shadows.

Then he is screaming: "I never agreed to this. I signed no consent form!"

The mumbled voices seem to coalesce into just two voices—one of which is oddly familiar.

"Let me up. I'm here against my will."

There is a sigh from the darkness, then a high thin voice, almost a whistle, says, "Not against Mine, though."

Somehow that voice seems to be coming from every direction.

He twists to see who has spoken. And when he does he is surprised to see that he isn't in a room at all but at a crossroads of two highways, and the surgical light is an intense desert sun.

"Where do you want this killing done?"

His father! Fuck, his father.

Seth again pulls at his restraints, which have somehow changed from metal to something soft—like lambskin. Then he senses the blood. He feels its stickiness—and he knows where he is: the portal at the dream temple at Epidaurus. He is wrapped in a sheepskin—the pelt of a recently sacrificed animal still thick with fresh blood.

For a moment the word "sacrificed" reverberates in his head, growing louder and louder until he hears, "Down on Highway Sixty-one." That thin, whistly voice again. "Yes, down on Highway Sixty-one."

"Father! Father!" Seth shouts.

Someone steps forward and momentarily blots out the sun.

"Seth."

Seth takes a breath and tries to stop the rising terror. "Father, what are you doing?"

"Doing?"

"Yes, doing, what are you doing?"

"Waiting. I'll be here waiting for you. I'll always be here waiting for you. I've told you that."

The sun glints off the blue edge of the surgical scalpel in his father's hand.

"Don't do this, Father. Don't!"

The scalpel scythes through the air. Seth yanks his hands, still bound as if in prayer, high enough to deflect the blade but not before it cuts both his hands—cleanly removing the baby finger from each.

He feels pressure on his chest. His father's right hand is there, pressing down hard. The scalpel in his left hand is in motion again.

A gush of blood fountains up from Seth's belly and bathes his face.

He swallows blood.

He gags.

His body convulses.

His two fingers fall to the floor.

Blood fills his lungs. He gasps for a breath, but no air—just the gurgle of the viscous thickness of his blood. He tries to scream but no sound comes.

And all the time his father just stands there, between the gas lamp post and the Joshua tree, silhouetted against the sun—and cries.

YSLAN AND GARRETH SENIOR

NSA SPECIAL AGENT YSLAN HICKS SAT SILENTLY AT THE FOOT OF the small bed in the darkened room in the New Jersey safe house and waited for the snoring man to awaken. He'd been taken from the San Francisco Wellness Dream Clinic and drugged so they could move him. For a moment she wondered why they hadn't just taken him to a San Francisco safe house and flown her out there. Then she dismissed it. He was here in New Jersey now and so was she. He'd been under for thirty-six hours. The drug would wear off shortly—and she waited, as she had done so many times before.

As she did, her mind slid back to the first time she'd used this safe house. It had been more than a year ago, and the man on the bed that time had been Decker Roberts—the man who had tilted her life into chaos.

The heavyset man on the bed snorted then stirred. Yslan signalled to her two assistants, whom Decker Roberts had given the monikers Mr. T and Ted Knight, to leave the room.

They did with a silence born of great practice. As the door shut behind them it occurred to her that she no longer knew their real names—they were now Mr. T and Ted Knight to her. How that happened she had no idea.

"Wha . . . ?"

Garreth Laurence Senior, former Toronto homicide cop, was awakening.

She watched as the man's eyes roamed the darkness. Yslan's eyes had adjusted to the gloom long ago.

She snapped on a gooseneck lamp and turned it towards him.

He flinched in the light and went to cover his eyes, only to find that his wrists were manacled to the metal railing of the bed. He gave one hard pull, then stopped.

Of course he stopped, Yslan thought. *He'd been a cop a long time; no doubt he'd seen people hurt themselves pulling against the reality of handcuffs.* A line of poetry slipped into her head that ended with the phrase "and adamantine chains." She shook her head to clear it. Before she'd met Decker Roberts she'd never had lines of verse leap uninvited into her head, but now they were coming at an ever-increasing rate. She made a mental note to check where the hell "and adamantine chains" came from, then shifted the light so it bounced off the wall beside the man on the bed.

Standing outside the rim of the light she said, "Garreth Laurence Senior, former homicide detective metro Toronto police force, re-tired—or was that forced into retirement?"

"Retired," the man said. His voice was hoarse. Thirty-six hours of drug-induced sleep will do that. But it wasn't just the drugs. There were years of drink here. A smoker—for at least several decades. She instantly craved a cigarette. At least that she under-stood. "Retired," the man repeated.

She nodded, then said, "Of course. Everyone retires twenty-two months short of his pension." Then without waiting for a reply she asked, "How do you like Seaside?"

Seaside, the elite planned community on the Florida Panhandle. The man sat back.

"So? I asked you a question. How's Seaside?"

"Fine, it's fine," he barked, just a tinge of his Scottish on the second hard *i*.

"A bit swanky for an ex-cop, wouldn't you say?"

"I wouldn't know."

"Sure you would."

"If you say so."

"I do." She picked up a folder from the table and read, "The house on Pensicola Street paid for in cash—six hundred and fifty thousand dollars—two bedroom, one bath, April 11, 2002." She closed the file. "Must be pretty damned special."

After a moment Garreth said, "It's adequate."

In the darkness she smiled. Garreth Laurence Senior was clearly a pro, and he was gaining his metaphoric footing. "Good. For that money I'm glad you like it."

She pointed the gooseneck lamp at the table and read from another file: " 'Born January 16th, 1954; Married August 17th, 1976, to Ellen Suzanne Jason; one son, Garreth Laurence Jr. currently on the metro Toronto police force; wife deceased February of 1990; promoted to homicide detective May 1985; left the force under a cloud on March of 2002.'" She put the folder down. "Any of this sound familiar?"

Garreth stared back at her. His almost translucent eyelashes batted just once, then stopped their motion: he was ready to do combat.

Yslan turned back to the folder and read, "Picked up in San Francisco in the Wellness Dream Clinic after an attempt to assault with deadly force one Decker Roberts, formerly of the Junction in West Toronto."

"A bloody murderer named Decker Roberts formerly of the Glencairn district of North Toronto." The man's voice was centred. He didn't know where he was or who had kidnapped him or who he was talking to, but he was clearly certain about this statement.

"Want to tell me about you and Mr. Roberts?"

"Nah—I think I'd prefer not to."

"Do you know where he is now?"

"No—but if you undo these cuffs I'll find him."

"Pretty sure of yourself, aren't you?"

"I'm more than able to track down a felon, yes."

"You didn't track him down, you tracked down his son."

"Seth."

"Yes," she said slowly. "Seth Roberts."

She'd only had information lately on the son, while she'd been accumulating data on the father for years. "So you found the boy and waited for the father to show up. Did you case the place?"

He nodded.

"What did you find?"

"A charlatan; a big-assed fake! I mean dream healing—"

"You mean the guy who ran it was a charlatan?"

"Who else?"

"Name?"

Garreth paused.

"What?"

"Couldn't find a real name. Couldn't find dick-all about him, really. Strange that. All I ever got was initials for him—assuming those initials were even for his name. Fuck, they could have been for his astrological sign for all I know."

"Initials?"

"Yeah, but I didn't care. I wasn't after him. I was after Decker Roberts."

"The one you claimed was a child murderer?"

"Bingo, lass."

Something about the curl in his voice annoyed her—that thing that said women have a place and the place wasn't here. She closed the folder, clicked off the light and left the room and Garreth Laurence Senior, still chained to the bed, in complete darkness.

• • •

In the modest kitchen she saw Ted Knight making coffee while Mr. T sat at the Formica-topped table and ate something that could clog the arteries of an entire city block.

They both looked up as she entered.

"Coffee, boss?" Ted Knight asked.

She shook her head.

"He giving you trouble?" asked Mr. T.

She didn't answer. Once again—as had happened so often in her dealings with Decker Roberts—she sensed that she was missing something. Something important.

She nodded at Mr. T. "A word?"

"Sure."

They went into the small fenced-in backyard. Ted Knight did his best not to be seen eyeing their exit, but both Yslan and Mr. T saw him trace their every move.

Once they were alone, Yslan turned to Mr. T. "Well?"

"Well what?"

"You were there."

"Yes, of course, keeping Decker safe. He's a valuable asset. That's what you called him. So yeah, when that ex-cop attacked him, I stepped in."

"Then you let Decker go."

"Like you told me to do."

A line from one of Decker's lectures to his acting class popped into her head: "We are never so messed up as when we mess up ourselves." She nodded, went to apologize, then shelved the idea and said, "Fuck it."

"What exactly is it that I'm supposed to fuck?"

She knew that either this guy or Ted Knight back in the kitchen reported her every move to Leonard Harrison, her boss at the NSA, but she didn't know which one.

"Something else, ma'am?"

"Yeah."

"What?"

"You call me ma'am again and I'll have you transferred to the Skagway office."

"We have a Skagway office?"

"Yeah. And I hear the four days of summer they have up there are delightful."

When she returned to Garreth's room, she was not surprised to see that the man was relaxed and ready to do battle.

"So," he said as soon as she clicked on the lamp, "which kind of fed are you? CIA, NSA . . ."

Before Yslan could answer, Garreth Senior snarled, "What are you, Decker Roberts' protector or something?"

"Let's leave it at 'or something.'"

"You know that he's a fucking murderer. You know that, right?"

After a pause she said, "Sure, we know that."

"You're a bad liar. A very bad liar, lass."

She thought about that. Before she spent those three days with Decker in this very safe house she could lie with the best of them. It was part of her survival kit. But now evidently she had lost that skill. *Could it have something to do with Decker? He was able to tell when someone was telling the truth, but he was a terrible liar himself. An irony,* she thought, then quickly a second thought followed: *Since when had that word "irony" become an important part of my vocabulary?* But she knew the answer to her question—since she'd had those three days with Decker.

She noticed the old cop's lips were moving again.

"A little girl. A six-year-old."

"What about a six-year-old?"

"That's who he murdered—a six-year-old girl."

"Please—"

"You ever notice him close his eyes then seem to scrape something off his hand? Ever notice that?"

She had but wasn't about to say so.

"I have no idea what the eye-closing rigmarole is, but wiping the hand? That's blood he's wiping off. A little girl named Kristan Ray. When he was a kid he cut her with a garden trowel and she bled out beneath the weight of the snow of the igloo they'd built."

She didn't say anything.

He shifted on the bed, his back resting comfortably against the wall, and said, "That's who you're protecting. A damnable child murderer."

But Yslan wasn't listening. She was remembering Decker wiping something from his hand—over and over—almost every time after she'd seen him close his eyes to find out if a person was telling the truth. He'd close his eyes. His breath would shallow, then he'd wipe his hand—his right hand against his pant leg—as if he were wiping away blood from his fingers.

The older man's lips were moving again.

"So I thought about your Mr. Decker Roberts, off and on, for years. There was something about him—something odd, and it just got odder as he got older. In his twenties he came on my radar again. You seen his website?"

Yslan had but didn't nod.

"Whatthefucksthetruth dot com. Well that, you might say, piqued my interest. You know that he rented himself out to rich corporations as a kind of human lie detector, don't cha?"

"A truth detector," Yslan said.

"What by all that's holy is the difference?" he shot back.

Yslan knew in her heart that there was a serious difference but didn't say so.

"Well, I followed him to a few of these little sessions of his and got the videotapes of him from the jerks who hired him. And every time right before he made a notation on the transcript, he

closed his eyes, then rubbed his right hand against his pant leg."
Garreth Senior paused, clearly pleased with himself. Then he
added, "That right hand—like he was wiping blood from his right
hand. Like the boy coming out of that damned igloo did—like the
fucking child murderer he is."

Yslan stared at Garreth Senior. The pupils of his eyes had narrowed to tiny black pinpricks. His face was contorted in a rictus.
Clearly from the moment he first met Decker Roberts he'd been
obsessed with him—maybe possessed was a better description.
But whatever the word, the man was sick—and the sickness
clearly had started on a cold day in the Glencairn section of North
Toronto when Decker Roberts emerged from a collapsed igloo
while a little girl had died inside—and wiped his blood-covered
right hand against his pant leg.

Without any explanation she flicked off the light and left the
room.

Late that night she awoke with a start. She'd figured it out—or her
dream had. She reviewed it again. Decker closing his eyes. His
breath shallowing. Then wiping his hand on his jeans—his right
hand. He wiped his right hand.

But he was left-handed.

If he'd cut that girl with a garden trowel as Garreth Senior
claimed, then he'd have blood on his left hand, not his right. A
left-handed person would only end up with a right hand full of
blood if he'd used his right hand to hold the victim down and
then plunged a knife or trowel or whatever into the victim with
his left.

But he couldn't possibly have done that under the weight of
all that snow—nor could a left-handed five-year-old boy have the
strength in his right hand to do the damage that Garreth Senior
claimed had been done to that little girl.

Yet there was something viscous on Decker's hand that he

wiped off—certainly something like blood. But whose blood? Who had Decker held with his right hand as he drew blood with a weapon in his left?

She tried to envision it—holding someone down. Why down? No, just holding. So the victim was still, and Decker had his right hand on his . . . chest! And the knife in his left hand—started over his head and thrust down, or out, through the heart. The aorta in shock contracted and threw blood up through the gash—and soaked Decker's right hand.

She got out of bed and threw open the curtains. A star-filled night greeted her. But she was not one for stargazing. If she had been, she'd have noticed that the stars over her head were out of place. Venus was above the moon on the eastern horizon, Scorpio was rising in the west with its tail raised and third star in its torso red and pulsing like a heart—then of course there was the four-star constellation that was so aptly named the Southern Cross. Yslan didn't know it, but she too was sliding and was now looking at the exact same sky as Decker was in Solitaire, Namibia—some seven-thousand-plus miles to the southeast.

Two worlds sliding—attempting to align.

Then her phone rang. It was the head of Homeland Security—he'd never called her before. As she heard his oddly detached voice, the hair on the back of her neck stood up and sweat popped out on her brow. "I need you to find a safe phone and call me." He told her to follow the protocol, then hung up.

3

DECKER ROBERTS BRUSHED THE SUDDEN GUSH OF TEARS FROM HIS cheeks. He was pretty sure that he was now standing beside his rented Jeep and looking at a large white man blowing the Namibian dust off his hands with an air compressor more traditionally used for inflating tires.

Yet he knew he had been fully alive only a moment ago thousands of miles away with a scalpel in his left hand, standing between the lamp post and the Joshua tree, his hand on his son's chest, and blood—so much blood—and his son's terrified shriek, "Don't do this, Father. Don't!"

He shook his head to try and clear it as he thought, *Sliding, I'm sliding*.

For the past three days, like Tom Hanks at the end of *Cast Away,* he had simply allowed the rented Jeep to lead him. Of course in Namibia there weren't that many choices.

He'd followed Highway 1 for days—sleeping in his vehicle with the Southern Cross above him and Scorpio rising. In the morning the Hindi people's oddly familiar mannequins appeared beside his car. In the dawn's light, with the pale moon on the horizon, he'd left money in the pouches of the statues then gotten back in his car and driven as Inshakha had instructed him to do all those months ago.

He'd been in Namibia before. It was his retreat from the world, and each time he'd been there Inshakha had, as if by magic, appeared at his side. They'd spent days and nights together—although never as lovers. When Yslan Hicks had come to drag him back to America to help her find who had planted those bombs at Ancaster College, she'd seen Inshakha and called her a whore. Inshakha had gone toe to toe with the powerful NSA agent and told her to "watch your mouth. You are a foreigner in a part of the world that takes slander seriously." Then she had turned, with such grace, and walked away.

The last Decker had seen of Inshakha she was sitting naked to the waist on the side of their rented cottage's bathtub pressing red mud into the beauty of her face, retreating from him—from them—into the deep private reality of an African woman, a place to which he could not even consider following her.

Decker drove and ended here—at the intersection of Highways 1 and 6—at a junction that consisted of nothing more than a petrol station, a small gift shop and a bakery that emitted the unmistakable smell of fresh-baked apple pies. There were three picnic tables but nothing else—except for miles and miles of desert in every direction.

The place's tattered sand-scoured tin sign hung at an odd angle and proclaimed its name: Solitaire. Solitaire, Namibia.

The large white man clicked off the air compressor, looked up and saw Decker—and his round face turned dark and stern. Then words came from his mouth. "I've been waiting a long time for your coming. I'm glad you finally found your path."

Decker had no idea what the big man was talking about.

"Yes, to Solitaire, to the junction of Highways Six and One."

"There's a song."

"Really?" the large man asked, clearly not all that interested.

"Yeah, really. But it's 'Highway 61 *Revisited*.'"

The large white man didn't respond, but Decker sensed

something moving behind his eyes. What, he couldn't even begin to guess. Then the man turned to him. " 'Highway 61 Revisited'?"

"Yeah it's the name—"

"Of a song. So you've said."

Then, not knowing exactly why he was asking, he asked, "Do you have music here?"

"Music is everywhere," the large man responded as he scanned the vast emptiness, "but you don't hear it—yet." Before Decker could question that, the man said, "You can call me Linwood," then he pointed to a small door behind the bakeshop. "This way. It's time you began to learn."

"Learn what?"

"Learn why you came here."

"I didn't come here. I just—"

"Of course that's what you think but you've been aiming to-wards Solitaire for a very, very long time. And I've been waiting for you all that time."

"For me? You don't even—"

"We all wait for someone."

"What—"

"Time to take what you would think of as a leap of faith."

"I'm not—"

"A believer? You only tell yourself that to keep yourself safe. But you came here for something quite different than safety, Mr. Decker Roberts of the Junction."

Then, without warning, Decker gulped. He hung his head and out poured howls of anguish. "I abandoned my son."

"The boy from the Junction?"

"Yes, abandoned him."

"Then find him, Decker. What are you waiting for?"

He looked up. It was his friend Crazy Eddie speaking. He was somehow back in San Francisco outside the dream clinic—and Seth was gone.

Decker mumbled something.

"What?" Eddie demanded. As he took a step towards Decker his foot lift brace clacked.

Decker mumbled again.

"Time to enunciate, partner!" Another step. Another clack.

"I'll kill him."

"What?"

"I'll kill Seth—I know it. I'll kill him."

"What the hell are you talking about?"

"I got close to that boy in Stanstead—I got close to that girl in the igloo. I'll kill him, Eddie."

Eddie saw real fear in Decker for the first time. "Seth is your son, Decker, you hear me—your son."

Decker looked at Eddie. He had his arm around his daughter, Marina. Her eyes roamed aimlessly. It occurred to Decker that it would be a life's work looking after this poor girl—it was going to be Eddie's path.

Eddie was speaking again. Decker only caught the last part of what he said: ". . . time for you to vacate the premises—maybe even the continent."

Decker looked at his friend, but it was not his friend—it was the large white man who called himself Linwood. And he wasn't outside the San Francisco Wellness Dream Clinic—he was in Solitaire, Namibia.

"Sliding!" he shouted as he slammed his hand against the side of the Jeep.

Linwood stood back and watched intently. When Decker finally seemed to have himself under some semblance of control, Linwood asked, "Are you finally ready to learn?"

Decker heard himself say, "Yes, yes I am. Please." But it sounded like someone else had answered Linwood. With a shock he recognized whose voice had come from his lips—that of his son, Seth.

Linwood pointed to the small door again.

"Apple pies?" Decker ventured.

Linwood nodded slowly, then looked at Decker from beneath his heavy eyelids. "Inshakha should not have told you."

Decker didn't respond, but he thought, *So Inshakha's part of all this. Whatever this is.*

"Are you ready?" Linwood asked.

Decker eyed the big man, then said, "I guess."

"Good. Give me the keys to your car."

"Why?"

"Commitment is the first step on the path that you are about to follow."

Decker hesitated, then tossed the keys to Linwood. Before they disappeared into the bear paw the man called his palm, they glinted in the fading sun. The unlikeliness of this place—this peculiar oasis in the midst of the vast nothingness of rock and brush and sand, of far horizons, of a thin moon high in the sky all day long—settled on his shoulders like a heavy wooden yoke on a draft horse.

Then in the distance he heard a lion roar, and it echoed in his head—and heart—and soul.

"Does that happen often?"

"The lions?"

"Yeah—them."

"Usually only after sunset."

"But it's not—"

"Yes, well, things are changing."

Sliding, Decker thought, but he asked, "How? How are things changing?"

They were outside the small door. Linwood pushed it open, revealing a tiny but immaculately clean kitchen. "Do you know the concept of one hundred thousand kowtows?"

"No."

"Well, you will."

"When?"

"After you bake some pies."

The big man opened the door and indicated that Decker should enter.

He did and was immediately adrift in the sweetness of apple preserves.

Over his shoulder he heard the big man say, "You will, Decker Roberts of the Junction, you will—and then you will hear the music."

4

VIOLA TRIPPING

IT WASN'T A LION THAT VIOLA TRIPPING HEARD, BUT SOMETHING that slithered—something malevolent, at large, released . . . and searching for her.

She parted the drapes by her small bed and stared out at the thick blackness of the rural Nebraska night.

It was out there, of that she was sure.

She slid off her bed and wrapped her robe around her shoulders—such a small robe, such small shoulders—and went into the hall.

It was cold. She shivered.

At the far end she cracked open the door to Sora's bedroom. In the glow of the new moon she saw her caregiver of almost thirty years sleeping on her back. Her steady breathing and gentle snores comforted Viola.

In the morning Sora awoke to find Viola asleep in the bed beside her, her cheeks stained with tears, her fingers interlaced on her chest.

She gently moved Viola to one side and slipped out from under the covers. A cold dawn greeted her. She looked back at her sleeping charge and made a decision.

In thirty years Viola had never crept into her bed. She'd been told to report any change—and this was a change.

She withdrew the cell phone she'd hidden in the shoe box in the recesses of her cupboard and stepped outside.

She'd only used the thing a few times before, but she remembered the instructions the woman with the southern accent had given her and entered the fourteen digits that corresponded to the date and prepared to wait—she'd been told a connection would take time. It had in her previous calls.

But this call was answered before the first ring. There was an odd background hum. A cool male voice said, "Yes?"

"It's Viola," Sora said. "Something's happening to Viola."

"Okay," the cool voice said, then repeated itself: "Okay."

Sora didn't like the voice. It was somehow neutral, way too neutral, too cool, but before she could say anything—before she could ask where the woman with the southern accent who answered all her previous calls was—the line went dead, and the cool voice was no more.

5

WILLIAM JENNINGS CONNELLY COOLLY POCKETED WHAT HE thought of as his "special" cell phone. *Good, very good,* he thought. The boy was still bound and asleep as anyone with that kind of sedation in his system should be.

William Jennings Connelly knew a lot about sedation—a lot. His first company patented and marketed a totally unique approach to sedation, and even after he sold the company he kept a large supply of its secret products. With the money he made from the sale of the sedation company he posted bail and then paid for the defence funds for three of the world's most notorious computer hackers. The four of them went into business together. He supplied the money and they taught him an eccentric new approach to systems integration.

He took out the phone, put it on vibrate as he saw his conductor enter the wings. He pulled back his long grey hair and snapped an elastic band around his ponytail. He shook his head to splay the lengthy grey strands across his back then stared out at the audience. As he did he slid his fingers across the well-oiled surface of his Andrea Amati cello and yet again sensed the ancient mystery within. An Andrea Amati cello was even rarer than a Stradivarius violin—and it, if not its mystery, belonged to him. To him, William Jennings Connelly. Well, not William Jennings

Connelly anymore. Now that his parents were safely in the caressing arms of dementia, the world knew him only as WJ—just WJ.

It took a lot of money to control personal information—De Beers money, Sung family money—but he had done it, and now he was just WJ to anyone and everyone who wanted to know. And they could search and search but they'd never find anything but those two initials. WJ was him—period.

His conductor entered, accepted the audience's applause, then stepped on the podium. He raised a baton and all twelve members of the chamber ensemble readied themselves.

The audience closed their programs and stopped rustling.

A moment of silence. Then, the conductor brought down his baton—and they played as one intricate, interlocking thing.

As the music rose, WJ looked around him. He was more pleased with the aural than the visual of the ensemble. In fact they were, on the whole, an odd-looking lot. He perhaps the oddest. His sinewy six foot four inch frame and grey hair down to the middle of his back drew many an audience member's eyes, but not as many as the pretty Chinese girl who played second violin—or was she Korean? He'd never spoken to her—or for that matter to any of them except to say hello and compliment them on their playing. He wondered if any of them suspected that it was his money that paid their salaries. Then he wondered if there were any female Chinese gymnasts who were also accomplished string players—a Chinese gymnast violin player, that would be perfect. He wondered if he'd respond to perfect.

After the initial crescendo he began the almost seventy bars of rest. He looked down. He wished he didn't have such tiny feet—size five shoes and over six feet tall? Ridiculous! Sometimes he wore bigger shoes with paper stuffed in the toes, but when he did he often tripped over his feet. Like a dumb clown.

The music modulated and the violas took the melody.

WJ knew that music at its heart had a "feel" and that, to his profound frustration, he could never feel the "feel," so he copied the others—with arithmetic precision.

He readied himself and made a perfectly timed entrance with the other cellist. They took the melody for six bars then the rest of the ensemble joined in.

It was for moments like this that he bothered with the cello—to be in the midst of the sound.

With the music all around him he could almost feel its magic. No—he could almost feel something.

As a younger man, WJ had tried to understand what was happening to him. Everyone else seemed to be finding partners and solace—and more than that, joy!—in the company of others.

He'd listen closely to the lyrics of love songs, but couldn't understand what it was they were singing about.

English literature had been his Waterloo in high school. He'd read what everyone else read, but he got nothing from the words on the page.

Movies left him cold whenever the plot degenerated to the love between the two leads. Even the hatreds in the films escaped him. He literally didn't get what the problem was. Sure, he saw the logical outcomes of being cheated or betrayed or abandoned, but he saw no joy in retribution, or hate, or love, or sex—or anything.

He was left especially cold when musicals, for no discernible reason, broke into song. *Glee* was the bane of his existence, and he'd smashed two expensive HD LED monitors when he turned them on only to find *Smash* mid yech. Yep, he'd smashed *Smash*—twice. He knew he should find that humorous. He didn't. He knew it was funny—had even read and annotated the Bergson book, *Laughter,* in an attempt to understand "funny"—but he never felt the joy of the joke.

Most confusing was that women found him attractive. At first he thought it was just because he had money and the things money can buy. But, much to his surprise, they found him a good bed companion. This stunned him, since he seemed more and more divorced from the act of sex as time went by. He seemed to float above it, marvelling at the look on his partners' faces—what he could only assume was a kind of ecstasy, but from what he couldn't begin to guess, let alone partake in. Yet the further he abstracted himself from the reality the more they seemed to adore him—so sexy, so alive, such a great lover!

The other cello player turned the page a moment late, which brought WJ crashing back to the present. He ventured a look at the man. The guy liked to interpret the music. WJ didn't approve of that, so Mr. Interpreter wouldn't be a member of the ensemble much longer.

WJ held his bow above the strings and allowed the bass, violins, and the violas to lift him—like the young monk he'd seen on the synaesthetes' website who sang single notes up to the dome of the chapel and then seemed to rise—no, did rise, encased in the music he sang.

And such a look of glory on his face!

WJ knew from the moment he saw him that that boy was the key to opening the door that all his life had been closed to him. Even as he put his bow back on the strings and joined the andante finale of the piece he knew that it was worth every penny he'd paid, every law he'd broken, every risk he'd taken to entice and then kidnap the monk from the video.

The monk: Seth Roberts.

He remembered nights before he'd captured Seth. After a concert, back in his three-storey loft, he'd turn out the deco lamps and stare at the towers of San Francisco, which stood out like beacons against the incoming fog.

He'd push aside the floor-to-ceiling glass sliding door and step out on the wraparound deck. He'd breathe in the dampness—and feel so entirely empty that the thought of simply jumping and ending it all would flash across his mind.

He'd quickly retreat to the warmth of his vast main room and turn on the six-foot-wide gas fireplace embedded in the west wall. Turning his back to the flames he'd take in his existence—he'd had the loft completely redecorated by the very best Bay Area designers every three months for the past seven years. It always pleased him at first—he'd get the sense that he was really seeing. But the pleasure always faded—and it faded more and more quickly with each new design.

He knew that eventually he would get no pleasure whatsoever from it—or anything else.

But now he had hope.

He had Seth Roberts.

Nine months ago on an idiot shrink's advice about "dreaming being a potential access portal to feelings," he'd started the Wellness Dream Clinic in San Francisco. It quickly drew a wide assortment of wackos, lookee-loos, and hypochondriacs—and even the odd surgery freak. A few people were genuinely interested in exploring dream healing. These folks were brought by his interviewer teams to speak to him. The most interesting of these was an elderly indigent man who claimed that, after being hit by a car, he was plagued by odours—odours that he'd smell every time he saw a primary colour.

"When you see what?"

"Primary colours, like I said. Hey you're lookin' funny—"

"No sir, I am not," WJ responded. "But if I was to show you a primary colour . . ."

"I'd smell a particular odour. I've become a synaesthete. Haven't you ever heard of synaesthesia?"

He hadn't and acknowledged as much.

"Well, educate yourself," the old man had said.

"And how would I do that?"

He spoke of a website for "people like me."

"But how does a—"

"A man like me? Libraries. This country still has libraries, and those libraries have computers for poor people."

WJ nodded and, after a little financial prodding, the synaesthete gave over the URL of the synaesthetes' private website—and after a bit more financial prodding, his password.

That first time on the website WJ saw the videos of Daniel Tammet and the Human Camera, and although impressive, they seemed no more important than a person able to keep a dozen plates spinning on sticks. He was about to abandon his search when up popped the video of the young monk singing notes up into the Duomo. And suddenly he knew there was a path—a way out of his "dark room."

After that WJ spent hours on that site hoping to see the young monk and that look of glory again. But no matter how often or at what hour he logged on, there was no monk video. Then one day he used the old man's password and the knowledge he'd gained from his hackers to get into the webmaster's section of the site. And although he didn't find any details about the young monk, he found something most peculiar—another person who seemed to be accessing the website exactly the same way he was, searching for the video of the young monk. And this user was also looking for three other people: a Viola Tripping, a Martin Armistaad and a Decker Roberts.

WJ began to search for the searcher. It took him a bit of time, but he eventually found the searcher's home URL and then a name: Leonard Harrison. This ghost in the machine was Leonard Harrison, the head of the NSA.

Now why would the head of the NSA be investigating synaesthesia? And why would he be using his own computer? he'd wondered. These questions occupied WJ's thoughts for an evening before he came up with the only possible answer: Leonard Harrison, head of the NSA, was using his own computer because he didn't want anyone at the NSA to know what he was doing. *Yes, but why and what exactly was he doing?* WJ asked himself.

He left an encrypted message on the site for one Leonard Harrison. Much to his surprise, he quickly got a reply. So he appended another note and shortly got a second reply. *A fellow traveller,* WJ thought. Then he thought, *I really ought to get to know you better.*

It took some doing to find Leonard Harrison and his daily routine, especially his 9:00 p.m. evening coffee at Seattle's Best on Wisconsin Avenue, but the rest was relatively simple—especially the musically inclined barista.

One night he even followed Harrison back to his house in Georgetown. It was a quiet house on a quiet street. A private place for a man with a private obsession. Unfortunately for this man, W.J. Connelly thought of the young monk in the video as his—and his alone. And W.J. Connelly never backed down from a competition—in this case a rival for the possession of the young monk, Seth Roberts.

6

A WORLD OF WONDERS—BEFORE

HE HAD EXPECTED SOMETHING, BUT NEVER SOMETHING LIKE THIS. It was all there, worked out for him. Yes, Leonard Harrison, head of the NSA, had shown him the way—the answer to all those questions that had haunted him since he was a boy attending Mass every morning with his mother.

He felt like laughing, but he didn't.

He turned on his hooded flashlight and slowly allowed it to bring this secret place to life.

Unlike the rest of the house, which he'd explored earlier, this hidden room was a relative mess. Well, not a mess, but not as anally clean and meticulously put together as the rest. As if Leonard Harrison had been somehow drunk when he—he didn't know what verb to use—"created" this place. Yes this place was a creation, a world of wonders.

The ceiling was painted black and had patterns of iridescent stars on it. The walls were bare, while the floor was covered by an unusually shaped map of the world upon which sat a heap of female clothing and possessions.

He lay on his back and took a wide-angled shot of most of the ceiling. He then entered it into an astronomy data bank and was surprised to see the response: *An accurate depiction of the sky of the Southern Hemisphere August through September.* He took more shots and identified some planets and constellations: the Southern Cross, Venus rising, and Scorpio with its third star blood red.

Finished with the starscape he moved to a corner of the room and pressed his considerable bulk against the wall so that he could see the entirety of the floor map. Africa was huge, while Europe seemed like a tiny afterthought.

He adjusted his camera with a perfectly manicured fingernail and shot the floor map, entered it into another data bank, and got back a surprisingly simple answer: *World Map from Southern Perspective. Most world maps are looking down on the Northern Hemisphere; this one is looking up at the Southern Hemisphere. Made sense*, he thought. *Southern sky, southern map.*

He wiped the sweat from the back of his liver-spotted hands.

Then he saw the chalk marks—no, chalk lines—spreading from beneath the pile of junk on the floor to various points on the map. One of the chalk lines led to the west bank of the Missouri River, on the Kansas side of the border. At the end of the chalk line was the number 4. Another chalk line led to southwest Africa and had the number 2 beside it. A third line led to a large circle that enclosed almost all of the U.S. Plains States and had the number 3 beside it.

He looked for the number 1 and finally found it up in the heavens beside the red star in the Scorpio constellation. With a large question mark beside it.

He moved from the corner towards the things on the floor and noted them: a handbag, a pair of high-heeled shoes, sweatpants and other articles all on a wooden pallet. Unlike the rest of the room it seemed incomplete—a work in progress. Something that Harrison hadn't finished, was still investigating.

He stepped back and tried to make some sense of the thing but couldn't. He photographed it from various angles and sent it to dozens of data banks—no matches of any sort were reported. He stepped back. All the chalk lines converged beneath the articles on the wooden pallet. He gave it a push with his foot and the thing slid easily to one side, revealing a circle on the world map from which all the chalk lines emanated. The circle was on the north shore of Lake Ontario on what seemed to be the west side of Toronto.

He photographed that and entered it into a general data bank. The response came quickly: *Toronto, Ontario, Canada—Exact Area: The Junction.*

He didn't know what to make of that bit of information. Most of the rest he thought he understood. Long before he'd broken into Harrison's house he'd spent exhaustive hours reviewing Harrison's searches on the synaesthetes' websites. From those searches he knew that number 2 was a man named Decker Roberts, number 3 was Viola Tripping and number 4 was Martin Armistaad.

He circled the room twice more before he satisfied himself that he had seen everything there was to see.

Then he noticed them—the vector arrows on all the chalk lines, all pointing towards what he now knew was an area of Toronto called the Junction.

All pointing?

Were Decker Roberts, Viola Tripping and Martin Armistaad— and perhaps the woman whose articles these were—all heading towards the Junction? And what would happen if they were all there at once?

It was then, at Shakespeare's proverbial "witching hour of the night," that he'd gone to the synaesthete website and up popped the video of the young monk singing single notes up into the ceiling of the Duomo—and down came chords of music that seemed to wrap around him. When the young monk turned to the camera, he gasped. The smile on the boy's face was so intense—so profound, so real—that he realized that all his life had led to this. All those early mornings in the church, then the cathedral. All those silences— and finally here in Leonard Harrison's hidden room, his world of wonders, there might finally be an answer. No—the answer.

7

DECKER AND PIES

DECKER FOUND HIMSELF SMILING. HE USED TO THINK THAT REP-etition was the bane of his existence. Awake every morning at six o'clock, sit-ups, morning supplements, flossing, cleaning the mirror with a damp tissue of what the thread had dislodged and deposited on the glass; steel-cut oatmeal with blueberries and almonds; coffee; morning paper. Margaret Wente first just to see what mischief she was trying to stir up; then the top editorial followed by world news; a check on the Jays fatal flaws; the TV and film reviews to see which of his students was doing what; and on Friday the real estate section to see what his empty burnt-out property in the Junction was worth.

Day after day.

He'd treat himself to pancakes on Sundays with his copy of the *New York Times* (which arrived on Saturday in the Junction), but even that was just a weekly rather than a daily routine.

And every day older, and although not deeper in debt, deeper in other ways—like in the ground, somehow deeper in the ground.

That was his regimented routine before he got to Namibia—to Solitaire—to Linwood. Routine was chains. But here, in the heat, in the bakery, every day precisely the same—exactly so, because as Linwood proved to him, baking requires precision. In the routine and precision he'd found a freedom he'd never known.

As his hands measured and weighed and kneaded and rolled and folded, his mind was unleashed, free to roam the memory chambers of his deepest secrets.

And roam it did. Memories of his mother were the first to flood him. By his bedside calming his fears, telling him that it didn't matter what others said, that they'd moved houses three times in six months because they wanted to, not because of "what happened." And your father will come around, he will, he'll come around. He remembered asking her why she loved that man, and her funny response: "He always kept so clean, his shoes, all of them always polished." He remembered her refusing to let him play ball hockey in the summer—"Hockey's for winter, Decker. Is it winter out there?" She'd put his hockey equipment in a cedar chest in the basement—with a lock. But on Labour Day, with school looming and Decker's anxiety about returning to class on the rise, she'd bring him into the basement and give him the key. He'd open the trunk and take out his hockey gloves and skates, and the smell of the cedar was on everything, in everything. To this day that smell brought a smile to his lips. Some years he'd open the chest and there'd be new hockey gloves or pads—those were special years.

His mother was in her forties when she gave birth to Decker, and when it came to musical taste their age difference was most acute. He'd catch her singing from Gilbert and Sullivan operettas. When he'd mention that these two were just a bit racist, she'd scoff and remind him that she'd sung *The Mikado* in high school with Wayne and Shuster.

Memories of his father were often less pleasant—and often intruded on other memories. A boy seldom forgets being called a freak by his father. Then there was the time he applied to five medical schools for Decker—without Decker's knowledge. He got acceptances to four. When he refused to go, what little communication he had with his father came to an abrupt halt.

He remembered the day he read them a short story that he had written. He was fourteen. It was about an autistic boy who threw a beggar a coin that landed on its side—and stayed there. The boy quickly gained intelligence until the beggar picked up his bowl and the coin fell, and the autism returned. He'd never forget their grim faces when he finished reading the story. It would be twenty-two years before he'd put pen to paper to try his hand at writing again. And although his parents loved the arts—especially the theatre— they were appalled that his career path headed in that direction.

And then there was the fact that there was no love lost between his wife and his parents. Even as she walked down the aisle to him he saw his mother shake her head.

And she had been right.

Sarah and he had made a child—made a life but only remotely clung to love. And when the ALS had set in—well, Decker had much to apologize for. Then he'd found Eddie sitting in the snow on Yonge Street trying to sell jewelry that he'd made. He'd brought him home, and Eddie and Sarah were almost instantly deeply in love. One night he had to cut class short because there was a blackout in the studio. He'd arrived home two hours early and opened the door to his bedroom—Eddie and Sarah were in bed. He was holding her. She was smiling. He'd carefully closed the door and never mentioned it to either of them.

At the funeral he really wanted to go up to Eddie and say, "Your love was the most important thing in her life—it allowed her to hope and carry on." But before he could even contemplate doing that he felt Seth's small hand drop from his as he said, "You're happy Mommy's gone."

"No Seth—"

"Don't lie. I can always tell when people lie. You're happy Mommy's dead."

And Seth wasn't completely wrong. "Happy" was the wrong word—but how much difference is there between happy and re-lieved?

Even here, with his hands buried in the dough, he could still feel Seth's small hand in his. It was the last time he'd held his son's hand.

He remembered touching his own father's hand in those final days in the hospital. How angry he'd been with him. A doctor who had made no peace with the idea that his life, like all lives, would have to end. Then that one lucid moment after the months of gibberish, when his father had looked him in the eyes and said, "All my life I denied the gift. Feared it. Then I saw it in you." Then no more—the clarity left his eyes and never returned.

And there were other memories—some sweet, some not. His parents arguing in their bedroom without realizing that the heating vent from their room led directly to his bedroom. Night after night he lay awake and listened to them arguing—often about him. The sweetness of a kiss at a school dance, a girl whose name he couldn't recall, but thin in his arms and warm, and lips so soft. The back stairway in one of the houses he grew up in that held so many secrets for him—and, of course, the horror on his father's face when he told him how much he loved the darkness there. Other memories, for some reason so vivid and clear: In a New York diner. A working-class guy—maybe fifty—clearly dragged there by his wife, who just as clearly wanted to be part of New York's "roar," to have something in her life that brought her a bit of joy. She'd gotten dressed up—overdressed for brunch at this place. But when the guy's eggs arrived, one of them had a broken yolk, and his words still echoed in Decker's head: "I can get fucked up eggs at home, I don't have to pay for crap like this." The woman's face floated across Decker's mind: So hurt. So lost. So trapped. So alone. As if this were her last hope of gaining a glimmer of joy. That idea somehow faded into the glare of the battle zone in New York in the time before Disney came and made the city safe for midwesterners. How he loved slipping from the apartment—from Sarah's bed—and pulling on his army jacket and roaming the night world between Thirty-Ninth and Forty-Eighth Streets and Seventh and Tenth Avenues. Its hawkers and hookers, its dope dealers and dopers, its seeming aliveness creeping out from beneath the rocks when the legit theatres that Decker worked in closed and this other drama took centre stage in all its garish and vicious vitality. That art in opposition to the other art he loved—the acceptable art. Not always so acceptable. He remembered the artistic director of the theatre in Shanghai that he'd worked in. He had just arrived in China—fresh from Broadway—and this artistic director's very first words to him were something he'd never forget: "You are to remember that you can be replaced!" Thank you and fuck you very much. Then he heard it and turned, and there was the old arhu player in the pedestrian tunnel down by the Bund—so much music from two strings, so much. And as the player pressed on the strings, its sound rebounded off the tile walls of the tunnel and led Decker to something completely else—a club. An older African-American man blowing sweetly into his flügelhorn—and the thought in Decker's head, that the air from this man's lungs went into the metal and came out as music. A magical transformation from the completely normal, banal, into something otherworldly—music. Then the music stopped and Inshakha turned to him, her face and whole upper body covered in thick red mud. He stepped towards her, but she shook her head and he knew he would never see her again. As she passed by him his eye was drawn to one side, and there was Viola Tripping, cowering in the corner of a windowless, locked room, demanding, "Are you of the clearing? Are you of the clearing?"

Just another thing Decker didn't really understand.

8

SLIDING

TIME DIDN'T SEEM TO MEAN ANYTHING. NO—IT DIDN'T MEAN ANY-thing as Decker slid through it and space, baking pies.

A remembrance of Seth's birth slipped away, and he was in a doctor's office in Manhattan as the man told him that his wife was not just tired but rather had a disease named after an old baseball player. As he relived that awful moment he looked down and there was a red ribbon of blood in the dough. He withdrew his hands and watched the blood on his right hand drip to the floor. He went to wipe it off but it wouldn't leave his skin—and the taste of fear filled his mouth.

He knew he was awake and in Namibia, but he was sliding again—he could feel it. There was the pretty blond secretary—and he knew where he was.

He was back in Charleston, South Carolina. It was two or three years back. He couldn't remember which, and he'd been offered a huge amount of money to watch an interrogation of a businessman.

And he was there—and in Namibia at the same time.

And he couldn't stop the sliding—or the remembrance of the first time he saw the hanging boy and he knew that this, all of it, somehow was leading back to that—a boy with painted fingernails, missing both baby fingers, slowly being strangled by a noose around his neck.

The starchy smell of old cigarette smoke assaulted him as he followed the pretty blonde into the small boardroom. The solid oak door closed behind him with a thunk, and an ominous click suggested that a dead bolt had been thrown.

For a moment his blood pressure soared, then he calmed himself and sat at the antique pine table. The monitor showed him a balding, middle-aged man in casual golf attire sitting across a formal desk from two executives—or at least the men's clothes screamed as much.

Decker watched the printer beside the monitor spit out a running transcription of the conversation on the screen.

He slipped on a set of headphones and flipped through the pages.

"Henry, we're not here to interrogate you," the elder of the two executives said to the balding man. His tone was more pleasant than his words.

Decker didn't need to close his eyes to know that this statement was a nontruth—nor did the balding man, who was evidently named Henry.

"Maxwell," Henry said, "cut the crap. That's exactly what you're here to do."

Maxwell put his hands in the air and announced, "Guilty as charged."

"So what have I done?"

"Nothing."

"Fine, so what am I doing here? I'm number three in sales in the firm, granted down from my number-one status last year, but still better than twenty-seven other guys."

"True," Maxwell said. "But that's not what this is about."

"It's not?"

"No." It was the younger exec. Decker found it hard to place his accent—maybe the Pacific Northwest. Whatever it was, the man's "no" broke the odd fellowship that southerners keep alive even in the most desperate of times.

Henry turned towards the younger exec. "You're not from here, are you."

"No. I'm from the central office."

"Henry meet Chas," Maxwell said.

"And where exactly is central office?" Henry asked. "This company's been bought and sold so many times that I don't even recognize the signature at the bottom of my paycheques."

"Do you recognize these?" the younger man said as he flipped three photographs onto the table in front of Henry.

On the transcript Decker read, "FIRST ENVELOPE."

Decker reached across the table and opened the manila envelope marked ONE and pulled out three photographs. Each had evidently been taken in an elegant restaurant with Henry sitting across the table from two Chinese men.

"I asked if you recognized these." Chas.

Henry nodded.

"You do recall that you signed a confidentiality agreement when you entered our employ, Henry?" Maxwell.

Henry looked away, then back at his interrogators.

"Up and down means yes, Henry." Chas.

Henry nodded slowly, then lowered his eyes.

"Come on, say something," Decker muttered.

But the man didn't say anything.

"Do you want a lawyer?" Maxwell prompted, his voice still soft and kind.

"Or maybe you'll just tell us what you were doing talking to these two Chink gents." Chas.

Finally Henry said, "I was on a wrong path."

Decker closed his eyes and was surprised to see two parallel lines cross his retinal screen—Henry was telling the truth. He indicated as much on the transcript, but when he looked at the monitor he got a shock. He leaned closer to the screen. For an instant Decker could have sworn that he saw a boy, not Henry. He cupped his hands over the earphones.

"Selling the company's secrets is sure as hell the wrong path." Chas.

"Not selling. Seeking," Henry said.

Decker closed his eyes again, and a single perfect triangle floated up onto his retinal screen—another truth.

"Seeking? What does that mean, Henry? Seeking what?" Chas again.

"Answers."

"To what?"

Henry looked away.

"We're over here, Henry, and we're waiting. Seeking answers to what?" Chas.

"To meaning."

Again the image of a young boy replaced the balding man. *The bald man as a young man?* Decker wondered.

"Try me again, Henry." Chas was demanding, not requesting, an answer.

Henry sighed, then said, "Those two men have a niece."

Decker closed his eyes. A single straight line—a truth.

"So this was about sex?" Chas.

"No—well, maybe—but no."

"What does that mean?"

Henry sighed again—more deeply this time—then put his bony hands on the desk and began to drum his fingers. The odd rhythm of the drumming drew Decker's eye. The man had a thumb but only three fingers on each hand—he was missing the baby finger on both. Decker also noticed that he had a circle of white flesh on the tanned fourth finger of his left hand—his wedding ring had been removed and his fingernails were oddly dark.

Henry finally spoke. "Have you ever felt that you're not really awake—that you're actually asleep?"

No response from the two execs.

"Well, that's how I felt. Then on my last visit to Hong Kong I met someone who told me how incredible Peking Opera was—and he happened to have an extra ticket for a performance in Shanghai."

"One of the two Chinese guys?" Chas.

Henry nodded, hung his head, then whispered, "That was where I met her."

Two rectangles floated across Decker's retinal screen—a truth.

"The niece of our two major Asian competitors? That her?" Chas.

Henry nodded, then said, "I didn't know that was who she was when I met her."

A square—a truth.

"All I knew was . . ."

"What did you know, Henry?" Maxwell prompted.

"That all my life I've waited to wake up, for my fake life to end and my real one to begin, and . . ."

"And what?" Maxwell demanded—no longer the kind friend.

"Somehow I thought that girl would start my life—awaken me."

Three parallel lines—a truth—and once again the young boy was present. This time Decker was sure he was the older man as a boy.

"And you didn't know who this girl was?"

"I didn't care who she was."

"But you knew that she was the daughter of—"

"No I didn't, but I wouldn't have cared. Don't you understand, I wouldn't have cared."

"Because she 'awakened' you?" Chas.

Decker ignored the young exec's sarcasm. He knew the central operational myth of the West was the Sleeping Beauty story—that we are all actually asleep and only if the right person kisses you the right way will you awaken.

He put his hand to the screen and watched as the balding Henry morphed into the boy he had been, then back again. Back and forth, sliding from then to now, then to now. When the image finally stabilized, Decker whispered, "Poor bastard." He took off the headphones, completed his notes on the transcript, then stood and knocked on the door.

He heard the deadbolt scrape and the door opened.

The pretty blonde.

He gave her the transcript. "The truths are underlined."

She handed him a thick envelope with one of his aliases, Gert Rose, on the front.

He took it and began to walk down the hall.

"Mr. Rose?"

He turned back to her. "Yes?"

"Aren't you going to count it?" she asked.

He shrugged.

"Okay," she said, "but answer me this: why did you say 'poor bastard'?"

He hesitated, not pleased that his room had evidently been bugged. "Once you are awake you can't go back to sleep. Once the blind see they can never be totally happy in the dark."

At her quizzical expression he turned and disappeared into the Charleston night—well at least, into its darkness.

Then Decker broke one of Eddie's ironclad rules, and although he left the building where he had witnessed the interview through a service entrance, changed cabs three times and posted his USB key recording of the session to himself in the Junction, he did not leave town.

He'd always liked Charleston. When he ran that theatre in North Carolina he took every opportunity to get to Savannah and Charleston, both of which fascinated him. Their physical beauty was undeniable, as was their despicable racial history, which was in evidence down every alley and back stairway. The clash of the two opposites fired his imagination.

So he barhopped in the old section of Charleston, allowing the liquor and the soft night to dictate his moves.

Leaving the third bar he leaned against a gas lamp. His world was spinning. He hoped it was just the alcohol, but he knew it was more than that—it was his worlds cascading together, sliding, trying to align.

Just past three in the morning he turned the corner at Meeting and Broad Streets and stopped in his tracks—suddenly cold sober.

The plastic cup containing bourbon and shaved ice slipped from his hand and made a gentle squishing sound as it hit the cobblestones—then somehow became glass and split into a hundred shards.

Decker stared at the glass, then saw something reflected in a large piece and looked up.

The boy at the end of the noose dangling from the gaslight across the road was squirming, although he evidently didn't have the energy to reach up to the rope around his neck or call for help.

A clatter of hooves drew his eyes away from the hanging boy. He assumed he'd see one of the hundreds of horse-drawn tourist carriages, but that wasn't what he saw. A dozen or more horses neighed from their hitching rail as eight or nine men in full Confederate army uniforms galloped down the street. Their uniforms were torn and covered in mud and dust. One of the men was missing an arm and had his shirtsleeve pinned up to his shoulder. Another was without a right eye. A third had a jagged cut on his left cheek that seeped blood.

Then Decker heard a new sound, loud but low—moaning—the sound of many, many beings in pain. He looked towards the source of the sound—the slave auction house.

He glanced down and saw his feet on the cobblestones. They were shod in knee-high boots laced with worn leather strips.

He tasted something in his cheek and realized that he had a chaw of tobacco tucked there. He spat a slick of brown onto the cobblestones.

The Confederate soldiers dismounted and strode towards the slave market. Decker followed them. When he crossed beneath the gaslight he lifted his eyes—the boy was now hanging limp. Something about the boy's face was familiar, but he couldn't place it.

Then he noticed the boy's dangling hands—he was missing the baby finger on both hands. The remaining fingers all had blackened nails.

He slid back to the present and stared at the vast desert behind the small reality of Solitaire, now lit to a ghostly sheen by the new moon. Then he heard it. Far off a girl crying—a girl—and he trembled.

He turned and was surprised to see Linwood. Tears were in his eyes. "It's begun. It's too soon, but it's begun."

"A girl's cry begins something?" Decker asked.

And Linwood nodded slowly and stared at Decker. Finally he said, "Yes, it will begin with the girl, you must be ready."

"What do I do?"

"You wait."

"For what?"

"The missing piece."

"The—"

"The agent of change—who will bring this nasty world to an end and usher in the new one. She's always been there but doesn't know the role she needs to play in this end game."

"End game?"

"End of time."

"What?"

"And you have your part to play, but in the meantime you

bake pies—you owe one hundred thousand kowtows. It's your role."

Decker nodded. Somehow this made sense to him. Then he heard the cry again—a simple, clean sound moving across the Namibian desert like a boundless grief loosed into the world.

9

MARTIN ARMISTAAD

EX-PRISONER 271403, NOW JUST PLAIN OL' MARTIN ARMISTAAD, didn't understand exactly what had happened that set him free, but he did know that you didn't take your dick out of a gift horse's mouth.

Speaking of mouths, his hurt like hell where they put in that prison tooth.

But he was out! Out! Unleashed and hunting. After six years in Leavenworth Penitentiary he was on his own, breathing air that had not been befouled by hundreds of other men's breath and body odour and fear.

And there were stars. "Stars, stars, stars and one Secony station," he whispered to himself.

And there indeed was a Sunoco station—"Thanks, Mr. Bruce, I'll take it from here," he whispered.

Martin took his makeshift garrote from his pocket as he walked into the store behind the gas pumps. He watched the cars come and go. It was just a few degrees above freezing, but he wasn't cold—he didn't get cold. He had been up more than twenty-four hours but he wasn't tired—he never got tired.

"Can I help you, mister?" the acne-afflicted youth behind the counter asked as he looked up from the sheet of paper he was working on with a drafting pencil and compass.

"Got any heroin?"

"Excuse me?"

"No. Excuse me." He walked over to the young man and asked, "What're you doing?"

"Working out a design problem. I'm going to be an architect."

"Are you?"

"I sure hope so," he said, moving the compass a half turn and noting the angle on a sheet of paper.

"How old are you?"

The boy smiled. "I'll be seventeen on Thursday, sir." His breath smelled of Juicy Fruit.

"A shame."

"Why's that, sir?"

As Martin Armistaad's garrote bit deeply into the boy's throat, tearing open the carotid artery, he said, "Because statistically speaking most boys get laid in their eighteenth year. Eighteen point eight four to be exact—six times pi."

The take from the register wasn't much, but the store had good road maps, and the boy's car keys led him to a 2004 Corolla out back—and of course he could pump as much gas as he liked.

He had already charted occurrences backwards from the bombings at Ancaster College, and sure enough they conformed to a factor of pi—*Like everything else in the devil's kingdom,* he thought.

He took out the newspaper clipping that had been mailed to him three days before his surprising release. It related the story of the memorial for the victims of the Ancaster College bombings. It featured a photo of Viola Tripping.

It had shocked him because he recognized the girl/woman.

He'd seen her in the clearing while doing what some called dreaming.

In the newspaper photo she was entering the church for the memorial. It was raining, but she was wearing sunglasses and holding some man's hand—her tiny frame like a child's beside him.

He'd been in the clearing often enough. But he was never able even to glimpse the glass house except for that one time with her.

He'd first experienced the clearing as a young man, right after he'd figured out the exact date of the beginning of the market crash in 1973. It was in what he later understood was a waking dream. A dream that always had a behind and an ahead. Behind was the dense forest with all those lost voices seeking in vain to find the clearing where he was. Ahead were the very few who had found their way out of the clearing and were on their way to the glass house. Ahead had always been out of his reach, despite his desperate searching for a path out of the clearing.

Then he'd seen this girl/woman in the newspaper photo, Viola Tripping, in the clearing, and a path opened. It was then that he caught his only glimpse of the great glass house. But, in an instant, the path vanished—as did Viola Tripping. He returned over and over again to the clearing, hoping to find the girl/woman, but to no avail. And he knew, like a parched man in the desert knows he must find the oasis, that he had to find the glass house.

Then the day before his release he'd seen the girl/woman shaken and frightened on the ground of the clearing.

"Who are you?" she'd demanded.

"Never mind that. Lead me to the glass house," he'd said.

"You don't know the way?"

"No, but you do."

"I don't. I've only seen it once."

"When you were with me."

And the two had stared at each other, knowing beyond knowing that only together could they ever reach the great glass house.

Martin drove the Toyota through the night—west, running from the dawn, farther into the heartland. As the sun rose behind him he took in the desolation of midwest America. Strip malls and small towns and everywhere a drab uniformity, as if, as Lenny said, "First morning you see the cannon, then there's nothing else to do."

At high noon he pulled over to the side of the highway and spread out the road map on the passenger seat. Taking out the pimpled boy's compass he placed one of the points on Ancaster College then extended the arm out, marking pi diameters in miles, then in kilometres. The concentric circles got bigger and bigger until they stretched from the mid-Atlantic to the California coast.

Then he put the point of the compass on Leavenworth Penitentiary and marked the same pi-generated arcs in miles and kilometres. He circled the intersections of the two sets of arcs. They marked a straight line to rural Nebraska.

He pulled the compass away from the map and looked at it. *So simple,* he thought—*but useful*. He folded it and put it in his breast pocket. "Never know when a sharp point may come in handy. A shame that it'll never design a building—but then again, once I'm in the glass house, there'll be no need for buildings ever again."

He didn't notice as he pulled out into traffic that he'd been speaking his thoughts aloud. Nor did he notice the cop in the unmarked police car who was punching his licence plate into his car's computer.

The cop looked at the notation on the computer and obeyed the order to call a number that was fourteen digits long. The call was answered quickly, and a cool voice told him not to pursue the car—that this was a federal investigation.

10

YSLAN AND HOMELAND SECURITY

YSLAN FOLLOWED PROTOCOL AND ENTERED HER PASSWORD—
mydad,whoIneverknew—and waited for a six-tone response.
When it came she entered her second password and then added
her identifier—Solitaire, the private name she had for herself when
she was a little girl. The phone did the digital equivalent of turning itself inside out as it moved to full encryption mode. When the
transition was complete it sounded a single tone—then silence.

But only for a three count, then the voice of Hendrick H. Mallory, head of Homeland Security, was cool in her ear.

"Where exactly are you and who's with you, Special Agent
Hicks?"

She told him about the safe house, Garreth Senior and her two
assistants.

"Are they trustworthy, your assistants?"

Yslan hesitated.

"Okay, I get it," Mallory said.

"I didn't mean—"

"Of course. But you don't completely trust them, do you?"

She downed the dregs of her cup of bad coffee and instantly
longed for a cigarette. *I should be over this already! Why's it coming back now?* but she said, "No. I'm afraid I don't."

"Then neither do I. Don't tell them about this."

"About what?"

"When did you last hear from Harrison?"

"Sir?"

"When did you last hear from him?"

A moment of confusion from Yslan, then she said, "I don't recall exactly . . ."

There was a long pause. Finally Mallory spoke. "Harrison's been poisoned, or so we think. He's in a catatonic state and the doctors can't seem to figure out what's caused it. All they know is that it's something he ingested."

Yslan's mind raced—Leonard Harrison, her boss at the NSA, poisoned and catatonic? But before she could find words, she heard Mallory speaking again. "Make an excuse and leave the safe house. Get back to D.C. Now. You got that, Special Agent Hicks?"

Yslan didn't answer.

"You still there, Hicks?"

"Yes sir."

"Another thing."

"Yes?"

"We want you to bring your synaesthetes files. All of them."

"Who's we?"

"Not your business. Just bring them."

"All right, but why do you want to see my synaesthetes files?"

Yslan could hear him take a long breath. Finally he said, "Things may be in motion."

"What things?"

"If we knew we wouldn't be enlisting your help, Ms. Hicks." Then he asked, "Was Harrison religious?"

"Harrison? I don't know. Why?"

"Did he ever talk about the end of days?"

"I don't know if he did or didn't."

Ignoring her evasion, he asked, "Are you, Miss Hicks? Religious?" Before she could answer that she understood a lot about religion but she'd be hard-pressed to call herself religious, Mallory moved on. "Do you too believe in the end of days?"

Yslan heard the swell of a strong current beneath his question—something in motion indeed! But before she could ask a question of her own, Mallory repeated his question; "Are you religious, Ms. Hicks?"

"What?"

"It's not a hard question. Are you religious?"

"Why is that important?"

"If you need to ask that question, you wouldn't understand the answer."

"Excuse me but—"

"Do you know where Decker Roberts is?"

"Southwest Africa."

"How about his son, Seth?"

"No. I don't, but I don't see—"

There was no reason to continue her question. Hendrick H. Mallory, head of Homeland Security, had hung up on her.

She gathered her wits together, then headed back into the safe house. Mr. T was lounging in the kitchen. He looked up and said, "You okay, boss?"

How do I answer that question? she thought. But she said, "Yeah, I'm fine." She hoped she hadn't emphasized the pronoun. She remembered one of Decker's lectures to his acting class stating that spoken English has only two rules—if you lift the end of a sentence it makes it a question; if you emphasize a word it makes it comparative. As in *I'm* fine—but someone else isn't. So she hoped she'd kept her tone level.

Ted Knight entered. He had a curious look on his face.

"I'm on to something else now," she announced. "Nothing

special, but it's time sensitive." She hoped the vague excuse she was offering her two assistants would be accepted at face value.

"And him?" Ted Knight asked, indicating Garreth Senior in the locked bedroom.

"Hold him for two more days, then drug him and drop him back in Seaside—in his six-hundred-and-fifty-thousand-dollar two-bedroom house."

The two men made no effort to cover their open looks of amazement.

Yslan didn't care. "Harrison poisoned, catatonic," "things may be in motion," "end of days" just kept going round and round in her head.

Just over three hours later Yslan found herself waiting in the office of the head of Homeland Security. As she glanced at her watch, Hendrick H. Mallory entered the office with his hand out.

"Give me the files."

She hesitated, then handed over the files on her synaesthetes—no, her Gifted. It surprised her how much real pain she felt doing it.

Mallory sat his considerable bulk in his desk chair and signalled her to sit across from him. He opened the topmost folder.

Yslan looked out the window. In the distance she could see the Vietnam Veterans Memorial, with the name and dates of the father she'd never met incised in it like a scar in the blackness. The father who according to her mother had loved bacon. That's about all that she knew about him outside of his military record. He loved bacon. When she looked back at Mallory she saw that he had already finished reading the first file and was halfway through the second. In less than two minutes he'd finished the third file, and a sound that could have been a laugh slid from his almost closed lips. He put Yslan's files to one side and reached into his desk.

He pulled out a stack of folders. Opening the one on top he flipped an eight-by-ten across the desk. It spun a full 540 then stopped in front of her—facing her full on. It showed her leaving Emerson Remi's apartment in the middle of the night—doing up her blouse. It was from almost eight years ago.

Another photo. It also spun a turn and a half, then came to rest facing her. Leonard Harrison eyeing her as she leaned over to pick up a briefcase. This one was more recent—about two months before the bomb blasts in upper New York State.

A third, also perfectly tossed—the guy must practice—of her sitting on the box seat in the window of the Lakeshore Ramada in Toronto with Decker Roberts very close to her. As if it were the moment before a kiss—although there had been no kiss.

"Glad to see that Homeland Security is up on my sex life." She wondered if maybe she'd been wrong when she thought this man was nothing more than a stuffed shirt—a chauffeured, bloated bureaucrat. The kind of moron who tossed around words like "cadre," as he'd done when she'd seen him last, three days after the terrorist attack at Ancaster College. He'd asked her and Harrison, "Could Professor Frost possibly have a cadre?" After he'd gotten back in his chauffeured car, she'd turned to Harrison and asked, "What the fuck's a cadre?"

Mallory opened another file. For the first time she noticed how soft his hands were—almost pudgy. His cuticles were perfect manicured half-moons, the liver spots on the backs of his hands slightly faded probably by the use of some expensive cream.

"Yslan Hicks—born February 6th, 1975, in Fayetteville, North Carolina; parents Helen Anne and Robert, both deceased. Father in Vietnam at age thirty-two. Mother died shortly thereafter. Raised by maternal grandparents, tobacco farmers, who lost their farm after the locust hordes arrived in 1987. Grandfather committed suicide eighteen months later. Grandmother died of cancer two years later to the day. High school, Sacred Heart Secondary. North Carolina State University, degree in criminology, recruited for Quantico training by one Leonard Harrison in 1999. Achieved rank of special agent 2004, been on the NSA's synaesthetes' file for five-plus years."

"Fine. But all that is public record. I've testified before a congressional committee every year since—can we get back to Harrison?"

"Soon. And you're rather testy when you testify, aren't you? No need to answer that." He put aside the folder from his desk and picked up the synaesthete folder that Yslan had brought. He flipped one open and read aloud in a bored monotone: "Viola Tripping, born 1967, 4 foot 3 inches tall, eighty-two pounds, blond hair usually worn long." Without looking at her he tossed three six-by-eights across the table. They each completed their revolutions and ended up fanned out facing Yslan: Viola in a slow spin speaking for the dead in a tent in Florida, Viola doing the same in south Texas, Viola doing it in the middle of the night at the blast site at Ancaster College.

In quick succession he tossed the remaining twelve photos of Viola on the desk. The last four were from Ancaster College.

He was speaking again. "Speaker for the dead. Special talent: the ability to, if standing on the spot where a person died, recite his or her last thoughts. Most recent NSA activity at Ancaster College, where she and Decker Roberts combined to identify Professor Neil Frost as one of the people behind the terrorist act."

Yeah, she thought, *the one who had no cadre.*

"Present exact whereabouts unknown but thought to be somewhere in Kansas or Nebraska. Only contact through NSA specially encrypted phone used by her caregiver. Why?"

"Viola's very private. She insisted and we agreed. We're not even sure it's Kansas or Nebraska. All we know is that it's somewhere in the American Plains States."

"You couldn't trace her cell?"

"No. We gave her the new model that you folks invented."

"The untraceable one?"

"Yeah, that one."

He nodded, then opened another folder and threw six photos on the table—Decker Roberts.

"Mr. Roberts was born in 1964 in the Glencairn district of Toronto but moved to the Junction of West Toronto, Canada, in 2001. His house there burned to the ground April 15, 2009. Currently sharing a house with a high school friend, Eddie Hundert—aka Crazy Eddie. Was working as a researcher for the Canadian Public Broadcasting Company, CPBC, on a documentary now called *At the Junction*." He looked up. "Have you seen it?"

"His TV show?"

"Yes. Have you seen it?"

"The first three episodes. I have the last three on my PVR. Apparently they got a renewal for another six."

"From CPBC?"

"Yes, I think that's the broadcaster."

"And they're all produced by Trish Spence?"

Yslan was tiring of this but answered, "Yes, I think so. And Theo Denman is the other researcher. He owns a used bookshop in the Junction around the corner from where Roberts used to live."

"Do you know that Mr. Denman is quite ill?"

"He coughed a lot when I met him but—"

"And that Ms. Spence has become a serious hoarder?"

"Really?"

"Why that response, Agent Hicks?"

"I spoke with her briefly when I was up there looking for Roberts. She seemed very, well, together, in charge of herself—and others."

"In public but not in private. Have you met the others?"

"Roberts' other acquaintances?"

"Who else are we talking about here?"

"Yes. Eddie Hundert is as crazy as his nickname, but he has advanced computer skills."

"How advanced?"

"Enough that he's ahead of us most of the time. And there's the girl."

"Marina?"

"Yeah, that's his daughter from a common-law marriage."

"Which is now over. And the girl's retarded."

"Mentally challenged, not retarded."

"Sure. Then there's Leena, Roberts' old girlfriend who had the terrible car accident."

"It was a long time ago. When she was a teenager."

"But the scars are still there, aren't they?"

Yslan nodded.

"Don't you think it odd that everyone Decker comes in contact with seems to have been harmed in some way?"

Yslan didn't want to answer that question, then decided to. "Why ask a question that you already know the answer to?"

"Right. Back to Decker Roberts. He runs a successful acting studio, Pro Actors Lab. Present whereabouts—somewhere in southwest Africa. Son of a Presbyterian doctor and an atheist Jew mother. Honours degree from University of Toronto in English literature, MFA in directing from the Yale School of Drama. Artistic director of North Carolina theatre, two Broadway shows, blah, blah, blah. Wife Sarah died of ALS. Special talent: the ability to tell when someone is telling the truth. Made a living sitting in on the final vetting of business executives and reporting back the truthfulness of their responses. Kidnapped from a bar in the Chelsea district of New York City and held for three days in a safe house in New Jersey"—he looked up, then added—"where you are currently interrogating Garreth Laurence Senior." Then he recited the vital statistics—height, weight, hair colour, blood type. When he came to "left handed," Yslan thought, *Yeah left-handed, so he couldn't have blood on his right hand from killing that girl in the igloo. Besides, he was only five years old. Right-handed, left-handed, bi—a child doesn't have the strength to do something like that.* Once again, the word "obsession" rose up in her head when thinking about former-homicide cop Garreth Laurence Senior. She admired due diligence and stick-to-it-iveness, but what Garreth Laurence Senior felt towards Decker Roberts bordered on a mania. Fuck, it *was* a mania. "Special Agent. Special Agent!"

Yslan looked up.

"Yes, sorry."

"Fine. Let me repeat my question. Care to tell me how he managed to escape from the safe house in New Jersey?"

"No." Yslan was icy cold.

"Okay, but you picked up his trail and tracked him to Cincinnati, Ohio, where you protected him, as a much-valued asset ought to be protected, in his confrontation in a synagogue—of all places—from the head of a pharmaceutical company who evidently intended him some harm." He looked up. "You want to add anything to this?"

"No."

"Then of course there was you fetching him from Africa to help Viola Tripping with your investigations into the terrorist bombings in upper New York State."

Again he looked up at her. There was something wrong with his skin—too shiny, like a frog's belly. And those soft hands and manicured fingernails.

"Then that unfortunate incident in San Francisco that sent him running back to Africa." He closed the folder. "Am I missing anything?"

Yslan thought, *Is it possible they don't know about the son? About Seth? If he knows, he hasn't mentioned him. And what about the Rothko Chapel?*

She heard the whisking sound of two photographs crossing the table to her—both spun and landed perfectly so that they faced her. The first was of Seth on a surfboard bobbing on the waves, probably off the coast of Vancouver Island. The second was of her sitting alone in the Rothko Chapel in Houston, where she had followed Decker.

When she looked up from the pictures she saw Mallory smiling. *Why was he smiling?* she asked herself, then thought, *Men with tiny teeth really shouldn't smile.*

He picked up another photo and examined it. Then he slowly turned it to her. It showed her sitting on the small cot in Decker's psycho single dorm room at Ancaster College. She had just un-done his handcuffs and the two of them were so close to each other that they were breathing in each other's expelled breaths.

He tilted down his reading glasses and looked at her. "Could he tell when you were telling the truth to him?"

After a sigh that she wished she hadn't let pass her lips, she said, "Yes."

"Then he didn't care all that much for you, did he? It's a fact that he's unable to use his special talent on those he cares about. Isn't that true?"

Yslan didn't say anything.

"He's unable to use his special talent on those he cares about. Right?"

"That's correct."

"Thank you."

He opened another of the folders. "Then there's Martin Ar-mistaad, born 1952." He threw three photos of the man onto the table. Perfect spinners again. "Mr. Armistaad's special talent has to do with pattern recognition, which somehow he always associ-ates with the mathematical realities of pi. He predicted to the day the peak of the yen in 1975, the bottom of the Dow in 2002, the rise of the Tea Party in 2010—and about thirty other world occur-rences that he had no right to know. Correct?"

"To the best of our understanding, yes."

"Any idea how he does that?"

"Not a clue."

"And how the others do what they do?"

"Ditto."

"Don't you think you should have shared this information with us at Homeland Security?"

"No. I think we have our area of expertise and you—"

"Are just a bloated government bureaucracy that rides around in chauffeured limos. Something along those lines?"

"If you say so."

He smirked then said, "Well, Martin Armistaad, ex-prisoner number 271403—"

"Hold on. *Ex*-prisoner?"

"Yes, Special Agent Hicks. We believe that thanks to your boss, Leonard Harrison, or someone your boss was working with, Martin Armistaad, ex-prisoner 271403, is in the wind."

Is that what he meant when he said, "Things may be in motion"? she wondered.

"Armistaad is dangerous," Yslan said.

"And you know this from—"

"I've interviewed him."

"At Leavenworth?"

"Yeah." It was hard to forget, but she had a video of their conversation. Not something she'd wanted to revisit, but she thought she might have to now.

Mallory stood. Just for a moment something that could have been concern crossed the chubby cheeks of his face. "Russian dolls, Special Agent."

"You mean—"

"Matryoshka dolls—one inside another inside another . . ." He paused, and Yslan was pretty sure he was going to say something more, then he added, "That's how security works."

It wasn't what he was going to say, but she replied, "The NSA is—"

"Just a subset of us at Homeland? No. I'd never claim that. But the NSA has real overlap with Homeland." He glanced at the extra files that he hadn't opened for her. Had he thought about showing her their contents? She didn't know because now he was on his feet, somehow no longer a soft bureaucrat. Now he was a general giving her marching orders. Then he tossed a set of keys at her, which she caught with an athlete's ease.

"And these are?"

"Keys to Leonard Harrison's house. Your partner wants to start there." Before she could respond "I don't work with partners," Mallory smiled and pressed a button on his desk console.

Yslan found it odd that he had such an old-fashioned gizmo.

The door behind her opened, and the handsomest man she'd ever seen entered. He wore a button-down Oxford shirt, cuffed and pleated taupe slacks, and cordovan shoes that must have cost more than a month's rent. He moved like an athlete yet was a bit fey—Princeton fey.

Mallory said, "Special Agent Yslan Hicks, you know—"

Before he could say the man's name, Yslan said, "Hi, Emerson." Then she laughed.

"I'm disappointed," Emerson Remi said.

"Why's that?"

"This time you laughed. In times past I believe I've elicited more intimate sounds from you."

"I prefer laughing."

"Now why is that?"

"Because knowing that you have been working for Homeland Security all this time, a lot of things that didn't make sense now do."

Then Hendrick H. Mallory dismissed her. At the door he called to her. "Special Agent Hicks?"

"Yes." She couldn't bring herself to add the word "sir."

"By the by, a cadre is a group—often a secretive group, but a group nonetheless."

Of all the shocks she had received in that room, this was somehow the most shocking.

11

VIOLA TRIPPING

"GO AWAY!"

Sora, Viola Tripping's nurse and protector for almost thirty years, was startled into waking by her charge's tearful, "Go away!"

Sora slipped out of her bed. She knew better than to turn on the overhead light. She had no idea what time it was, but through the opening in her bedroom curtains she saw the deep darkness of the rural Nebraska night.

"Go away! Please go far away," Viola cried.

"Why Viola? What's happened?"

Sora saw Viola straining to get words from her brain to her mouth. She'd seen her have this struggle before and had read about it in the Cassandra myth. After the god spat in her mouth she was able to see into the future, but when she went to tell anyone, out came nothing but gobbledegook.

"Come on, Viola, tell Sora what's wrong."

Something in the room crashed to the ground. Sora assumed it was her antique full-length stand-up mirror. She steadied herself, then stepped out into the darkness. She felt the glass cut deep into her feet, but she didn't care. The girl/woman she'd looked after for all this time was clearly coming apart.

"I'm going to turn on a light, Viola, so cover your eyes. I know that light hurts your eyes, so cover them with your hands, sweetie."

She waited, but Viola didn't say a word.

"You ready? Cover your eyes."

Sora punched the wall switch and the overhead snapped on.

And there Viola was.

Curled up in a ball in the far corner of the room, her long hair a rat's nest—and wet. Wet and matted with blood, which seemed to be pouring out of her in dozens of places.

Then Sora saw it—the razor blade.

Viola squirmed to a sitting position. She raised the blade to slash down at her exposed thigh.

Sora threw her body at the girl/woman and the razor skittered a few feet away.

A beat.

Then Viola, slick with blood, lunged towards the blade, but Sora kicked it across the room and flopped on top, trapping the girl/woman's hands beneath her body.

Sora heard Viola breathing hard beneath her and felt her blood seeping up through her nightgown.

Slowly Viola gave up the fight and at last lay still beneath the weight of her caregiver.

Finally Sora said, "Enough?"

Viola nodded.

"If I let you up you'll behave?"

After a breath, Viola nodded again.

"All right, but first tell me what this is all about."

And Viola tried, but all that came out of her mouth was, "Go away. Go far away. Go far away now."

"Yes, I hear you, Viola, but why? Why should Sora go far away now?"

Viola took three trembling breaths and finally managed, "Kill. He—will—kill—you."

It took the rest of the night for Sora to clean up her diminutive charge, but she was unable to get from Viola who exactly was supposed to kill her.

As the sun rose, Viola, with bandages on every limb and six stitches on her upper arm, finally closed her eyes and slept.

Sora saw the girl/woman slowly shallow her breath, and then her eyes began to move rapidly beneath her barely closed eyelids. Although Sora had seen this hundreds of times before, it always shocked her—eyes in motion, lids partially open, fast asleep.

Sora reached down and pulled the antique crazy quilt up to Viola's chin. As she did, Viola slid her tiny hand into Sora's and said, "Don't hate Viola, please don't hate Viola."

"Never, sweetie, never would I hate you—ever."

Viola sighed deeply and turned towards the wall.

The quilt slipped a little and a wound on Viola's neck opened, allowing a thin stream of crimson to work its way down her back.

Sora took a tissue and blotted it, but the cut was stubborn and would not clot. She contemplated getting her sewing kit again to stitch it up, then she saw Viola's left hand snake around and feel for the gash. When she found it she put her index finger deep into the wound, and the bleeding slowed, then stopped.

Why not? Sora thought. *Considering the other things I've seen her do, why shouldn't she be able to stop her own bleeding?*

Sora returned to her room and began to clean the mirror glass from the floor. When she went to right the antique oval frame it came apart in her hands. She held back tears. The mirror had been the very last gift her mother had ever given her.

It was Viola's reading of her mother's final thoughts before her death—*Tell Sora that I will always love her and I'll be waiting for her*—that had convinced Sora to commit her life to looking after the diminutive speaker for the dead. She hadn't planned to, it just happened. As if it was meant to happen. Meeting Viola Tripping had completely changed the path of her life.

Little did she know that everyone who was close to one of the Gifted had his or her life profoundly altered. And not always for the good.

As the dawn came, she found the razor blade that Viola had used to cut herself and wondered where she had gotten it. She'd bathed Viola for years and had never used a razor on her silken skin. What few strands of hair she had on her arms were almost transparent against the blanched whiteness of her skin. Her legs were hairless, as were her private parts. Sora had wondered what she would do when Viola began to menstruate—but that eventuality had never come into being.

She heard the girl/woman cry out from her bedroom, the words painful but piercingly clear: "Please don't hate Viola, please don't hate me! Please!"

An hour later Sora took the cell phone from the shoe box in the back of her closet and dialed the number again—and again that hum in the background and the too-cool voice.

"Something's happening," Sora said, trying her best to control the scream that was building in her chest.

"Yes, yes it is. I know it is," the cool voice responded. The line went dead.

Sora dialed the number again, but this time no one answered— just that odd hum. When she tried again there was no dial tone on her phone.

12

A TAPE OF MARTIN ARMISTAAD

"TURN LEFT," YSLAN SAID.

"Georgetown's to the right," Emerson said.

"I want to see Harrison before I see his house."

Emerson turned left. Yslan sat back and switched on her iPad.

"Whatcha' gonna watch? Cat videos?"

She shot him a look. "How far to the hospital?"

Emerson's deep grey eyes turned to her. "It's a long-term facility, not a hospital."

Yslan pulled herself away from the depths of his eyes. "Already? Already they moved him?"

"Apparently he didn't warrant the expense of a hospital bed."

"But they need to do tests."

"They've done the tests. They're stumped."

Yslan smacked her palm against the window. "How long?"

"Till we get there?"

"Yes."

"Ten minutes or an hour."

"What—"

"D.C. traffic, ten minutes or an hour." He shrugged.

Yslan turned back to her iPad and summoned up the last prison shots of Martin Armistaad. They'd been taken two days before his unexpected release. He was smiling, clearly knowing he was

being photographed. His teeth were surprisingly good for a con-
vict six years into his sentence. She saved the pictures in a file of
their own, then switched to the video of her last interview with
the man—and hit play. She braced herself. Before his arrest Mr.
Armistaad was number one on her Gifted file. She had met him
twice before his incarceration and had thought of him as a vital,
and charismatic, if eccentric, individual.

But the creature on the video who ambled into the prison interview room appeared to be nothing more than a thin, balding man
with a greying beard and a vicious case of psoriasis that coated his
left arm and shoulder and reached up to his cheek.

"Thank you for seeing me, Mr. Armistaad," she heard herself say.

She steadied the tablet on her lap and activated the split-screen
function.

The man across the table from her sat and hung his head. He
scratched a red patch on his flabby left forearm, and it extruded a
yellowish fluid.

"I know you didn't have to agree to this meeting, sir." She remembered feeling queasy then. Now she just wanted to vomit.

Armistaad said nothing.

Finally Yslan asked, "How's the food in this joint?"

With his head still hung low Armistaad said, "The restaurant
leaves something to be desired, but if you're really bad you get
room service, so . . ." Armistaad allowed his remarkably light voice
to trail off as he raised his eyes to meet Yslan's. "Pretty eyes," he
said, then corrected himself: "hider's eyes." His voice was deep-
ening, no longer light. His head no longer down but rather held
proudly.

Yslan watched herself do her best not to be repulsed. And although she obviously wanted to deny this man a view of her eyes
she remained facing him straight on.

"You don't know, do you, Special Agent Yslan Hicks?"

"Know what, Mr. Armistaad?"

He winked at her then said, "About the clearing."

"The what?"

"Nothing. Nothing that I could tell you. Something you'll just have to figure out for yourself." Before she could respond, he added, "So what do you say we start again. You pretend that I didn't have to agree to this meeting—I believe we were at that lie, weren't we?"

The man's eyes blazed. The old magnetism was back in full force.

Armistaad reminded her of Hannibal Lecter, but she dismissed the thought, reminding herself that Hannibal Lecter was a fiction. Then she stopped herself from such sophistry—the man on the iPad screen was as otherworldly as Thomas Harris's nightmare creation. And he clearly knew it.

For a moment she wished that she'd never been introduced to the idea let alone the reality of synaesthetes—that the ground she walked on was the solid terra firma that she thought it was before she met the likes of Martin Armistaad. That the world was a real place with real rules. Not the shifting miasma of Martin Armistaad, Viola Tripping—and Decker Roberts.

Yslan watched herself on the screen take a breath and then say calmly, "Thanks for taking this meeting, Mr. Armistaad."

He opened his arms and then laced his fingers behind his head, shimmying down in his chair so that his pelvis was aimed more directly at her face. "What can I tell you, Ms. Hicks? My social calendar is very full, but I was able to sneak it in—as I did the last time we met." He smiled, the antecedent for his "it" obvious to both of them. He was missing a front tooth.

"Thank you for seeing me again."

"Not a problem." More scratching.

"In your early essays you state that all your thinking is purely mathematical. That there are natural cycles in the world that are generated from the mathematical reality of pi."

He stared at her. No more scratching.

"Do you still believe that, sir?" To her ears, she sounded way too much like Jodie Foster—no, Clarice Starling.

"Yes . . . and no, Ms. Hicks. I think I believe, as you are learning, that there is something else at work in the universe. Something that Hamlet sensed when he saw the ghost of his murdered father, something that great artists see—something other."

"I see."

"Not yet you don't." He smiled again then added, "Do you?"

"No. Not personally. No I don't see 'something other.'"

"That's why you are here, isn't it, Ms. Hicks. You could read my writing online—everything I've written is immediately in the public domain. You see, I'm not allowed to charge for anything I write in here—am I?"

"I guess not."

"I'm not." This last was very hard. Angry. "So I ask again, Ms. Hicks, be honest with yourself and answer my question: Why exactly are you here?"

"To understand what I can about how you worked."

His surprisingly thin tongue licked his lips, leaving a glistening sheen as he whispered, "Liar."

"Tell me how it works, Mr. Armistaad."

"Fine," he said. Then just as Yslan was about to speak again, Armistaad added, "I close my eyes, Ms. Hicks, and the clearing comes into view, then I am there and this world aligns—with the other world, that is."

She snapped off the video and closed her iPad as Emerson pulled the car to a stop in front of a smallish whitewashed building.

"This the hospital?"

"No."

"No? I thought we—"

"As I said before, it's a long-term facility." He looked at Yslan's grim face. "At least it's not a hospice."

After taking a deep breath, Yslan said, "Yeah, we can be grateful for that."

Emerson nodded and got out of the car.

13

VISITING HARRISON

FIVE YARDS OUTSIDE HARRISON'S ROOM, YSLAN SMELLED THE sharp aroma of cheap antiseptic. She breathed through her mouth and opened the door.

Leonard Harrison was propped up by pillows in a wheelchair facing the window of his small room. A thick leather belt around his upper chest that buckled behind the backrest stopped him from falling forward. He had a large bandage on his forehead. There was a food tray attached to the wheelchair. *Like a highchair tray,* she thought.

A large African-American nurse was finishing cleaning Harrison's face with a soft cloth.

The baby food on the tray—apricot—brought the terrible reality home to her. Apricot baby food for Leonard Harrison's lunch. She recalled periodically sticking her head into his office around noon—he always ate at his desk, wearing a large linen napkin around his neck to protect his Savile Row shirts and ties. He ate nothing but organic food that he prepared at home. He was careful, fanatical, about anything that entered his body.

Except for his 9:00 p.m. cup of Seattle's Best coffee, which he picked up on his way home.

When she started at the NSA, on occasion she would get him

his coffee when he worked late. Hardy blend, tall, no milk, no sugar—organic, fair trade only.

As the nurse finished her work and removed the tray, Yslan heard Harrison pass gas, then she heard him strain as he passed a stool—into a diaper, no doubt.

She turned, not wanting to see his face. "Can't you help him?" she demanded.

"Yslan, don't—" It was Emerson, stopping her from making a fool of herself.

"That's right. You tell your girlfriend to watch her manners in here," the nurse said.

As Yslan left that antiseptic-tainted room, the image of her boss—her mentor—Leonard Harrison catatonic, apricot baby food fed, diapered, poisoned, rose in her head like a cobra ready to strike. Then a new thought hit her—slugged her. *He was on a different path—just a different path.* Where had she heard that?

She passed by Emerson. He was looking a little grey around the gills. Tough.

14

IN HARRISON'S HOUSE

THE DRIVE TO HARRISON'S HOUSE WAS TWICE AGAIN AS LONG as it had been to get to the hospital or long-term care facility or whatever it was. Neither spoke. Both still had the image of Leonard Harrison shitting in his diaper in their heads.

Emerson finally pulled the car to the curb in front of a neat Georgetown row house, now festooned with yellow tape and watched over by two young cops. A forensics truck was parked across the road. Two middle-aged techs were taking in the sun and smoking.

"There's no number."

"Yellow tape, two cops, forensics truck—I'd guess this is the place."

"But you don't know? He was your boss."

"Yeah, but I've never been here before."

She got out of the car before she had to elaborate, badged her way past the cops and entered Leonard Harrison's home.

A taped outline marked the spot where Harrison had fallen. The photos that the cops had given them as they entered showed him stretched out on his side in the front hall, a blood patch on the hardwood floor where he must have banged his head.

"If he fell here, how did they know to come for him?"

"He managed to call nine one one," Emerson said.

Yslan nodded and said, "Okay."

"Okay what?"

"Get the nine one one tape. And tell the cops outside to stay there."

"And the techs?"

"Outside till I call for them."

Emerson went to the door and told the cops. When he came back into the hallway he was surprised to see Yslan standing in the midst of the living room, dead still.

"What exactly—"

Yslan held up her hand, stopping Emerson's question. She walked slowly down the hallway to the kitchen in the back. She was literally following her feet. The kitchen held few surprises—except for its excessive cleanliness. She didn't know that pots could actually shine like that.

The refrigerator proved predictable for a food nut. All organic, all organized, all labeled with dates.

"What's with the dates?" Emerson asked.

"You ever bought organic produce?"

"No. Can't say I've ever indulged."

"Well, if you had you'd know that it goes bad quickly. Sometimes it feels like it's bad before you get it home."

"So they're best-before dates?"

"Yeah," Yslan muttered but she had already bent down and was pulling out the packaged vegetables, fruits and exotic grains, putting them on the counter. "Write down the dates, Emerson, then get them to the lab. I want them tested for toxins." She turned from the kitchen and headed up the narrow staircase to the second floor. Halfway up she stopped and looked back at the first floor. What bothered her about it? She couldn't say, but something was wrong.

A bedroom on the right, prim to the point of prissy—perfectly made bed, toiletries in the en suite bathroom, all made from natural products and lined up with military precision, lamps on either side of the bed, no overhead with the low ceiling. Even the oval hooked rug at the foot of the bed was perfectly placed so that it was dead centre in the room. She lifted the rug and pulled it to one side. She ran her palm along the floor to check for ridges that could indicate the presence of trap doors, but there were none. Besides, there was so little space between this floor and the ceiling below. *Is that what bothered me on the stairway?* she wondered.

As she backed out of the bedroom an odd image popped into her head—herself coming out of the en suite bathroom wearing nothing but a pair of men's boxer shorts and approaching the bed. But it wasn't Harrison on the bed—it was Decker Roberts. And somehow she was watching herself approach Decker. And as she did she sensed someone else watching Roberts from the other direction. She turned towards the shadowy figure. "Seth," she said aloud, but before the figure could turn to her, it evaporated. The room stabilized.

She had no name for what had just happened, but had she mentioned it to Decker he would have told her that she'd just experienced what he so often experienced—sliding.

She took a long slow breath and approached Harrison's armoire. Six suits all pressed and ready to go, ten pairs of pleated, cuffed slacks, eight pairs of shoes all polished to a high gloss. She parted the clothing and pushed against the back panels. "Lion, witch and wardrobe, here we come," she whispered—but nothing gave under her pressure.

She quickly went through his dresser drawers—folded underwear, correctly matched socks, a single widow sock to one side. She picked it up. It was torn. *Harrison had kept a torn solo sock.*

She closed the drawers of the dresser and headed back into the hall.

Across the way was a closed door. She tried it. Locked.

"Let me," said Emerson.

How he'd managed to sneak up on her was a matter of concern, but she just nodded. With surprising expertise he manipulated his pick and probe with his long, tapered fingers. It took him some time but eventually the door popped open. He stepped aside and she entered.

The small bedroom had been converted into a study. The antique desk was as neat as the rest of the house, his Lenovo laptop dead centre.

"Why's his computer still here?"

"The techs got everything they needed from it without having to touch it."

"What did they get?"

"Not much; apparently it'd been monkeyed with by experts."

"Dust it."

"I'll call a tech."

"Okay." She waited until Emerson had left the room and closed the door behind him, then she opened the desk's two drawers. She found nothing but high-quality writing paper, an expensive pen, a box of chalk and a well-worn family Bible that was printed in Edinburgh in 1691. She looked at the family trees on the front four pages and was surprised to find that Harrison had a twin who had died almost thirty years ago.

Beside the date of the brother's death were the words "We'll meet again at the End Time." Yslan recognized Harrison's beautiful penmanship.

She stepped back and looked at the window. An overhanging willow tree obscured the view, but the window itself was so thick that it blurred her vision. She tapped the glass—bulletproof. The locking device on the side, the best money could buy. Harrison evidently didn't want anyone in this room. She assumed it was because of what was on the computer and turned to go.

A tech entered.

"Your guys really found nothing on his computer?"

"Not nothing, but what we found was pretty much useless."

"Why?"

"Usually people try to erase things—that we can almost always undo. But whoever worked on this computer used a completely new strategy."

Yslan prompted him. "And?"

"How computer literate are you?"

"Some."

"Well 'some' isn't enough to understand what happened to that computer. Look, think of it as a crime site."

"Okay, I can do that."

"Good now think of a crime site where someone imported a herd of five thousand cows to walk and shit all over it for a year—then you've got what we have with that computer."

"Explain 'imported.'"

"Someone got access to that computer from an external source, that much we know."

"So the lab can—"

"Find out who that someone is? No, we can't. Not a chance of that happening."

"What—"

"Sifting through the five thousand cows and cleaning it up? Probably not. They say maybe—which usually means no."

"But maybe sometimes means maybe."

"Sure. You want me to dust that thing or not?"

"Yeah, dust it."

She heard a chuckle—it was Emerson at the door. She stared at him. Within the door frame his perfectly symmetrical body gave Leonardo da Vinci's drawing of the perfect man a run for its money. He gave her a big smile and a thumbs-up. But now she wasn't watching him. He noticed. "What?" he demanded, but she was already past him and running down the stairs.

When he caught up to her she was across the street looking at Harrison's house.

"So I repeat—what?"

"How many storeys do you see?"

"Two."

"Really?" She crossed the road and hurried down the lane at the side of the house. Emerson followed her.

"And for the third time I ask, what?"

"It's a false ceiling." And she was moving quickly again.

When he caught up to her she'd dismissed the tech and was standing on Harrison's desk, prying open an overhead panel. Then she leapt up and levered herself into the hole in the ceiling.

It took her eyes several long moments to adjust—then the hair on the back of her neck stood up.

"What?" she heard from down below. But she wasn't ready to speak, not just yet. She took out her cell phone and turned it on. In the bluish light she saw the stars painted on the ceiling, then four numbers drawn in chalk, then further chalk marks on a map of the world that covered the floor. Chalk marks with vector arrows on them. All the lines converged under what was in the centre of the room. And what was there shocked her. A perverse shrine. At the very centre of which was a single nude photograph of her. She grabbed it and noticed there was writing on the back— what seemed to be a chemical formula of some sort followed by a Bible citation: Deuteronomy 34:1–4. She used her cell phone and snapped off thirty photos of Harrison's "private place," then pocketed the nude photo and called out, "Emerson, call your boss, he's going to want to see this."

Two hours later the small room above Harrison's study was awash with floodlights. Yslan stood outside the house with the head of Homeland Security at her side.

"Did you know?" he asked.

"Only what most women know."

"And what's that?"

"That some men find them attractive, want more from them than they are willing to give."

"Harrison wanted more from you than you were willing to give?"

"Yes, that's what I meant."

"Just that? Nothing else?"

"Nothing more than that."

But as Mallory walked back to Harrison's house, followed by a steady stream of techs in their white Tyvek suits, Yslan knew there was much more here than that. She was pretty sure that Harrison was trying to figure out the secret that she'd first sensed existed when she was twelve, standing in her grandfather's tobacco field with locusts all around her, the otherness she felt every time she ran her fingers over her father's name on the Vietnam Veterans Memorial and somehow smelled bacon—the otherness she'd felt when she was close to Decker Roberts. Harrison was after that—what she assumed he thought of as the End Time—when he would meet up with his dead twin.

She checked her cell phone for the pictures she'd taken before she allowed Emerson up into the secret room. She went through them one at a time. Etched on the underside of the roof the Southern Cross with Scorpio just rising—the third star in its thorax bright red. Then the chalk lines on the floor map—one line to Leavenworth Penitentiary, another to a large circle in the Plains States and then a third line to southwest Africa. And numbers—beside southwest Africa the number 2, beside Leavenworth the number 4, beside the Plains States the number 3 and the number 1 with a question mark beside it beneath the red star in the body of the Scorpio constellation.

Then there was the shrine. It had an old purse that she'd thrown away, an empty bottle of her perfume and a pair of her sneakers that she'd "lost" at the office and dozens of other personal items of hers, all neatly balanced to form a rough pyramid. She'd removed only one thing: the nude photo of her with the chemical formula, which she hadn't yet deciphered, and the Bible citation on the back.

That night she applied her considerable computer skills and found out, much to her surprise, that the formula outlined the use of a catalyst in a chemical reaction. On further searching she found the basics. A catalyst was a freak of nature. An entity—an element—that needed to be present to allow a chemical reaction to take place between two or three or four others. The other entities changed—but the catalyst never changed. Yet without the catalyst the entities could come into contact, could be heated or mixed and nothing would happen. But put the entities together then add the catalyst and an entirely new entity would come into being—although the catalyst remained unchanged. The catalyst was simply used by the other entities to do their work. *Moses leading the ancient Israelites to the promised land but never being allowed to set foot in it,* she thought. *He caused the change but would not experience the change.* So she wasn't surprised when later she checked the Bible citation from Deuteronomy 34:

1 And Moses went up from the plains of Moab unto the mountain of Nebo, to the top of Pisgah, that is over against Jericho. And the Lord shewed him all the land of Gilead, unto Dan,

2 And all Naphtali, and the land of Ephraim, and Manasseh, and all the land of Judah, unto the utmost sea,

3 And the south, and the plain of the valley of Jericho, the city of palm trees, unto Zoar.

4 And the LORD said unto him, This is the land which I sware unto Abraham, unto Isaac, and unto Jacob, saying, I will give it unto thy seed: I have caused thee to see it with thine eyes, but thou shalt not go over thither.

She re-created the image of the room in her mind, then viewed it from the opposite direction and reconfirmed what she had seen before. All the chalk lines radiated from the picture of her. She was somehow the very centre, the epicentre of all this—whatever this was.

That night sleep evaded her. Odd images of Decker and Harrison and the perverse shrine kept pummelling her like pop-ups on a computer screen.

At four in the morning she'd had enough. She got into her car and just drove—although she knew where she'd end up.

At dawn's light she was by the Vietnam Memorial in D.C., her hand touching the name of the father who had died in the swamps of the Mekong Delta, the father she'd never met. As the sun peeked over the horizon a single beam of light crossed the memorial, and she was able to read her father's dates—and realized that she was now exactly ten years to the day older than her father had been when bullets ripped through his body and pinned him to the thick mud of a South Asian river.

She allowed her fingers to trace his name and whispered, as she had so often done in the past, "Your little girl's in over her head, Dad. Way over her head."

An hour later she grabbed a coffee. *Crap, at a place that should have been called D.C.'s Worst*, she thought and made her way to Mallory's office. She badged her way through security and was met by Emerson, who seemed as fresh as someone who'd had ten hours of sleep. Maybe he'd had ten hours of sleep.

"You look—"

"Fresh? Yes I do. You, on the other hand, look like a somewhat worn dishrag."

"Thanks."

"An attractive dishrag who's in trouble."

"Why's that?"

"Because I found it."

"It?"

"You'll see."

"Enough. Where's the meeting?"

"This way, Your Highness."

As they walked, Yslan noted that government buildings were built like warrens—hives. She shivered as she realized that they were built that way to defeat an invading force—modern castles.

Emerson opened a door and stepped aside for her to enter ahead of him.

She did and was greeted by a sight that surprised her. Overnight the techs of Homeland Security had recreated in exacting detail the room above Harrison's study and were just now adding the final touches. She turned to speak to Emerson, but Mallory was there.

"So what did you take?"

"Excuse me?"

"What did you take?" He grabbed her by her upper arm. His manicured nails bit into her flesh. He guided her to the shrine and pointed to the place on the pyramid of things that had formerly been occupied by the catalyst formula and the Bible citation. "There. Emerson says there had to be something there. What was there?"

"A picture."

"Of?"

"Me."

"And you took it?"

"Yes."

"Why?"

"It was lewd."

He stepped back to get a better look at her. "Lewd?"

"Yes. I don't know how he got it but it was . . ." She allowed her voice to trail off, and she shook her head. When she looked up, Mallory was staring at her. Then he turned to Emerson.

"Are you sure?"

Emerson walked up to the shrine and spent a long time looking at the objects there. It surprised Yslan that Mallory waited patiently—but waited for what? For Emerson to do what?

Emerson turned to Mallory and said, "It wasn't just a photograph."

Yslan stared at Emerson, who raised his shoulders. "It's a special talent of mine." Yslan thought, *Decker could tell when people were telling the truth, Viola Tripping could stand on the spot where someone had died and tell you what had been in his mind and Martin Armistaad could predict events based on the mathematical reality of pi. What is it that Emerson—*

Emerson said simply, "People called my grandmother a witch. I was with her when she died. I was six. She taught me how to see patterns—even in her crazy quilt."

Yslan vaguely remembered Decker talking about a thing that he called semblant order—was that what Emerson was talking about?

He was pointing at the pyramid again. "It looks random, where he put the objects, but there's a pattern—and a nude picture of you, however charming that might be, doesn't totally complete the pattern."

"So what does?" It was Mallory, and he was openly angry.

Yslan reached into her pocket and took out the photo, formula and Bible quotation side up.

Mallory called out, "Henderson." A classic tech raised his head. If there were still pocket protectors he would have had one, maybe two. He had a coffee stain on his wrinkled white shirt. The man left his task and his cup of Seattle's Best coffee on his table, then approached. "What do you make of this?"

Henderson glanced at it and quickly said, "Standard formulation for a catalyst, sir. Why?"

"No particular reason." Taking back the photo he said, "Thanks," in a manner that those with power are comfortable using to dismiss a subordinate—and Henderson ambled obediently away.

Mallory took out his BlackBerry and expertly navigated to a Bible search site, entered the citation, read the text and grunted.

Mallory turned to Yslan and stepped inside her personal space. "Explain. You have two minutes to explain why I shouldn't have you locked up for interfering with a federal investigation."

Yslan took the photo from Mallory, walked over to the shrine and put it where it belonged, then turned back to Mallory and Emerson. "Because somehow I'm part of all this—whatever 'this' is. And I don't mean just as an investigator or agent for the NSA—but part of all this. I've felt it for a long time."

"Since you met Mr. Roberts?"

"And before."

Mallory stepped forward and raised his voice. "That's enough— every nonessential out. Now. Out." And after a bit of scurrying the room was empty except for Yslan, Mallory, Emerson and the tech who had decoded the catalyst formula.

"Explain."

"I can't."

"Why?"

"Because I don't know why myself. But I believe it's true."

"The house was immaculate but this room was by comparison somehow chaotic. Why?"

Yslan thought, *Because the chaos allowed him to feel closer to the 'other.'* Instead, she said, "I have no idea. Maybe because he never thought anyone would find his hidden room."

Mallory looked at Emerson, who had a profoundly lost look on his face. "Makes no sense to me, sir. If there was a pattern then I'd have found something in the rest of the house that would have preambled this."

"Preambled?"

"Foreshadowed. Patterns always have predecessors—always. And there were those three sets of prints we found."

"Three?" Yslan asked.

"Yours, Harrison's, and an unidentified set."

"You've run—"

"Of course, and no hits."

"Were there any—"

"Dozens. Hair samples, clothing fibres, enough that whoever it was might have been up there for quite some time."

"How could that be?"

"I don't know."

It seemed clear to Yslan that Mallory had rarely, if ever, allowed those words out of his mouth.

The tech approached them, his coffee cup in his hand. Yslan grabbed it from him, hot coffee splashing his already coffee-stained shirt.

"Hey!"

"What the hell?" Mallory demanded.

"Something was snuck into Harrison's food, right?"

"That's about the extent of what forensics is willing to commit to."

"Yet, Harrison was a maniac for preparing his own food. He had a real thing about that."

"So?"

"Except for coffee—from Seattle's Best."

Mallory watched Yslan and Emerson leave, then turned to the tech. "Out."

The tech quickly left the room. Mallory allowed his eyes to trace the chalk lines to the four chalked numbers, then back to the shrine—just as he had done when he was in Harrison's hidden room all those months ago.

Well before anyone else had seen Harrison's creation, his world of wonders.

He'd arranged for Harrison to attend a conference in Malaysia, which gave him lots of time to follow up on the doings of one Leonard Harrison. That's when he'd found the man's family Bible—and chanced upon the hidden room that Special Agent Yslan Hicks thought she had been the first to discover. The third set of fingerprints were, of course, his.

He stepped into the midst of the reconstruction and stared at the photo of Yslan Hicks. "Find him, Special Agent Hicks—find number one."

SEATTLE'S BEST

THE SEATTLE'S BEST ON WISCONSIN AVENUE WAS THE NEAREST one to NSA head offices and looked pretty much like every other Seattle's Best. Yslan didn't enter, she just stood outside looking in the window.

"Waiting for something?" Emerson asked.

She had to get used to him being by her side.

"Yeah," she said, "till nine o'clock."

"It's almost—"

"But not exactly nine."

She waited for the digital clock behind the coffee bar to register 9:00. When it did she stepped into the coffee bar. The barista behind the counter was talking to his customer. "She'll ring you up." He took off his apron, and another young barista stepped out of the back room, smiled and approached the cash register.

Yslan watched the shuffle closely. Watched the coffee cup on the counter—and saw quite clearly that in the nine o'clock switch it would have been easy to reach over and lace Harrison's coffee with whatever it had been laced with.

The music changed from early James Taylor to something classical.

Yslan approached the cashier.

"Hi, what can I getcha?" the barista asked.

"Information," Yslan said, flashing her NSA ID.

"About what?"

"Do you usually work the nine o'clock shift on your own?"

"For now—until they replace Jason."

"Where's Jason?"

"Who knows. The guy up and quits and leaves me to deal with the crowds."

"When?"

"When what?"

"When did he quit?"

"Last Friday, and I really thought he liked working here. It's why we got the dumb classical music—for him."

"Not a fan?"

"Hell no, not me."

Yslan smiled. The barista smiled back.

After that it took Yslan only three minutes to get Jason's address, four to find out that a barista only makes $405 a week, five more to find that Jason had made a $500 deposit to his savings account last Friday. Fifteen minutes later she was standing outside his apartment door and signalling to the cops carrying the battering ram to use the damned thing.

The door gave with a nasty screech and Yslan found herself in a small apartment that clearly belonged to classical musicians. A string quartet was playing on the iPod dock, two music stands were set up with scores opened and annotated. There were posters of classical music concerts on the walls.

Jason's two roommates made some noises about warrants, police brutality and Nazis but shut up when Yslan told them that they could go, that they should go, that it was only Jason who she wanted to talk to.

Once his roommates were gone, Jason looked around wildly. He wore an old pair of pleated and cuffed Dockers and a large cardigan sweater that failed to hide his bulk. A long strand of hair fell across his eyes, and the cello bow in his right hand vibrated like a hummingbird's wings.

Yslan lowered her voice and said, "Five hundred dollars isn't nearly enough to commit a murder."

"Murder!"

"Yes, a murder, Jason." She heard the cops behind her shuffling, but she didn't care. Dead, catatonic—what's the difference? "So, who gave you the money?"

"He said it was just a sedative, to counteract the effect of the caffeine. That the guy was his partner and hadn't slept for days. That I'd save their marriage if I'd just put the powder in the coffee so he could sleep."

"And you believed him?"

"Yeah."

"Really? Why would you believe that?"

"Well, he's a musician like me."

"How do you know that?"

"He'd brought in his cello before. He showed it to me. It was incredible—an Andrea Amati."

"A what?"

"Some think it's the finest string instrument ever made. There are only three still extant," Emerson said.

She looked back at him. "And you know this why?"

"Because such things interest me."

Yslan shook her head and returned to Jason. "What about the five hundred dollars he gave you?"

"It was a surety."

"A what?"

"He promised me that if I put the powder in his guy's coffee that he'd let me have the Andrea Amati for a week. A whole week! But since he didn't have it with him that time he gave me five hundred dollars as a show of good faith."

"What's this guy's name?"

"I don't know."

"Can you describe him?"

"I can try."

Yslan turned to the cop who still had the battering ram in his hand and said, "Get a sketch artist in here, now."

There was a long moment of silence. Jason sat heavily on a straight-backed chair. The cello bow fell from his hand to the floor with a thin clatter.

"What happens now?" Jason asked.

"Now you talk to the sketch artist."

"And then?"

"You get yourself a lawyer because you're going to need one."

Down on the street, Yslan pulled out her BlackBerry.

"What now?" Emerson asked.

"That cello."

"The Andrea Amati?"

"Yeah, that one. It's rare, right?"

"Yeah."

"Get in the car." She looked at her BlackBerry and said, "Twenty-One Eighteen South Dakota Avenue. Go."

"What's there?"

"Maybe a place to start."

16

A MUSIC SHOP

THE SHOP DOOR HAD A SIGN STATING "APPOINTMENTS ARE RE-quired, please do not ring the doorbell" and gave a phone number.

Emerson leaned on the doorbell, and eventually a light came on inside the shop. Through the dust-covered front window the place looked like something from a Dickens novel. The man who eventually opened the door was also right from one of Mr. Dickens's extraordinary inventions. Since he was much closer to seven feet in height than six and could not have weighed 120 pounds, he probably would have had a name like Pennyfeather or Pifflewanger or the like, although he introduced himself as Theodore Ross. They introduced themselves then asked if he would answer a few questions.

"Okay but I'm afraid I've become just a teensy bit literal in my old age. I hope that's okay with you?"

Neither Yslan nor Emerson had any idea what that had to do with anything, so they launched right in. "Have you ever sold an Andrea Amati cello?"

"An Andrea Amati? Goodness gracious, no. And I don't know anyone who ever has."

"So you don't—"

"I've only seen an Andrea Amati in this shop once before."

"And when was that?"

"July third, 1994."

"And you remember that date why exactly?"

"Well, it was the only time I'd seen an Amati cello."

"So you said."

"That literalism I warned you about."

"Yes."

"And my wife died the very next day."

Yslan stared at this strange creature. Was he pulling their collective legs? But Emerson was unfazed and said, "I'm sorry to hear that. Do you happen to remember who brought you the Andrea Amati cello?"

"Certainly."

Yslan and Emerson waited for the details, but none were forthcoming. "So?" Yslan demanded.

"So what?" Theodore Ross asked, clearly lost.

"So," Yslan asked carefully, "can you describe the person who brought you the cello?"

Theodore Ross smiled, greatly relieved, and said, "Yes."

Yslan and Emerson waited—nothing. "Well, would you please?"

"Please what?"

"Describe the person who brought in the Andrea Amati cello."

"Oh, that. But I'm not good at describing—"

"Please try, it's important."

"There's an easier way—"

"Excuse me?"

He indicated an old poster behind them on the wall. It announced a classical string concert by a group called the Path. No other names appeared on the poster. The date was almost two years ago. The poster did have a small photo featuring the twelve musicians fronted by a conductor. Theodore Ross crossed to the poster, leaned down and put on a pair of glasses with Coke-bottle lenses. Then he pointed to the grey-haired man in the back row and said, "Him."

Within twenty minutes they had enlargements of the man's image sent to every Homeland and NSA office, and the most advanced facial recognition software in the world was parsing the image.

Jason ID'd the grey-haired man as the one who gave him the five hundred dollars.

An hour later Emerson and Yslan were in the office of the concert promoter who had staged the event where the Andrea Amati cellist had played.

17

MR. LEVINE

THE THIN BALDING MAN HAD DELICATE HANDS. HE'D CLEARLY earned every wrinkle on his seventy-plus-years face. He sat behind a huge desk. Yslan wondered if his feet touched the ground. She doubted they did.

A poster over his shoulder announced, "Nothing mars perfect beauty like missing a Levine concert."

"Thanks for seeing us, Mr. Levine."

"I was told that if I knew what was good for me I'd make time to see you."

"And that you'd cooperate with us?"

"Yeah, that too."

"That's good advice, Mr. Levine," Emerson said.

The man's face suddenly lightened—as if the clouds had cleared. "Call me Arnie, like the golfer."

"Okay, Arnie, who gave you such good advice?"

"A flutist who owes me some money, whose brother's wife's sister is a legal aid attorney."

Emerson nodded. Yslan produced a copy of the concert poster from Theodore Ross's shop and laid it out on the desk. "Arnie," Yslan said, "you promoted this concert."

"That's against the law? Since when?"

"It's not against the law, Arnie. Just take a look at the poster."

Arnie took a pair of wire-rimmed glasses from his desk and looked at the poster. Then he muttered, "Very smart, very smart." He took off the glasses and took out another pair that looked exactly the same, put them on, looked at the poster and said, "Ah." He noticed Yslan's inquiring look and said, "Silly me—I bought regular and reading glasses exact the same."

"Why? Was there a sale on frames?"

"There was one, but I missed it by a week. My kind of luck, if you know what I mean."

"Yeah, that kind of thing happens, Arnie."

"To others, seldom—to me, all the time."

"Yes. Arnie, can you take a look at the poster. Do you remember this group of musicians?"

Arnie leaned forward so that he was almost on top of the poster. Yslan wondered what good the glasses did if he had to be so close. Then Arnie smiled. "Yeah, I remember. They were great."

"How so?"

"They paid up front—great."

"Do you remember anything else about them?"

"The Path, they were called the Path—or at least that's what they called themselves then." He took off his reading glasses.

"Classical groups change their names?" Yslan asked as she rolled up the poster.

"All the time—helps them get away without paying the promoter."

"What?"

"Nothing—a joke, just a joke, jeez."

Yslan thought for a second then asked, "Why the Path? Why that name, do you think?"

"Classical groups need to sound, you know, hip."

The word "hip" sounded archaic coming from this man's mouth—archaic, white, fifties.

"Do you know where we can find the Path?"

"You fans?" Before Yslan or Emerson could reply, he continued, clearly happy that this was no more than fans wanting info. "Hard to find them in stores—ain't that many record stores left. Online I guess, if you're lucky. That's it? That's all you want to know? Thanks for coming—"

"No, Arnie, I mean find them. The actual musicians of the Path."

Arnie deflated. "Nope. Haven't got a clue how to find them."

"How do you communicate with them?"

"E-mail."

"We'll have to have our people look at your computer."

"Okay. Do I get a loaner? I'd love an iPad."

"No you don't."

"Hey! That's not fair; I'm cooperating here."

"Yes you are, but you're dealing with the federal government—and they're not always fair. Our guys are outside, they'll be right in."

Emerson and Yslan headed towards the door, where Yslan stopped and turned back to Arnie. "How do they pay you?" The little man's face crinkled into a smile. "Cash? They pay you in cash, Arnie?"

"A man has to make a living and classical music—"

"Isn't that popular anymore," Yslan completed his thought. "Do you happen to declare this cash to the IRS?"

The man smiled and shrugged. His narrow shoulders almost reached his ears as he said, "I'm such a small fish, who would notice?"

"I would, Mr. Levine," Yslan said.

"Now it's Mr. Levine. Was Arnie before, but now it's Mr. Levine."

"Right," Yslan said, "So, Mr. Levine, maybe we can help you keep your secret."

"That would be good, since I'm cooperating. And you're a nice person." Then as if it were a revelation he announced, "Hey, I'm a nice person—"

"Yes." Yslan returned to the desk and spread out the poster again. "Put on your reading glasses, Mr. Levine." He did. Yslan pointed to the man holding the Andrea Amati cello. "Tell me everything you know about this man."

"The Freak?"

"Why do you call him that?"

"Because he looks like a freak—so the Freak."

"You wouldn't happen to know how we can find the Freak?"

"No idea where to find WJ."

"WJ?"

"Yeah, that's all I've ever known him as—WJ. He comes, gives me the cash, plays the concert, then poof—gone."

"What does WJ stand for?"

"For WJ I guess."

Yslan stared at Arnie for a moment, then picked up the poster, turned and headed towards the door, where she said to the waiting techs, "He wants a loaner for his computer."

They all—except Arnie Levine—had a good laugh about that.

"Very funny. You folks are really a hoot. Yessiree bob."

Something about the slurring of the s in "yessiree" made Yslan turn back.

Arnie smiled at her, a big sarcastic smile. "A real pleasure doing business with you people," he said.

She hadn't noticed that he was missing a front tooth before.

"Now get your ass outta my office."

"Sure, Arnie. But, you know, you ought to get that tooth replaced. That space in the front of your mouth mars your perfect beauty."

"Will do, officer, just lend me the twenty-five hundred buckos."

"Twenty-five hundred dollars?"

"Front teeth—they have to screw in. Twenty-five hundred buckos."

Back on the street, Arnie Levine's phrase "twenty-five hundred buckos" kept going round and round Yslan's head. She walked right past their parked car.

"Hey! Car's back here."

"Yeah I know that, but—"

"But what?"

"I don't know what—but it's something." *Twenty-five hundred buckos*, she thought, *twenty-five hundred buckos*.

Yslan awoke with a start and switched on the bedside light. She grabbed her BlackBerry and quickly found the prison photos of Martin Armistaad taken three days before his escape, two of which had him smiling a big tooth-filled smile. Then she called up the video of her interview with him. She fast-forwarded to the one moment Martin Armistaad smiled at her, and there it was—he was missing a front tooth.

She grabbed the phone and called Emerson.

"What?" he answered, his voice deep with sleep.

"We're going to Leavenworth."

"Why?"

"Because a new front tooth costs twenty-five hundred buckos."

18

TEETH

THE PRISON DENTIST MADE THEM WAIT. YSLAN TOOK THE TIME TO check up at the office. There was a note that they were having trouble contacting Viola Tripping. Yslan tried Sora's private line—there was no connection. Not no signal—no connection.

The elderly inmate who acted as a receptionist approached them and said, "The doctor will see you now."

To Yslan the prison dentist looked more like a well-fed country vet than a DDS, although he had all the arrogance of a head of surgery at a big city hospital. "Look here, I'm an educated man—"

Yslan cut him short. "There's no patient confidentiality between a dentist and a patient—especially a federal prisoner patient—if that's where you are going with this."

"I'll need a lawyer to confirm that," the large man said.

Yslan was about to respond when she felt Emerson's hand on her shoulder. He whispered, "A word?"

Yslan turned to the dentist and said, "We'll be back in a minute. Give me your cell phone."

"Why?"

"I don't want you making calls while we're out there." The man reluctantly handed over his cell phone, and Yslan stepped out into the hall. Emerson was leaning against the wall as relaxed as if he were on a street corner in the West Village. "Well?"

"He learns that we are here to see him."

"Yes?"

"He makes it difficult for us to get an appointment, busy and all that."

"He has patients."

"Convicts don't have busy schedules. They can be rescheduled; what else have they got to do?"

"Okay."

"Then he doesn't show up when he's supposed to meet us."

"Yes."

"Then when we find him—"

"He's not thrilled."

"Then he is about to claim dentist-patient confidentiality."

"Then wants a lawyer. Think he has something to hide?"

"I think he has a twenty-five-hundred-bucko secret."

"Get Homeland to access his bank account."

"Already done."

"And?"

"Two weeks before Martin Armistaad disappeared, one day before his tooth implant, the good DDS deposited ten thousand dollars in a three-year certificate of deposit at his local credit union."

Without knocking they crashed back into the DDS's office and handcuffed him to his dental chair. The man began to shout for help, but his cries were drowned out by the sound of the old-fashioned drill that Emerson operated with a foot pedal.

The man's eyes grew huge as Emerson approached him with the spinning, chipped thing.

"Okay, okay!" he shouted.

Emerson took his foot off the pedal. The drill whined as it slowed—as if it were upset that it didn't have the chance to grind into something.

"Good," Yslan said. "Where did the money come from to pay for the tooth you implanted in Martin Armistaad's mouth?"

"Who?"

Yslan shook her head, and Emerson started up the drill.

"Yeah, yeah, Armistaad, I remember him."

The drill whined to a stop.

"Good," Yslan said. "Now, where did the twenty-five hundred dollars come from?"

"Twenty-five hundred dollars?"

"Yes, the cost to implant a front tooth."

"Is that how much it costs?"

Yslan looked at Emerson. "Are you as tired of this as I am?"

"Yep."

Yslan stepped back and said, "Well then."

Emerson hit the pedal hard. The drill seemed thrilled to be back in business.

"Okay, okay!" the dentist screamed.

"I repeat myself: Where did the money come from?"

"There was no return address. Not even a postmark. Just a note with a request to implant the tooth and ten thousand dollars."

The drill once again whined to a halt, clearly upset that it wouldn't be cutting into enamel—or perhaps gum tissue, if it was lucky—today.

"Who sent you the cheque?"

"No cheque."

"No cheque?"

"Just cash and the tooth."

There was a pause. Yslan looked at Emerson, then the two of them looked at the dentist. "You were sent the tooth?"

"Yes, and a note that said, 'Use this tooth and make it fit tight.'"

"Why that particular tooth?"

"I have no idea."

Emerson asked, "And did it fit?"

"Well no, not well, but I made it fit—tight."

"By shaving down the tooth?"

"No. The note was specific. The tooth was not to be meddled with. So I trimmed the teeth on either side—quite a lot, actually."

"That must have hurt."

"Well yes, but Mr. Armistaad got an expensive new tooth."

"Do you still have the note?"

"It's in a safe deposit box."

"Key."

He indicated a set of keys on a small table. Emerson slid the entire key ring into his pocket, turned and headed out.

"Hey!" the dentist called out, rattling the handcuffs.

"Oh, yeah," Yslan said. "When you prove to me that you've given that ten thousand dollars to charity I'll send the key to the warden—and, by the by, I think your employment here is now formally terminated."

"How am I supposed to send the money to charity while I'm handcuffed to this chair?"

"Hey," Yslan said, "you're an educated man—figure it out."

As she caught up to Emerson she said, "Jason gave us the Amati cello; the Amati cello gave us the Path; the Path gave us the name WJ; Arnie's smile gave us teeth—"

"Careful. It's two different cases, isn't it? What do Armistaad's tooth and Harrison's poisoning have to do with each other?"

She nodded agreement, but she didn't agree.

She didn't agree because she'd seen the numbers in chalk in Harrison's secret room. Armistaad is number 4 and he's in the wind. Viola Tripping is number 3—and now no one answers her phone.

An hour later she was on the phone with Mallory. "Any answer from Sora, Viola's caregiver?"

"No."

"Have you been able to find the farm?"

"You folks at the NSA hid it even from yourselves."

"I know. It was part of our deal with her."

"Swell."

"How's Harrison?" she asked. The phone line momentarily went silent. "Sir?"

"Yeah," Mallory eventually answered.

"So how is he?"

"Who knows?"

"The doctors should know!"

"They're completely stumped—his tox report is gobbledegook. They're at a complete loss as to what happened to him."

"Well we know what happened; the barista put something into his coffee."

"Yes, Special Agent Hicks, we know that, but the barista doesn't know what it was and neither do we. All we know is that Harrison is in a living vegetative state."

The horror of that sat between two of them. Finally, Mallory spoke. "He's in his own world now, and the doctors don't think he's coming back to ours."

Or he's on his own path, Yslan thought, then without saying another word, she closed her cell phone.

Yslan slumped onto the sagging bed in her motel room. She was so tired of cheap motel rooms, but that's all the federal government was willing to cough up for.

She flipped on her cell phone and quickly went through the pictures she'd taken in Harrison's hidden room till she got to the one that showed the back of the nude photo.

She glanced at the catalyst formula and the Bible citation yet again, then went through the photos of the hidden room slowly, one at a time.

Clearly Harrison had found something about the Gifted that she hadn't found. Some knowledge that she didn't have. What he no doubt thought would lead to the End Times—when he would get to see his brother again.

She went through it again—chalk lines to Martin Armistaad and Decker and Viola, then arrows pointing to her in the Junction. Then there was the question mark beside the number 1. Someone she hadn't discovered. Not one of her Gifted.

The question mark clearly indicated that Harrison didn't know this person's identity either.

If Harrison was right, then when all of them followed the chalk arrows and met up in the Junction—with her as the catalyst—something momentous would happen. Something that Harrison wanted to be part of. Something important enough—no, personal enough—that Harrison kept it secret from the agency, from everyone. Everyone except whoever owned the mysterious third set of prints in the hidden room.

Her phone rang. "Hicks."

"We finally got something from his computer."

"Harrison's?"

"Who else?"

"What did you get?"

"A repeated visiting of a website."

"Which one?"

"The synaesthetes'."

"Yes, of course, we've known about that for—"

"He was corresponding through the website."

Yslan was on her feet. "With whom?"

"We don't know."

"Well, what the fuck *do* you know?"

Back in Hendrick H. Mallory's office, the tech looked over his shoulder. His boss stood very still.

"The password he used to correspond through the synaesthetes' website."

Yslan let out a sigh. "Great. What's his password?"

The head of Homeland Security nodded to the technician, who said into the phone, "The number sign, then the numeral one, then an equals sign, then the name Seth. His password is #1=Seth."

She hung up.

So did the tech, who looked to Mallory. "Something else, sir?"

"No, that's enough for now." When the tech was gone, Mallory said aloud, "That should prick the sides of her intent."

Yslan immediately called Ted Knight. "It's Yslan."

"What time is—"

"Who cares? Send me the tapes we made at the safe house in New Jersey."

"Of the Toronto cop?"

"Yeah."

"When?"

"Now. Send them fucking now."

Ten minutes later they arrived on her BlackBerry. She played back her first interrogation:

"A bloody murderer named Decker Roberts formerly of the Glencairn district of North Toronto."

"Want to tell me about you and Mr. Roberts?'

"Nah—I think I'd prefer not to."

"Do you know where he is now?"

"No—but if you undo these cuffs I'll find him."

"Pretty sure of yourself, aren't you?"

"I'm more than able to track down a felon, yes."

"You didn't track him down, you tracked down his son."

"Seth."

"Yes, Seth Roberts."

"So you found the boy and waited for the father to show up. Did you case the place?"

Yslan clearly remembered him nodding in response to that question.

"What did you find?"

"A charlatan, big-assed fake! I mean dream healing—"

"You mean the guy who ran it was a charlatan?"

"Who else?"

"Name?"

"Couldn't find a real name. Couldn't find dick-all about him, really. Strange that. All I ever got was initials for him . . ."

When, five minutes later, she played it for Emerson, he demanded, "And you didn't ask about the initials?"

"No, I was stuck on his claim that Roberts was a murderer."

"That was—"

"Dumb, I know."

Emerson looked at her closely, then said, "You've changed since you met that Decker guy. You'd never have missed that before."

"Yeah, I guess," she said.

"It's not a guess," he said.

"We can still catch the late flight."

"To?"

"Seaside, Florida—so I can ask about those initials."

19

SEASIDE, FLORIDA

FORMER TORONTO HOMICIDE DETECTIVE GARRETH LAURENCE SEnior was wearing only a pair of ill-fitting Bermuda shorts as he stared through the screen door of his Seaside, Florida, porch at Yslan and Emerson.

"What's the pretty boy?" he growled.

Emerson stepped forward and extended a hand to open the screen door.

"I really wouldn't do that. Florida has a stand your ground law, and you'd be best to think that I not only have a weapon but know how to use it." His words were a bit slurred.

"A little early to be drinking, don't you think?" Yslan said.

"Not aware that my alcohol consumption was of any interest to the American government."

"It's not," Yslan said, "but we have other concerns."

"Hey, why not just drug me and haul me off to some safe house and beat the crap out of me?"

"You were never beaten, sir."

"Quibble, quibble, quibble."

"Can we come in? Open the door, please."

"Once you answer my question."

"Which was?"

"What's the pretty boy?"

"Emerson Remi," Emerson said.

"Not his name. I couldn't care less what he claims his name is—it would be just lies anyway. I want to know 'what' he is."

"I don't—"

"Is he muscle? Muscle's never that pretty. What is he?"

Yslan took a breath, then said, "His name is Emerson Remi, he works for Homeland Security."

"Oooow—bloody Homeland Security—now I'm afeared, I am." Garreth's native Scottish accent was reemerging.

"Open the door or we can get a court order. We know you're a Canadian living in this country without proper documentation." It was a minor technicality, but she was anxious not to involve the local authorities, even the local NSA office.

Garreth paused for a moment, then flipped the latch, turned and retreated into the house's interior.

Emerson and Yslan followed him.

Yslan had been in the homes of many a drinker—her grandfather had a serious habit—and they all had certain things in common. A staleness, a casual approach to cleanliness and an air of things falling apart. Even though much of the furniture was new, it didn't really fit together, and comfort rather than style seemed to rule all the choices. The La-Z-Boy couch was a classic—as were the ring stains on side tables and couch arms.

Garreth was pouring himself a drink. Bourbon. "My neighbours taught me to put sugar in it—which I like," he said, adding a heaping teaspoon to the amber liquid in his juice glass. "They also encouraged me to add a sprig of mint, but I couldn't manage that without thinking there should be a tiny umbrella and a cookie—so I passed on the mint." He took a long pull on his drink. "Come to apologize, lass, or are you going to drug me and—"

"We need some information, Mr. Laurence."

"Sure, always happy to help the federal constabulary for a price."

"You want money?" Emerson demanded.

Garreth did a full turn, his arms wide. "Does it look like I need money?"

It looks like you need a good cleaner is what it looks like, Yslan thought, but she said, "What price?"

"Decker Roberts, the child murderer. Decker Roberts."

Yslan wanted to say, He's no child murderer, then explain about him being left-handed, but instead she said, "When we find him, I'll inform you."

"Are you saying you don't know where he is?"

"We know he's in Africa."

"Then for the love of Christ get a plane and haul his fucking ass back here."

That one she could agree to, so she said, "I will."

"Good. Bring him here, then I'll answer your questions."

"No," Emerson said. His "no" left no ground for contradiction. "Answer our questions, Mr. Laurence. And answer them now."

"That sounds like a threat."

"It is," Emerson said, then in rapid succession he knocked the drink from Garreth's grasp with his left hand and broke the man's nose with his right.

Yslan was as shocked as Garreth—she'd never seen Emerson do anything like that.

From his knees, his hand over his face, blood dripping between his fingers, Garreth said, "Pretty muscle, who woulda thought." Emerson took a step towards the man and Garreth said, "Make me a drink, then I'll answer your questions."

Emerson moved to the counter and poured three fingers of fine bourbon into a glass that smelled of fermenting orange juice.

Garreth had struggled to his feet and sat heavily on a chair at his dining room table. The blood had slowed to a trickle. His nose was quickly swelling and now had a sharp crook to the right that had not been there before.

Emerson held out the drink and Garreth took it. After one long swallow he reached up and felt his nose—then yanked it to the left, then sharply down.

Yslan heard the scrape of cartilage and was amazed that Garreth didn't even wince.

Garreth put a finger on one nostril then blew hard. A wad of mucus and blood splatted to the dark hardwood floor. Garreth nodded and said, "Good. Just a broken nose—no sinus damage."

"San Francisco," she said. Her voice was hard as honed steel.

Garreth looked up at her. His eyes were blackening. "Nice city. They have a homeless problem."

"You were there."

"No kidding. That's where your people drugged and kidnapped me."

"What were you doing there?"

"Waiting for Decker Roberts to come and claim his kid."

"Seth?"

"Yeah, that's his name."

"And you cased that place?"

"The Wellness Dream Clinic? Can you believe that nonsense?"

"Yeah, that place. You cased it?"

"Yeah, sure." He made air quotes with his fingers as he added, "Cased it."

"What did you learn about it?"

"It was a sham! Dream Wellness, what crap!"

"What else?"

"The patients weren't even patients, neither were the help. They all arrived at six in the morning and left at ten at night."

"Why?"

"They were actors or something."

"Actors?"

"Look up an ad in the *San Francisco Chronicle* for a TV show called *The Institution*. They were auditioned then hired to play parts."

"By whom?"

"The grey-haired freak who ran the show."

Yslan tensed. She took out the blowup of the members of the Path. "One of these people?"

Garreth pointed an unsteady finger at the tall grey-haired cellist.

"Name?"

"Is that what this is all about?"

"Name. Just give us his name."

"Give me the murderer Roberts and I'll give you the freak's name."

"He's not a murderer—"

"Wrong, lady!"

"Right, you old drunk. When you found five-year-old Decker Roberts, was there blood?"

"A regular ton of the stuff."

"And where was the blood?"

"On the boy's right hand. It was covered in it."

"His right hand?"

"Right again, lady."

"Well Decker's left-handed."

"What?"

"He's left-handed. Has always been left-handed. So how the hell could he have ended up with blood on his right hand? More to the point, even if he was right-handed, he was only a little boy. A five-year-old kid! How could he have been strong enough to kill that girl, with a garden trowel, in his wrong hand under the weight of all that snow? Isn't it more likely that he took the garden trowel from her and tried to dig their way out? Isn't that a more likely scenario? You're a cop, or at least you were a cop. And according to your records, a darned good one before you met Decker

Roberts. So isn't what I just said the probable truth? He took the trowel from the girl, he tried to dig their way out and he cut her somehow. Isn't that probably what happened?"

Garreth sat very still for a long time then muttered, "Probably."

"What's the man's name in the photo, Detective Laurence?"

"The grey-haired freak?"

"Yes, him."

"WJ something or other."

"WJ what?"

"I'm not a cop anymore, so I don't have access to the resources, you know what I mean?"

"Not exactly."

"I copied all the data from his computer—"

"From this WJ guy's computer?"

"Who the fuck we been talking about?"

"You still have it?"

"Hey!" he said, standing unsteadily. "I'm still a copper—still a copper."

Shortly he produced a USB key. "Here," he said. But his voice was little more than a whisper. He turned and walked away from them towards the bourbon bottle. As he did it seemed to Yslan that he got smaller and smaller—till there seemed to be little left of Garreth Laurence Senior.

Emerson plugged the key into his laptop and shipped the data off to Mallory.

Outside Garreth Laurence Senior's $650,000 two-bedroom house, Emerson looked at his iPhone. "It was the computer that was corresponding with Harrison through the synaesthetes' website."

Yslan nodded and said, "Maybe this WJ didn't like a competitor."

"A competitor for what?"

Yslan ignored Emerson's question. She wasn't going to get into that with him. "We can assume that WJ poisoned Harrison—maybe to get him out of the way—and we know that he has Seth, who Harrison, from his password, evidently believes is number one."

Spartacus, Yslan thought—*fucking Spartacus.* She stood in the early morning heat, turned her right palm upwards, then slammed it into her forehead and swore, "*Spartacus!*"

"What about *Spartacus?*"

Yslan looked at him, but she wasn't going to tell him that she was being flooded by the images on her tape of one of Decker's acting lessons. The lesson stood out because it was the only time Decker ever mentioned another acting system than his own. And it was one of the few times that Decker actually cracked himself up as he talked to the actors in his class. The image of him giggling uncontrollably made her smile.

He was explaining the origin of the presentational method of acting that had for some time dominated Canadian stages and had stopped Canadian actors from making major inroads into the American film and TV industries. Some of that presentational act-ing grew out of the Delsarte acting system, which was a classic of its kind. It postulated that there were an exact number of human emotions and that each one was represented by one and only one specific gesture.

Yslan remembered laughing aloud as she watched Decker il-lustrate some of them. Then he had added, "But the system hasn't really died. If you've ever seen the movie *Spartacus,* Olivier uses one of the classic gestures when he is told that the upstart Sparta-cus leading the revolt was the same man he saw refuse to kill the black gladiator in the forum. When he receives this information he takes his right hand, turns it palm up, then slams it into his fore-head—the Delsarte gesture for the emotion of "I am astounded.""

"I repeat," Emerson said, "what about *Spartacus?*"

"It was right in front of us all this time—right in front of us. We find Seth, we find the guy who poisoned Harrison—WJ. Get us on the next flight to San Francisco."

Emerson stopped and turned back to Garreth Senior's house. "And what about him?"

"A month," Yslan said.

"Till what?"

"He ends it. Believing Decker Roberts killed that girl gave him the excuse he needed to not fall off the face of the earth. Now he has no excuse."

"Hence a month?"

She glanced at the house and was pleased that she didn't hear a gunshot, although she knew it would not be all that long before Detective Garreth Laurence Senior took the bullet train. Then an odd thought struck her: *Garreth Laurence Senior was just another person hurt by his contact with one of her Gifted.*

20

HENDRICK H. MALLORY AND HARRISON'S
WORLD OF WONDERS

HENDRICK H. MALLORY, HEAD OF HOMELAND SECURITY, LOCKED the door to his office. Out the window the lights of D.C. blinked and bobbed in the humid heat of the night. He turned on what he called "my snooper" and waited for the electronic all clear.

It dinged and he crossed to his printer and pressed the decrypt code.

Emerson Remi's latest report slid onto the tray. He admired his manicured fingernails as he picked it up. He read it quickly. *So they're on their way to California. It's about time,* he thought, *although that's fine, it gives number four enough of a head start. They all have to get to the Junction at the same time, damn it!* He put Emerson's missive to one side and turned to the far wall, whose twelve foot by sixteen foot surface was covered by a blowup of the interior of Leonard Harrison's secret room. What he thought of as Harrison's world of wonders. For the hundredth time his eyes sought out the numbers on the photo that he'd taken well before Special Agent Yslan Hicks "found" the secret room. He chuckled as he thought of Hicks chasing after the third set of prints up there. He had long ago had all his prints removed from the data banks.

From his techs' deciphering of Harrison's searches on the synaesthetes' website, he knew who the numbers represented.

Number 4 was Martin Armistaad, whose release from Leavenworth he effected with remarkably little effort, complete with tracking tooth. Number 3 was Viola Tripping, whom he first saw at Ancaster College shortly after the bombing and who now was hidden somewhere in the American Plains States. Number 2 was Decker Roberts, who he knew was a long way from the Junction, somewhere in southwest Africa.

He went to his desk and opened a bottom drawer, then unlocked the safe that was secreted there. He pulled out a large file, some of whose folders went back forty years to when he first began to suspect that there were others who sensed the world—the other world—more deeply than he did. He'd gone through the normal routes to find the "other," the religious routes—the Catholicism of his birth, studies in the Tibetan Book of the Dead (the bardo idea dominated his thinking for years), the Kabbalah—but he eventually came to the conclusion that all religious systems sensed something out there but none had even an inkling how to access "the other."

It was his Introduction to Botany class at the University of Chicago of all things that opened his eyes to another possible access point. His elderly professor claimed to be a synaesthete. He memorized large sections of ancient texts through his sense of touch. He claimed that different sounds induced different feelings in his body. The man's condition didn't interest Mallory, but a phrase he used certainty did: "Nature always seeks a balance. When it takes away something it always—always—supplies something else in its place."

He'd raised his hand and in that huge lecture hall asked, "Do you consider your synaesthesia a gift?"

"I do," the old man had replied.

"Well, where is the ungift?" he'd asked.

There were titters in the class, but the professor ignored them and asked, "Can you explain yourself more clearly?"

"Yes I can. If nature always seeks balance and you have been given a gift, doesn't that mean that someone else has to have something taken from him?"

The old professor had done a little Texas two-step and metaphoric tap on his head, then moved on without answering his question.

But it had begun Mallory's search, and now as he spread out the files on his desk of the forty-seven individuals throughout history that he'd identified as having a "gift," he reached into another drawer and withdrew a much larger folder—those who had the matching "ungift." Nature's balancing act was often incredibly cruel.

He flared out the files like two large fans, one above the other, then lifted his eyes to Harrison's world of wonders. He knew that his seeking of the Gifted had proved yet again the cruelty of nature's response.

He stood and approached the world of wonders.

It was number 1 that he concentrated on—up in the sky by the blood-red star in the body of Scorpio.

He was a Scorpio both by birth and inclination, but he knew number 1 was not him. He knew who number 1 was. As Harrison's password so elegantly pointed out: #1=Seth. Yes, but where in this wide world was Seth? And what exactly would happen when all four and the catalyst—Hicks—were together in the Junction, as Harrison's world of wonders indicated?

He glanced out the window a second time and dismissed what he saw out there: the cars, the people, the city—dismissed it all as nothing more than illusion. He pulled Leonard Harrison's Bible out of his desk drawer.

The spine of the old book creaked as he opened it. He found the sound reassuring, he found the heft of the book exactly right and the phrase—end of days—so perfect.

"End of days," he said aloud to the empty space. He looked

back at the blowup on the wall and concentrated for a moment on the shrine in the centre. A shrine to a catalyst.

He pressed a button on his desk and a large LED screen with a map of the United States slowly lowered from the ceiling. He centred his cursor on the end of the faint dotted line and zoomed in three times. As he did, the line on the map added another dot—it was now a straight line of dots moving into deepest, darkest rural Nebraska. "Number four seeking number three," he said aloud. "I knew it. I knew you could find her. Now get her."

He smiled.

Sending Martin Armistaad that newspaper clipping showing Viola Tripping in sunglasses in the rain waiting to enter the church after the bombing at Ancaster College had, he was sure, set the man on his path.

He had no doubt that once Armistaad found Ms. Tripping they would head to the Junction—just as Harrison's masterpiece indicated.

In the still darkness he allowed his mind to wonder.

To be done with it all—to have it all, all done. The end of days—a future devoutly to be wished, one he had longed for since he was a boy sitting in the silence of the cold church waiting, always waiting. Now he knew what he was waiting for.

And Special Agent Hicks was on her way to San Francisco—where she'd find Seth's drawing, just as he'd done right after Harrison left and Detective Garreth Laurence Senior was removed from the Wellness Dream Clinic. And she won't be able to decipher the clues Seth left behind any better than he could, so she'd have to seek out the help of the boy's father. So off she'd go to get the father, number 2, and together following Seth's clues they'd find the boy, number 1. Then they all would head, as Harrison's masterpiece indicated, to the Junction, where Viola Tripping, number 3, and Martin Armistaad, number 4, would shortly join them. Then with all four there—with their catalyst—it will happen. The end of days.

He called up an overlay on the North America map. This one had pi-diameter arcs in both miles and kilometres using Leavenworth as one locus and Harrison's secret room as the other. And sure enough, the points at the crossing of the arcs produced a straight line to the west end of Toronto—to the Junction.

He went to pick up the Bible and found that it was open to a section of Corinthians. For a moment he held his breath, then read where his finger had landed: "For now we see through a glass, darkly."

He closed the book and left the room. All that night he lay awake hoping, praying, that when this was all, all over, he would not be on the dark side of the glass—looking in.

21

DECKER WATCHES PIE KIDS

DECKER WATCHED THE TWO YOUNG BOYS IN THE PICNIC AREA BE-
hind the bakery hide their pieces of apple pie beneath the table.
Their parents were busily perusing a map. *We're at the junction
of Highways One and Six,* he thought; *not that many choices from
here. West to the coast, east to the Kalahari, north to Angola, south
to . . .* Decker didn't know what was south of Solitaire, but he
didn't really care. Whatever was to the south couldn't be more
interesting than the two pieces of pie the boys held beneath the
table.

The older boy, maybe eight or nine, smiled at the younger boy,
maybe six or seven. Conspirators "R" Us.

Decker knew that Stanislavski, the famous Russian acting
teacher, often went to the beaches of the Black Sea to watch chil-
dren play. He claimed that it revived his soul, renewed his faith in
the species.

The boys allowed their paper plates to fall to the ground. Another quick smile between them.

"Wasn't that great pie, boys?" the mother asked rhetorically.
"Anyone need to use the restroom before we go?" she asked, this
time not rhetorically.

The boys shook their heads and hid their smiles.

"Chat nicely with Charles while I'm in the loo."

So it's Charles, Decker thought. *Both boys look like their mom and not even a little like Charles. So is this guy their mom's boyfriend or stepfather, or is it just one of those families that allowed their kids to address their parents by their first names?*

Then he saw the gleam in the boys' eyes. *Boyfriend for sure,* he thought.

"What are you two scamps up to?" Charles demanded harshly.

Then the older boy tapped the table twice and the boys attacked. Apple pie was the weapon, Charles's face the target, revenge the motive.

And Decker saw it as pure. No hesitation, no tentativeness—in acting terms, no swing—just pure intent.

Decker smiled. A little pie wash was good for the soul, for all concerned.

But suddenly images of his own son as a boy flooded him, and Seth's voice, as if he were shouting in his ear, crying, "You're happy Mommy's gone. You are!"

"No Seth—"

"Don't lie. I can always tell when people are lying or telling the truth. Always."

Decker held his hands to his ears to try to stop Seth's voice. Then he felt someone staring at him.

He knew he was sliding and couldn't stop it.

It was Trish Spence, back in the Junction. She was yelling at him: "Decker, call home! Fuck, I need your help with this. Canada's Public Broadcaster is being a pill about the hanging boy in our documentary. Remember our documentary—*At the Junction* that we've been working on for two years? Remember? We got a renewal for six more episodes—remember? At any rate, for some fucking reason they are insisting that we cut the hanging boy. And I can't figure out why. So wherever the fuck you are, pick up the damned phone and call home!"

• • •

Trish pocketed her iPhone and opened the door to her three-bedroom condo on College Street. She'd never been a great housekeeper, but the stacks of newspapers everywhere and the pots balanced precariously on every table were now completely out of control.

"When did this start?" she asked the massive accumulation of clutter.

22

WJ AND SETH

WJ FINGERED THE ANDREA AMATI CELLO'S STRINGS AND ONCE again sensed the deep magic within the ancient instrument. And once again understood that he didn't really know that magic. He could sense it but could never really know it, be part of it, soar with it.

Movement on the flat-screen TV on the wall drew his eyes. The young man manacled to the gurney was awakening.

WJ knew he was already miles deep in felony land—fraud for the Wellness Dream Clinic, and then there was kidnapping of the kid and, of course, the permanent sedation of his rival, the NSA guy. All from following a casual comment from that dumb shrink. That comment led him to start the Wellness Dream Clinic, that led him to the old synaesthete, that led him to the website, that led him to the monk video.

He'd hired IT expert after IT expert—spent a fortune. At one time he had twenty-two experts working around the clock, but no one could trace the origin of the video. No one that is until he sought out one of the original hackers he'd bailed out of jail. A strange slender man who was nearly twice the age of any of the other IT experts—and he wore overalls, had a thick beard and thicker glasses. Petronius Chumley, PhD. He looked like a tall, thin version of George R. R. Martin. In less than twenty minutes he'd found not only the origin of the video but the young monk's name: Seth Roberts.

Until then he'd felt he wasn't living his life, just passing through it. All his life he'd waited for his life to begin. But now—now he had hope. He had Seth Roberts.

He tapped his fingers on the broad body of the ancient cello, and it seemed to echo the hollowness of his life.

He rosined his bow and put a Yo-Yo Ma recording on his Transrotor Artus turntable and carefully lowered the needle.

Bach's Cello Suite, Number One filled his room, pouring from his six speakers like honey from a jug.

He opened the sheet music and followed along, marvelling at how Mr. Ma found so much more than just the notes—the arithmetic—of the music. How the man found the secrets buried in the music, the magic.

He lifted the arm from the record, placed his bow on the strings of the Amati cello. His mind played back exactly what he had heard Yo-Yo Ma play, then his fingers and bow duplicated it—perfectly.

But even as he approached the midpoint of the first movement, disgust was rising in him. He wasn't playing music. He was aping the music that someone else had discovered. He was nothing more than a mimic—a joke to any real artist. Worst of all, he knew he was a joke.

He remembered when, five years ago, he couldn't bear it any longer and tried to "solve" the problem by seeking professional help. That's when he'd met the shrink who'd set him on this path.

"What does WJ stand for?" was the first question Dr. Crasni had asked him.

"For me," he'd answered. "What does your name stand for?"

The doctor did a very good impression of a smile, then said, "What I mean is, what do the initials WJ stand for?"

"They don't stand for anything. They're me. I'm WJ, simple as that."

"Fine." Dr. Crasni adjusted his butt in his chair and crossed his legs at the ankle. "So, what's your family name, WJ?"

"My name, my whole name is WJ, okay? Got that?"

"Got it."

"Good. Now can we move on?"

"Sure. So WJ, what brings you to my office today?"

Without hesitation WJ replied, "I think most other people feel the world more deeply than I do."

Dr. Crasni did his best to hide his surprise at the statement, then asked, "And why do you think that?"

"Because I hardly feel anything about anything."

WJ watched as Dr. Crasni shelved his initial plan of attack and decided for a bit of history, which WJ supplied: thirty-eight, single, never married, parents both in advanced stages of Alzheimer's in an expensive home up in Marin County—which he paid for—head of the North West Aggressive Hedge Fund, lived in the very heart of San Francisco for seven years, played the cello in a chamber ensemble.

"Are you good?"

"At what?"

"Playing the cello."

WJ shrugged. His long grey hair fell across his forehead, and he swept it back.

"Are you?"

"Some think I am."

"And you? What do you think?"

"I play metronomically; I never make mistakes."

"But it doesn't please you?" the doctor asked.

WJ shrugged again. He looked down at his tiny feet.

"Would you bring your cello to our next session?"

"If there is a next session, Doctor. I'm a busy man."

"And a lonely one?" Dr. Crasni ventured.

WJ's head shot up, and his eyes narrowed. "I assumed that you provided a service."

"I think that's a credible assumption."

"Then what does my loneliness or lack of loneliness have to do with this?"

"I have no idea. I just met you, WJ."

"But already you have surmised that I am lonely. I have people around me all the time. My bed is a regular Grand Central of the most desirable women in the Bay Area."

Dr. Crasni nodded for WJ to continue.

"That's it." WJ looked around wildly, as if he were caged.

"Do these people who surround you and populate your bed bring you any joy?"

"Not much."

After a longish pause the doctor asked, "Any? Do they bring you *any* joy?"

"No," he said. Then WJ blurted out, "I don't feel things the way other people do. I see them all around me, people stupider than myself who find real joy, feel real passion for things and people."

A silence followed.

Finally, Dr. Crasni said, "But you like music."

"Don't know how to answer that question."

"It wasn't a question."

"It should have been."

"Okay—maybe music's too close. What about films. Do you like the movies?"

"Some, if they're not too . . ." His voice petered out.

"Name me a film you liked. That you'd want to see a second time."

"*Company of Men.*"

The doctor stared at him. *Company of Men* was several years back—it was a deeply disturbing movie about a man who so completely couldn't feel that he caused chaos all around him in order to get close to the source of feeling, like a deaf person standing right in front of the loudspeakers at a rock concert. Abruptly WJ stood and headed to the door.

"Do you dream, WJ?"

"Why?"

"Sometimes our dreams are a portal to our feelings."

WJ lifted his bow from the strings.

That's where it had begun. A casual suggestion from a man WJ thought was a pretentious fool—that sometimes our dreams are portals to our feelings—began this voyage, set him on this path. He looked up at the image on the monitor and stared at Seth Roberts.

WJ rested his cello on the floor and mentally surveyed what he thought of as his "realm." Since the doctor's weird suggestion, for the first time in his life he had followed what others would call a whim. All his life his decisions had been rational—arithmetic—but they had led him to a sterile cul-de-sac, staring at forty with nothing ahead of him except more of the same, followed by a lonely death. A death before he had actually lived. At least that's how it had been until he followed the doctor's advice that had eventually led him to Seth—as a monk, in a video, touching glory.

He remembered seeing a French film, *La Femme Nikita.* In its opening scene, a fifty-year-old cop who thought he was happy with his life realized in a shocking moment that he had in fact been asleep all those years. A young murderess had inadvertently awakened him, and he began to act in a way WJ now called living.

WJ spun a full circle in his swivel chair, taking in each of the screens on the four walls of his room. He stopped and turned his chair slowly in the opposite direction—once again taking in each of the four screens. Four images of the monk Seth Roberts, slowly awakening.

WJ nodded, then said aloud, "If it all begins with dreaming, then let's start."

Seth didn't know if he was awake or dreaming. He knew he'd been under the influence of a strong sedative for some time—how long he had no idea. Evidently long enough to move him from the Wellness Dream Clinic.

This new place—his new room—had a single window high up in what looked like a dome. He closed his eyes and did what he used to do on Vancouver Island. He forced himself to be very still and allowed his brain to examine the air he inhaled.

It took a while, but slowly he began to collect information. Dry—the place was dry. So he wasn't in San Francisco any longer. And the air was cool, not cold. Cool and dry. He'd have to guess, but he assumed 14 or 15 degrees of Celsius.

Then he smelled the eucalyptus and the slightest tang of orange—so they'd moved him south. From the low temperature he assumed they must be near the moderating effects of the cold Pacific current. So probably south of Los Angeles.

He'd surfed down here at a place called Swami's near Encinitas, so he knew the south coast.

He hoped to hell they weren't in Mexico.

But then again, they could well be.

He wondered if it would be hard to get a sedated man across an international border.

He assumed that with enough money anything was possible.

He pulled hard on the handcuffs and leg restraints. They rattled against the metal sidings of the gurney.

Then he shouted, "What the fuck is going on?"

23

WJ—SETH AND DR. CHUMLEY

THE LIGHT FROM THE OPENING OF THE SMALL DOOR DREW SETH'S eyes. Then the light was obliterated as a man's silhouette filled the space. The man stepped into the room and went from silhouette to figure. He was wearing a white lab coat and had a stethoscope around his neck.

An unusually syrupy voice came from his almost perfectly circular face, but the words were spoken with a severe lisp. Seth thought the man said, "Ah, you've returned to the land of the living," but he couldn't be sure. Then the man flicked a wall switch and lights climbed the tall conical walls to the dome some forty feet above.

"Better?"—or did he say "setter" or "letter"? No, he asked if it was "better."

Better than what? Seth wondered.

"I asked you a question, young man." Seth's hearing was adjusting to the sounds coming from the man's mouth. "Impolite not to answer your elders. Impolite." The man's mouth was a tiny slit in the roundness of his face. Like one of those tropical fish that always seems to be kissing.

The mouth was doing that puckering thing again, but Seth had no idea what the man said. There, he was doing it again.

"Unlock these fucking handcuffs," Seth demanded.

"Language!"

That Seth heard clearly enough.

"Such language and from such a young man." The man's enunciation was suddenly perfect. "You were agitated and we didn't want you to hurt yourself in your sleep. Show me your hands."

Seth did and the man unlocked his cuffs. Seth went to rub his wrists, then noticed that the cuffs were well padded. *Someone didn't want me hurt,* he thought. *Then why did I go to rub my wrists? Because you've seen it a dozen times on TV.*

"I'm Doctor Petronius Chumley . . ." The man waited for Seth to supply his name in return. He didn't. "And you are Seth Roberts, the synaesthete, aren't you?"

Again Seth said nothing. He hadn't heard the term "synaesthete" for years—certainly not since he had handed over his father's twenty thousand dollars well over a month ago at the San Francisco Wellness Dream Clinic. "I'm not a synaesthete, I'm a bladder cancer patient."

"Really?" Dr. Chumley said. "Well, we have a profound interest in you as a synaesthete but not much, I'm afraid, in your run-of-the-mill bladder cancer. None, to be factual. Besides, it's advanced markedly since your arrival—in fact, a major tumour has entered your bladder wall. Not good that. Very dangerous—very."

"What do you want from me? Why have you moved me here? Where the hell am I?"

"It's all part of the wellness discipline."

As Dr. Chumley launched into a long sermon-like speech praising the practices of the Wellness Dream Clinic, WJ watched from his closed-circuit feed and smiled. He thought of Dr. Chumley as his Dulcolax—a softener.

Dr. Chumley entered WJ's viewing room. "Anything else, boss?"

WJ looked at the man and thought, *It's a shame he'll have to go, but a loose end is a loose end.* Then he said, "Sit, have a drink before you leave."

The good doctor poured what he thought was an aged single malt scotch and took a long sip.

WJ glanced at his wristwatch: 4:17. By 5:17 the man across the table from him would be unable to move, speak—or anything much else. "Good?" he asked.

"Excellent. Really excellent." He took a second sip, this one longer than the first.

WJ smiled and said, "Glad you approve. So Seth's ready for me?"

"As ready as an advanced cancer patient can be."

"And he has how long before—"

"I'm no medical doctor, but I assume not long unless you get him treatment."

WJ turned from Dr. Chumley and looked out the window at the brilliant Southern California sun and realized that it warmed other people, made them feel alive, made them feel glad to see the day and happy—and that it did nothing for him.

"Are you going to get him treatment?"

WJ didn't answer.

"Just asking, not my concern."

WJ tossed the man an envelope stuffed with hundred-dollar bills. "No, it's not. I assume that settles us."

Dr. Petronius Chumley riffled through the bills. "Generous. Very generous."

24

THE INSTITUTION—WJ AND SETH

WJ WATCHED DR. CHUMLEY LOSE HIS BALANCE AS HE WALKED TO-wards his car. Somehow he managed to get in and drive away in the direction of I-5.

Alone, WJ reviewed his situation one more time before he took the next huge step.

He couldn't continue to live this nonlife. He couldn't. So he'd take the leap.

He knew that most people thought that he was a mathematician, and he let them think that, but it wasn't true. What he was, was an arithmetician. At the heart of mathematics is an elegance—a "feel." He didn't have that. He was an arithmetician—a detail man.

Also a successful seducer. Long ago he'd used his arithmetic sense to break down the pickup into its component parts.

That's how he had looked at his initial attack on Seth Roberts back at the Wellness Dream Clinic in San Francisco—like a pickup in a bar. A very private, very special bar—for a very special pickup.

Step One: Can I stand near you? If you don't move away, then the answer is yes.

The boy had been eating—nibbling actually—at a vegetable

sandwich in the cafeteria, which WJ had stocked with actors who were paid to have lunch and not talk to anyone. It wouldn't be right for Seth to realize that he was the only patient in the institution.

There were actor patients, actor nurses and of course his paid doctors who asked the questions WJ wanted asked—and performed periodic cystoscopies to make sure that Seth felt he was actually getting medical care.

WJ entered with a tray of food—exactly what Seth had on his plate—and took a seat at the end of the long metal table. He chewed around the edges of his sandwich, removed the tomato, which he loathed, and looked up at Seth.

The boy's body canted away from WJ, but the boy didn't move—didn't get up and leave—so the answer was yes.

Step Two: Can I talk to you? If you talk back, the answer is yes.

"Food's better today," he said.
Seth nodded, then said, "Couldn't be much worse."

Step Three: Can I mention something a bit off-colour? If you don't object, then the answer is yes.

"This place sucks. It's not doing me any good," he said.
Again, Seth nodded. "I'm giving it time."

Step Four: Can I buy you a drink? If you accept, then the answer's yes.

"Can I get you a refill?" WJ said, pointing at Seth's empty Perrier bottle.

"Sure," Seth said and held out the bottle, wondering when he had started drinking Perrier. It was his father's favourite.

WJ almost touched his hand—if it were a pickup he would have—but this was way more important than any pickup, and the answer was yes.

WJ made his way to the front of the room, gave the counter person Seth's empty bottle and pointed towards him, then left.

Oh, yes, WJ had been pleased—pleased with how things were going and how easy it had been.

He'd used Craigslist to recruit people to populate his Wellness Dream Clinic. What they'd been told was that it was a reality television show called *The Institution. No experience required: Apply to the address above.*

Then he'd added this to his listing: *About the Show: Each actor will be assigned a role in the institution, some as orderlies, some as cooks, some as cleaners, some as patients. Each will be given a scenario, which they must follow faithfully. Every moment will be filmed by more than three hundred hidden cameras. Anyone acknowledging that he or she is playing a role—at any time—will immediately be taken off the show and forfeit the thousand-dollar payment. Please read the release below and sign it before applying.*

He'd been inundated with folks anxious for their fifteen minutes of fame. So he'd cast his show, then with the help of his hacker business associates lured its star—Seth Roberts—through his Gmail account.

From the first night in the San Francisco Wellness Dream Clinic, WJ took to watching Seth sleep, although the fact that the boy slept with his eyes open was disconcerting. And then there was all that rapid eye movement—the kid seemed to dream from the moment he fell asleep then on and on through the entire night.

But then his video cameras caught that cop breaking into the clinic, so he'd packed it up and moved Seth here to Southern California, to Carlsbad.

He played his copy of the video of Seth in the Duomo again

and marvelled, for the thousandth time, at the joy on the boy's face.

His Dulcolax had softened up the boy. It was time.

He picked up his Andrea Amati cello, then took a deep breath and said aloud, "It's now or never." Or had he just thought that? He didn't know.

WJ MEETS SETH

THE DOOR OF HIS ROOM OPENED, AND SETH SAW AN ODD SIGHT. The grey-haired man he'd met once in the cafeteria back in the Wellness Dream Clinic was there. He had an old cello in his hands.

"Seth Roberts?"

"Yeah. Who are you?"

"I'm your doctor, and in a way you're my doctor."

Seth immediately knew that both statements were true and untrue. It confused him.

WJ saw the confusion track across the boy's face. *Good*, he thought. He smiled. "Your treatments are going very well."

"Are they?"

"Yes, I'm very pleased."

Seth knew this was a truth—but wondered exactly what truth. "Where am I?"

"We're in Southern California, by the ocean." Seth nodded. "Did you figure that out?"

"Yeah."

"How?"

Seth ignored the question and asked one of his own. "I'm not here to be treated for my cancer, am I?"

WJ didn't say anything.

"I'm not being treated for anything, am I? This is all some kind of bad joke."

"No it's not, of that I'm sure."

Seth looked at the grey-haired man. The man wasn't lying, but he wasn't telling the truth either. More confusion.

The man opened a laptop and turned it to Seth. With a few keystrokes he brought up a shot of Leonard Harrison. "Ever met him?"

"No. Who is he?"

"Now? That's a good question."

"What does that mean? I've had enough of this, so if—"

"You're Decker Roberts' son, aren't you?"

That surprised Seth. He hadn't filled out anything that would identify him as Decker's son. In fact, he didn't mention who his father was to anyone—ever.

"Aren't you? No need to answer that, because I know you are. Where is he?"

"I don't know and I don't care."

"Okay."

WJ stepped back and looked at the young man—boy. His colour was not good, and he was clearly confused by what had happened to him.

"Did you have me handcuffed?"

"We had to move you here as part of your cure, and you're a very rough sleeper—you call out in your sleep and thrash about and seem to dream all night long. Do you know that you sleep with your eyes wide open? And they are in constant motion. REM sleep they call it. Deep dream sleep. So you see, padded cuffs were only there to keep you safe." Confusion once again registered across the boy's face. Clearly he wanted to believe that all this was for his health, and yet everything he saw or heard said that something else was going on.

"Look here." WJ called up a website—the synaesthetes' website. "Do you know what this website is?"

Seth stared at it. It was little more than a jumble of skittering lines and whorls.

"Is this another joke?"

If it is, WJ thought, *someone's going to pay big-time for the gag.*

WJ typed in the entry code he'd learned from the indigent synaesthete who'd first appeared at his Wellness Dream Clinic in San Francisco almost six months ago.

The screen went blank, then a runner appeared from left to right: *Welcome, fellow traveller.* WJ looked at Seth. "Are you a fellow traveller, Seth?"

"With whom?"

"What?"

"With whom would I be travelling?"

"This gentleman," WJ said, then selected a video that came up quickly. It was of the famous British synaesthete Daniel Tammet.

Seth watched intently. Every word this Mr. Tammet said was true. This guy evidently had learned Icelandic in less than a week and had recited pi out to more than 20,000 digits. Both immensely impressive feats, but as far as Seth was concerned, they had nothing to do with him.

"How's about this guy?" WJ said and selected another video. This one showed a middle-aged black man who was taken to the top of the Eiffel Tower and for ten minutes scanned the Paris cityscape. He was then locked in a circular room, where within twenty-four hours he painted in astounding detail the entirety of what he had seen in those ten minutes—right down to getting the colour of the window shades and the hanging laundry correct.

"Impressive, no?" WJ asked.

"That's hard to deny."

"What, that it's impressive?"

"Yeah, that," Seth snapped. "So what has this got to do with me?"

"Never been to this website, Seth?"

"No. Never."

"So you're not a synaesthete?"

"What's a synaesthete?"

WJ ignored the boy's question and pointed at his laptop, "Never seen this website? You're sure?"

"I told you I've never—"

"I need you to see one more video."

"Swell. Is there an NFB short before it?"

"NFB?"

"National Film Board of Canada. Socially relevant cartoons and boring birds are their specialities. The sex life of the tribreasted warbler was their big hit."

"Sounds fascinating."

"Yeah, your tax dollars at work."

"Your tax dollars—not mine."

"Right."

"Wanna see one last video on your site?"

"My—"

"Wanna see it or not?"

"Sure."

Using a remote he drew from his pocket, WJ turned off the lights in the room. They blinked off from ceiling to floor in a conical cascade.

Then he hit a single key on the laptop.

At first there was nothing—just darkness. Then the darkness gave way to a silhouette of a slender man dressed in what looked like a monk's robe with its hood up. He was walking away from the camera as he entered a very large, completely circular room.

The figure moved slowly—the word "glided" came to Seth—to the very centre of the large space. *The exact centre of the space,* Seth thought.

The figure, still with his back to the camera, stopped and seemed to find an utter stillness. Was he breathing?

Then he reached up and pulled back his cowl.

He shook his head, and his hair fell free, well down his back.

He rearranged his feet, then tilted his head back and sang a single note up into the dome.

He waited.

The echo of the note came down in loops, one note after another, each exactly the same.

He waited until all the sound had disappeared, then he tilted his head back again and sang the same note up to the dome.

Once again the note came down in loops.

But this time, before the sounds dissipated, he sang a second note—a third above the first—then quickly followed with a third note a fifth above the first note.

Then he opened his arms wide and full chords of music looped down to him.

Again he waited for all the sound to dissipate.

Once he had complete silence, his back tensed. He turned his head towards the dome and sang eight distinct notes at two-second intervals. And the chords came down. The first a diminished seventh, the second a minor fifth.

The young man spread his arms, accepting the loops of music as one accepts a gentle rain in the desert, a moth's breath.

He bent his knees and leapt into the air—then, somehow, buoyed by the echoing chords, he stayed some six feet above the ground.

The chords began to mesh, forming more and more complex chords and, as they did . . .

Seth pointed at the screen.

The young monk had inverted in the air—his head towards the floor—and spread his arms wide. He began to spin slowly. And as he did, the young monk's face finally came into view, and on that face were etched moments of glory. That face with glory so deeply imprinted on it clearly belonged to Seth Roberts—cancer patient, master dreamer.

WJ snapped the computer off.

Seth felt a surge of longing deep in himself, as if his heart were being pulled forcibly from his chest, as if his true soul's mate had been wrenched from his arms.

WJ positioned the cello between his knees and quickly rosined the bow. "You like music."

"Says who?" Seth felt himself somehow falling.

"Me. Says me." He locked eyes with the boy.

"I'm sick."

"Yes. Yes, you are. But you're gifted, too. You're my point of access."

"To what?"

WJ didn't answer the question. Instead, he hit a button on his remote and all four walls and the ceiling began to glow.

Seth stared at them. They were massive LED screens. Seth slid off the gurney and stood. "What the—"

"Look down."

Seth did. The floor was a screen too, and as he looked an image formed under his feet. He was standing on ancient paving stones. "Now look up," the grey-haired man commanded. Seth did. The walls were somehow curved into a tall cylinder, and the ceiling was a perfect dome.

"Here's your first note," WJ said, playing a B flat. "Now sing that."

And to Seth's surprise a perfect B flat flew from his mouth up to the ceiling and then its echo descended. But before it got to him, WJ played another note and commanded, "Sing that."

"You don't know what you're doing!"

"Sing that!"

And Seth did.

Then a third.

The echo of the notes surrounded him in a pure chord, and he felt a huge smile cross his face. He stopped resisting, raised his arms, and lifted off the ground.

Instantly he was in his favourite dream, gliding out of the clearing, moving towards the glass house. But even as he saw the figure in the doorway—the figure whose face he'd never been close enough to see—open the door for him, he felt himself sucked from one dream reality to another.

Sliding—sliding in his dream.

Without a whoosh or any sense of motion he found himself in a large, solemn interior space.

Seth stared at the black painted canvases on the walls—fourteen huge paintings—and although he'd never been there before, he knew where he was: one of the accesses to the forest—a portal—the Rothko Chapel in Houston, Texas.

Then he saw him, standing alone in a corner, crying. And he knew it was Mark Rothko—the artist who created the panels that occupied every wall. He had committed suicide shortly after the completion of his masterpiece.

A hand landed on his shoulder, and without looking he knew it was his father's.

"I thought this was a portal," Decker said.

"Someone's forcing things. It's not ready. Not everything's in place."

"What do you—"

"You said you thought this was a portal."

"Yes."

"*Was* is the operative word."

"Now what is it?"

"A cul-de-sac, a dead end—just ask Mr. Rothko."

"But why are the portals—"

"Because they've forced us to the end. Almost everyone who can get to the clearing has already gotten there or is through the

forest and approaching it, so there's no reason left for the portals—no need for a way to get to the woods."

A cry of anguish turned their eyes to the artist.

The man raised his tearstained face and shrieked at them, "Is it
really art? I mean, is it really art that I do?" then he broke into a
cackle. From beneath a bench he withdrew an old record album,
slid it out of its cover and placed it on a turntable that had not existed five seconds before.

Bob Dylan's "Highway 61 Revisited" came up and filled the
space.

Decker recalled a documentary on Dylan where one of the
talking heads had said something like, "It's as if God blew in his
ass and out of his mouth came poetry." *No,* he thought, *out of his
mouth came truth.* He looked at his son.

"You aren't—"

"Surprised? No, Father, I'm a much better dream traveller than
you."

"I just heard the lions and—"

"And here you are."

"You speak as if—"

"I'm the father and you are the son?"

"Yes."

"We've met in dreams before, Father, but you don't remember
them. I do. I remember all my dreams—I always have. I've seen
the glass house, and you don't even realize that you're in the
clearing. Do you remember the last time we met in dreams?"

"Why are you being kind to me? You haven't been kind to
me—"

"It's a dream, Father. When did we last meet in dreams?"

"The temple at Epidaurus?"

"Yes, the dream temple. I was covered in a bloody skin—on a
raised platform."

"I remember."

"Another cul-de-sac. No doubt it's closed now, too. Listen to the music. Remind you of anything, Father? Come on, you're Bible-read. And of course you love early Dylan. And where exactly is Solitaire?"

"At the junction of Highways Six and One."

"Right. Come on, put two and two together. Find the fucking semblant order here."

The words flew from Decker's mouth: "Come on, Abe, now kill me a son."

"Right, Father—and the next important line?"

"Where do you want this killing done?"

"And the last?"

"Down on Highway Sixty-One."

An angry cry drew their eyes. Rothko was screaming at the huge triptych on the west wall. Then his screams were drowned out by the roar of fire.

"What . . ."

"I'm surprised it took them so long," Seth said.

"Took who?"

"The believers."

"But why would—"

"Because if this is a path, then only one of two things can be true. Either there are more paths than they subscribe to, or their path is wrong."

The benches in the centre of the Rothko Chapel burst into flame as all fourteen paintings exploded into rectangles of fire.

Rothko slumped to the floor and held his head in his hands.

"Why aren't—"

"—we able to feel the heat, Father?"

"Yes, that."

"Because we are not really here."

"Is this really happening, Seth?"

"A foolish question."

"Why?"

"Because this is a dream; besides, "really" is a child's word. And only a child uses it, because an adult knows that real is a totally relative idea. What's real to you need not be real to me—in fact, it's unlikely that it's real to me. Like that scalpel in your hand."

Decker looked down and was shocked to see a surgical blade in his palm.

Seth held up his hands. Where his baby fingers should have been there were only bloody stumps.

"Tell me what to do," Decker demanded.

"Help me."

"Anything. I want to help you. I need to help you."

"You will. Before we get to the end, I have a battle to fight. And I'll need your help."

"Tell me how."

"Are you waking dreaming yet?"

"Like this?"

"Yes, like this."

"Sometimes."

"No good. Can you waking dream on command?"

"No."

"Then figure out how, dammit."

"Okay."

"When I need you I'll find you there, in a waking dream. Now pick up the scalpel, Father."

Decker hadn't realized that he'd dropped it. He reached down and picked up the thing. He held it out to Seth, who took Decker's right hand and put it against his own heart, then with his right hand grabbed his father's left hand, his knife hand, and plunged the blade hilt-deep into his own chest.

Blood covered Decker's right hand.

"Seth."

"Don't cry, Father, we are not really even here."

Decker stumbled back and looked past Seth. Two giraffes were outlined against the rising sun, and a herd of oryx were moving slowly to the east.

Linwood came up behind him and put a huge hand on his shoulder.

"Did you see—"

"What you saw? No. But I felt the shift."

"The sliding, you mean," Decker said, suddenly calm.

"Sliding? Yes, why not call it sliding. It's worlds trying to align themselves. The one I see and the one you just came from. And the place of meeting—the junction—is always complicated."

26

THE SLIDING—NEBRASKA

LINWOOD WAS NOT THE ONLY ONE WHO FELT THE SLIDING OF worlds.

In the Nebraska cornfield in which he had slept, Martin Armistaad felt the movement and knew his time to act was short. He took a long piss, painting a seven-foot-high cornstalk with his urine. Then, after a grateful sigh, he began to work on a dangling piece of barbed wire fencing. Back and forth, back and forth until the heat came and the wire broke free in his hand. He headed towards the farmhouse where his pi-generated calculation told him Viola Tripping had to be.

The sliding literally threw Viola from her bed. But when she hit the floor, she made no effort to rise. She skittered like a crab across the coarse floorboards of the farmhouse to the corner, pressed her tiny body against the walls and allowed her thoughts to splay out across the landscape. She sensed him out there, moving towards her like a monitor lizard after an injured fawn.

Sora came in and saw Viola on the floor. She'd seen Viola agitated, but never like this. "Viola."

"Shh! He's coming."

"Who is—"

Then Viola was crying.

"Why are you—"

"Because, dear Sora, you will—"

She never got out the word "die" because Martin Armistaad's barbed wire garrote slipped around Sora's neck. The woman struggled and managed to land an elbow to Martin Armistaad's face. Martin spit a tooth to the floor, then applied real pressure. The wire bit and cut so deeply that her head fell to her shoulder.

Viola did not move or cry out.

Martin Armistaad tossed his blooded garrote wire aside, cleaned his hands on his pants and spat another tooth to the floor. But he wasn't concerned about his teeth. He turned to Viola. "You feel it?"

"Of course."

"Do you know who I am?"

"Not by name. But yes, I know you are of the clearing."

"As are you."

Viola nodded.

"Do you know the way to the glass house?"

"No, I only saw the path once."

"When we were together?"

She nodded.

Armistaad crossed the room to her and held out his hand.

Viola didn't take it.

"Only together can we find the glass house—isn't that true?"

Viola got to her feet. "You are the enemy."

"Perhaps."

"You are the enemy of the clearing."

"Again, I say perhaps. But for sure, you are stuck in the clearing as I am. Only together can we find the glass house."

Viola knew it was true, had known it for a long time. She was stuck in the clearing and could not find the glass house by herself. She'd hoped that Decker Roberts could lead her out of the clearing to the house. That's why she'd agreed to help after the bombing at Ancaster College, but he didn't seem even to know that he was in the clearing.

At least this man knew that. She watched him as he knelt down and picked up his teeth. One he tossed aside. The other he pocketed. Seeing her questioning look he smiled, a gap-toothed smile, and said, "Damned thing hurt like hell to put in my mouth, so I'm keeping it." Then he grabbed Viola by the hair and dragged her towards the door.

"Where are you taking me?"

"Away. Away from here."

"But where?"

"A portal. Don't we need a portal to get to the clearing then the glass house?"

She freed herself from his grip and said, "Yes, but they're closing, can't you feel that?"

"Yes, I feel that—all of us from the clearing feel that." He thought for a second and then said, "Then we go to where the two worlds meet, the source—the one portal that never closes."

She nodded, freed herself from his grip, then headed towards her bedroom.

"Where do you think you're going?"

"To get a shawl. I hear it's cold up there."

27

THE SLIDING—MARINA AND HER FRIENDS

AS MARINA FELT THE SLIDING SHE PULLED A SWEATER OVER HER head. She now knew that it was finally time to begin, so she said to her father, "It's our turn."

Eddie sighed deeply—*Fourteen years old and still with the imaginary friends*, he thought. Then he corrected himself: *Fourteen and on her own path. But at least we are together here on Indian Road—in the Junction.*

He allowed his mind to drift to his friend Decker and wondered where exactly he was. He hadn't seen him since their brief time in San Francisco when he'd saved him from that cop. Of course he'd also removed the hidden transponder he'd placed in Decker's copy of that odd little play *Love and Pain and the Dwarf in the Garden*, so that, as he had so cleverly put it, *Now, Decker, you're finally really on your own.*

He thought back to Decker in high school—what a snot—then to Decker finding him homeless on Yonge Street and offering him a place to live, then to Sarah, Decker's wife, whom he had nursed through her final torturous months on this plane.

"It's our turn," Marina said again.

"So it's your turn now, is it?" he asked the empty air.

"No, *our* turn," Marina said.

Eddie turned from his computer to the door of his study, and there stood Marina, gangly and blond. To her left was a grossly fat young man with the clear facial markings of Down syndrome, while to her right was a tall thin boy, maybe eighteen or nineteen, whose head moved in a constant figure-eight pattern as his feet tapped on the hardwood floor. His eyes were closed. All three held hands.

"And who are—"

"Friends, Dada. These are my friends."

He smiled. "Your friends are always welcome here, Marina."

Then she said the oddest thing, "Of course—because it's our turn."

"Your turn for what, Marina?"

Instantly he was sorry that he'd asked. She was retreating, her shoulders turned in, her head down. "Sorry, Marina. Daddy's sorry, sweetie. Of course it's your turn."

"Sad," she said.

Carefully Eddie asked, "Why, Marina? Why is it sad?"

"Because, all that you in your heart of hearts believe is true . . . is all not true, Father."

Eddie didn't know what to say. He'd never heard Marina put together a sentence anywhere near as cogent as this one, nor had he any idea what she meant—and, oh yes, it was the first time ever that she'd called him Father.

28

DREAM CRASH

WJ WATCHED AS SETH LITERALLY FELL FROM THE SKY AND LANDED with a hard thud on the LED floor.

The boy's eyes snapped open—and he smiled.

"What?" WJ demanded.

"Nothing. Nothing the likes of you would ever be able to understand."

"Is that so? You underestimate me."

WJ stood. The boy watched him closely. Then without saying another word, the grey-haired freak flipped off the lights. In the total darkness the thunk of the deadbolt sliding to had an ominous sound.

But Seth didn't care. The battle lines were drawn—and now he had to prepare. Besides, darkness had always been his ally.

29

YSLAN ON THE WAY TO SAN FRANCISCO

ON THE PLANE TO SAN FRANCISCO, YSLAN CALLED UP THE SYN-
aesthetes' website and was quickly greeted with the pop-up videos of Daniel Tammet learning Icelandic in less than a week and
the Human Camera painting the Paris skyline from memory. She
waited for a prompt to use Harrison's private password, which the
forensic guy had given her. She waited for several minutes, but
there was no prompt, just random lines and swirls crisscrossing
the screen. She closed the website and called it up a second time.
She closed down the two pop-ups when they came up. But she
still couldn't find a box to enter Harrison's password. In frustration
she closed the website.

She looked out the window at the clouds over the Rocky Moun-
tains. She saw them swirl and crouch as they obscured her vision
of the peaks. She watched them closely, her mind automatically
trying to find a pattern, but there was none—at least no pattern
that she could discern.

She thought about that—no pattern that she could discern.
But that didn't mean that there wasn't a pattern—only that she
couldn't find it.

After a moment's hesitation, she tapped Emerson on the shoulder.

He leaned across her to see the screen, his body way too close
to hers. "At your service, Mistress."

"Cut it out."

She pulled up the synaesthetes' website for the third time and once again quickly closed down both of the pop-ups. "Can you see a pattern on the screen?"

Emerson watched closely for almost a full minute, then said, "The pop-ups didn't just blink out—they both vacated the screen to the lower right-hand corner. Move the cursor there."

She did and hit enter.

Nothing.

Emerson pulled the computer over to his tray and watched the patterns moving on the screen. As he watched he slowly pieced together the formations that the zipping and zapping lines were making. "They come from all directions, but they all cross—sometimes after exotic patterns—at a point on the left side of the screen," he said.

She watched closely to be sure that he was right. He moved her cursor to that spot and hit enter. A dialogue box came up: *Welcome Fellow Traveller. If You're One of Us You'll Know What to Do.*

Then the box disappeared. Yslan was lost.

"Patterns sometimes have two nodes. Usually in diametric opposition to each other," Emerson said.

Yslan took back the computer and watched the lines continue their seemingly random patterns on the screen. She placed her cursor where she had before and after hitting enter got the same message. But she wasn't looking at the message. She was looking at the place on the screen the dialogue box had come up. She moved her cursor to the exact opposite position on the right part of the screen and hit enter. An empty dialogue box came up, then the instruction *Enter your private code. If you make a mistake you won't be able to access the site for a calendar month—so type carefully.*

"What a team we are," Emerson said.

Yslan ignored him and typed *#1=Seth* into the box, then waited.

Another dialogue box popped open dead centre: *It's been too long since your last visit—supply your second identifier to enter the site.*

Yslan pulled her fingers away from the keyboard.

"Did the techs give you a second password for Harrison?"

Yslan shook her head.

A digital clock appeared in the dialogue box and began to count down from twenty.

When the counter hit three Yslan typed *end of days*—and waited.

Nothing.

Then the entire screen seemed to do a backflip. When it re-oriented, a video came up slowly: a monk—singing notes into a domed ceiling—chords coming down—him rising—turning upside down—spinning in midair. And as he turned Yslan finally saw his face, and blanched. It was Decker Roberts' son, Seth—number 1 by the blood-red star in the thorax of Scorpio.

30

LINWOOD AND DECKER—CONVERSATIONS

IT HAD BECOME A NIGHTLY THING.

As the sun set and Decker finished the last of the pies, he left the small kitchen and headed towards the stack of tire rims. Beside it was the compressed air hose, which he used to wash the dust from his hands. He then removed his clothing and cleaned the rest of his body with the compressed air.

Several of the African workers had taken to smoking and applauding him as if he were disrobing for their entertainment. Even from the start it didn't bother him because as he felt the air push against his skin he was watching the sun set over the desert and hearing the movement of the lions waking for the nightly hunt. To the west in the hills he sensed the leopards rousing and stretching, the bat-eared foxes slinking from their caverns and the oryx moving carefully as the sunlight, their greatest protector, sank below the horizon.

He'd put on the clothes that Linwood had given him. They hung off his body like Spanish moss on an ancient oak.

But he didn't care.

He'd had a day of several hundred kowtows, and with each— each pie—he somehow felt lighter.

He didn't remember eating.

In the first days he had eaten some of the pies he made, but that quickly stopped. The smell of apples never sickened him, but it no longer attracted him either.

As the last red strokes of the day shot skyward in a farewell to the living, Linwood would enter his tiny room, and without a word they would leave and begin to walk—at night, without protection, without a weapon—amongst the beasts of the desert. But they were never approached. Even the wild dogs seemed to know to give Linwood a wide berth. As they walked, Decker often heard the dogs' muffled coughing in the brush and always saw their eyes, red rimmed and piercing, watching—always watching.

Some nights he and Linwood sat on the petrified logs by the dry riverbed, other nights on the red boulders that were stacked against the rise to the west. Some nights they didn't stop anywhere and simply walked till the dawn.

Decker couldn't remember when he'd last slept—or felt tired for that matter. He'd broached the subject with Linwood, but all he ever got back from the big man was, "If you're tired you should sleep."

"But I'm not tired. I'm never tired."

"Then surely it would be foolish to sleep." Decker had nodded. Then Linwood surprised him. "But you've learned that you don't have to sleep in order to dream."

He'd never thought of it that way, but yes, he'd been dreaming while awake for some time now.

So he nodded. Linwood kicked at the ground, and a puff of the vast desert rose to his knees. He said, "Some call it the bardo; it's just being inside the forest."

When he'd asked him to elaborate, he got the usual response from Linwood; "Silly questions don't deserve answers."

That night, though, Linwood didn't speak for several hours, and they walked miles to the north. Finally they saw the brimming of dawn and Linwood turned to him. "So, when Eve ate the apple, what happened?"

Decker almost fell on his face. Linwood had never even indicated that he knew the basics of religion before.

"So what happened when she bit into that apple?"

"There was no Adam or Eve."

"Of course there was no Adam or Eve. They're a metaphor—the whole book's a metaphor. A metaphor to help us understand where and what we are. So what were the Bible writers telling us happened when Eve bit into that apple?"

Decker hesitated.

"There was a before the apple and after the apple," Linwood prompted.

"Time," Decker said. "There was no time before Eve bit into the apple."

Linwood nodded. The man never smiled, but this particular nod seemed to be approving.

"And with the beginning of time what else comes into existence?"

"Death," Decker said.

Again that approving nod, then Linwood said, "And with the arrival of death, what else was born?"

It took Decker a moment to figure it out. "Ego. Your death versus my death. Time leads to death. Death leads to ego."

"Right. That's why they chose an apple—a thing in two identical halves perfectly joined into one thing, complete in and of itself. Then it is bitten into—and it is separated from its wholeness. Just as you and I are separated by ego—yourself versus myself." He hesitated, then said, "But you have felt the healing of that rift in your time here." Then he said the most extraordinary thing: "You love music but are not even remotely musical yourself. You can't carry a tune. You have almost no sense of rhythm. You are separated from it—or you were till you started working here. But now you could harmonize without thinking about it."

He sang a single lovely bass note, and before Decker knew it he'd sung a perfect third above it. Linwood stopped and sang a note two steps above Decker's note, and Decker immediately responded with the tonic. And so they sang in the rising of the sun over the African desert and welcomed the day.

The next night Linwood surprised him with another bit of knowledge—or insight, or bias. "Do you believe in miracles?"

"No."

"Really?"

"No. Nor angels for that matter."

"Do you know why you don't believe in miracles?"

"Because they don't exist."

"No, because you mistake the entire idea of miracles."

"And how do I do that?"

"You think they have to do with doing good."

"And they don't? Miracles aren't about good being done?"

Linwood asked, "Do you know your World War Two history?"

"A bit."

"What would you say was the most world-changing thing that happened in the Second World War?"

"The Holocaust, the bomb, the slaughter of twenty million Russians?"

To each of Decker's statements Linwood shook his head. "No. Not even close."

"Then what?"

"The bombs to doves in Croatia."

"What?"

Linwood continued to walk. Neither his pace nor the tone of his voice changed.

"The Allied forces were moving north through Serbia fighting against the Croatians, who were as committed Nazis as the Germans. Well, the Allies had encircled them inside a medieval fort. When they had sealed off all the exits, they ordered in the bombers—and they came and they dropped their bombs. And in the full view of hundreds of Allied soldiers, those bombs turned to doves. There were hundreds of reports—maybe thousands of them—but all were suppressed."

"Why would someone suppress—"

"Because those Croatian soldiers were as vicious and savage a group of racist assholes as have ever existed." Decker had never heard Linwood swear, and it threw him off balance. "So how could a miracle happen to save such evil men?"

"I don't know."

"Yes, you do."

After a pause Decker said, "Because miracles have nothing to do with the doing of good?"

"Yes, that is not their purpose."

"Then what is?"

"To remind us that there is an other out there. Neither good nor bad—just an other, he or she or it just is. Like winter after autumn, just a fact, neither good nor bad. It's a mistake every religion makes. They assume the 'other' keeps score, that if you gain enough points you get a reward. And of course only they know what's a credit and what's a demerit. As if they had a rule book— the only rule book! Folly! Ignorant, self-righteous folly."

A cloud moved at that moment, and the full brilliance of a desert moon illuminated the craggy realities of Linwood's face. Suddenly it hit Decker.

"You were there. You saw it."

As if on cue, the cloud reasserted itself. Decker was not able to see whether Linwood's face betrayed what Decker knew to be the truth.

"Are you of the clearing?" Decker asked.

Linwood moved away, and the shadows seemed to follow him.

"Are you a friend of the clearing?" Decker persisted.

Linwood nodded slowly.

"But not *of* the clearing?"

The big man slowly turned to Decker. "They also serve who only stand and wait."

"So you know your Milton."

"Who?"

"Nothing. But you aren't of the clearing?"

"Sadly not *of* the clearing."

"But you know of the clearing?"

"Everyone who breathes knows of the clearing. People who call themselves religious sense its existence but are not even in the forest, let alone in the clearing. But the clearing draws them. The aggressive atheists call it 'the religious gene.'"

"I'm not religious."

"As you've said, but you sensed the existence of the clearing."

"I didn't."

"Yes you did, you just wouldn't allow yourself to believe in it." It took a moment for Decker to digest that, but before he could reply Linwood continued. "It's the real promised land, but some of us only get to see it from across the Jordan." Linwood looked more closely at Decker. "The Jordan?"

"Not a river, a metaphor."

"Right. Enough talk, let's walk."

And so they did—till the sun rose and brought the desert back to life.

It never occurred to Decker to truth-tell Linwood. He knew beyond knowing that the large man always spoke the truth, or at least the truth as he understood it.

One night they stopped in the midst of a dry riverbed and Linwood slowly turned and turned in the light of the full moon. When he finally ceased his circling he stooped and picked up a large handful of dusty river sand and slowly cascaded it onto Decker's head and shoulders.

It was only after the sand stopped that Decker realized that he was kneeling in the riverbed—at the feet of the large white man who called himself Linwood.

"You asked me if I was of the clearing."

"Yes."

"I prepare those who enter the clearing to try to find the great glass house." He dropped more sand on Decker's head. To Decker it felt like cool river water washing away his old self.

Another night they sat on the great boulders and Linwood asked him, "So, do you know why you're here yet?"

"No."

"You are a very bad liar, Mr. Decker Roberts. A very bad liar indeed."

"I don't know why I'm here. If you do know, why don't you just tell me?"

Linwood shook his head. His lips did not move, but Decker clearly heard him say, "If I had to tell you then it wouldn't be your path, it would be mine."

For a moment Decker made himself believe that Linwood had spoken those words, but he had been watching the man's lips and they hadn't moved.

They did not share a single word more that night.

Two nights later, Decker didn't wait for Linwood to speak but shouted at the large man's back; "So? Why exactly am I here?"

To his surprise, Linwood turned slowly, almost elegantly, in the bright starlight and said simply, "To put an end to this old world and usher in the new one. But you know that you can't do that alone, don't you? Don't you!"

Decker felt his head nod without intending to.

"You know that you can't do that without the boy from the Junction. Where is the boy from the Junction?"

"I feel like an autistic child beside you."

"Neither true nor relevant. An autistic child is merely on a separate path."

"Than me?"

"You are the man from the Junction. You have found your path."

"To what?"

Linwood ignored the question. "Where is the boy from the Junction?"

"Why do you want to know that?"

"Because the man from the Junction must be together with the boy from the Junction."

"To do what?"

Linwood stared at Decker and finally said, "You know what."

"Tell me, dammit!"

Linwood sighed deeply. For a moment Decker almost saw the weight of time itself on the big man's shoulders. "We've already talked about this."

"When?"

"What happens when Eve bites the apple?"

"Time begins."

"And when time begins what else?"

"Death."

"And with death, ego—your death versus my death—and so our present nasty world."

Decker thought about that for a moment then asked, "So what happens when Seth and I are together?"

"You put a stop to it."

"To what?"

Linwood spread his huge arms and said, "To all this. You bring this nasty tired world to an end and begin the new one."

31

AT THE ARCHIVE

TRISH INVOLUNTARILY SHIVERED AS SHE CROSSED ANNETTE STREET in the Junction and climbed the library steps. She turned and looked back at the place where the gaslight had stood from which the boy with eight fingers, each nail painted black, had been hanged in 1902.

She entered the library and went to the basement, where Theo had told her to meet him. She opened the door to the Junction archives and didn't see him.

Then she heard him cough.

"That's nasty, Theo."

"Yeah, and then we die. Thanks for coming, Trish."

"Sure. You found something in this place? I thought you'd been through here a dozen times already and found nothing of interest."

"Yeah."

"So why'd you want me to meet you here?"

Theo hesitated, then stifled a cough.

"What?" Trish demanded.

"When are you meeting with that Public Broadcaster guy about the hanged boy?"

"Later today."

"Too bad."

"Why's it too bad?"

Theo hesitated again. This time he didn't bother stifling his cough.

"Come on, Theo, we've worked together on this doc for almost two years. No one knows more about the Junction than you. So what's up?"

Theo spat something dark into a handkerchief; its multiple stains showed that it had received such deposits before. He pocketed the filthy thing, then asked, "You ever gone to a place over and over again—thought you knew every twist and turn—then one day you go back to that same place and it's like you've never been there before? Everything's changed?"

"Are you talking about this archive?"

"Yeah. It's like I've never been here before—but I've been here over and over again."

"So what's changed?"

"Everything. Nothing's where I left it, and there seems to be all sorts of new stuff—stuff I've never seen before."

"Anything interesting?"

"I honestly couldn't tell you. I have to go through it all—from the beginning."

"Is that why you asked me to meet you here?"

Theo coughed, then spat, then said, "I'm not sure why I asked you here."

"Theo!"

"Okay, okay, I'm sorry. It's just that . . ."

"What?"

"Somehow it's all changed. Everything's changed."

For a moment, Trish felt that she should hug Theo, then she thought better of it, turned and left the dusty little man in the dusty room—by himself.

32

A CALL FROM OCEANSIDE, CALIFORNIA

AS YSLAN GOT OFF THE PLANE, HER PHONE RANG. "HICKS."

"Special Agent Yslan Hicks?"

"Yes, who's this?"

"Carpenter, from the Oceanside office. Do you hear an odd hum on the phone?"

"A bit. But I'm in an airport so—What is it, Carpenter?"

"Your guy back east—"

"Are you referring to Leonard Harrison, head of the NSA?"

"Yeah, sorry. I meant no disrespect."

"Can you get to it, Carpenter. Why are you calling?"

"We found a man slumped over the wheel of his car, lucky as hell he ran out of gas. Could've killed himself and a lot of other people."

"What about the man?"

"He's displaying the same symptoms as Mr. Harrison. Totally vegetative but nothing out of the usual on his tox report. Just in a permanent deep sleep like Mr. Harrison."

A thought leapt into Yslan's head: *Is he dreaming?* She asked, "Have you got an ID?"

"Dr. Petronius Chumley, PhD in computer science."

She relayed the information to Emerson, who punched it into

the Homeland Security database: "Convicted of computer crimes in 2006, released four years early."

"How long is the drive to Oceanside from here?"

"Six hours or twenty—depends on getting around L.A."

Yslan thought about it, then said, "Get us a car."

Emerson's phone rang, and he picked it up. "Is she with you?"

"If she was I wouldn't have answered. She's in the ladies' room."

Mallory stared at the map on his office wall showing him where exactly number 3, number 4 and the catalyst were. "*Pilgrim's Progress,*" he muttered.

"Excuse me, sir?"

"Nothing."

Emerson quickly explained about the call from Oceanside and ended with, "Do you want me to cancel this?"

"No. She'll suspect something. But be quick. Catch a flight— there're private airports all over Southern California, there has to be one near Oceanside. Take a damned plane, it can take hours to drive around Los Angeles."

33

A HANGED BOY

"YES, HIS FINGERNAILS WERE PAINTED BLACK AND HE WAS MISS-ing the baby finger off both hands," Trish said to the Public Broadcaster vice president. Over his shoulder she saw the CN Tower and wondered for the umpteenth time what the point of that thing was. Part of this city's obsession with being world class, she assumed. Whatever that was. She felt it was like previous governments' arts councils that backed new plays—as if money could provide the depth needed for art. Then of course to control the money they'd established a bureaucracy of the world's most unimpressive people. People who did not threaten the real power—the hidden power.

She watched the CPBC exec, a charter member of the "unimpressives," hit two buttons on his remote. The two flat-screens behind him came alive with a reality series called *Hoarders*.

Trish blanched

The man smiled, then said, "Your first six episodes did okay, but in the new season, the hanging boy with eight fingers, be they painted or not, is out."

His pronunciation of the "ou" in "out" was even more deeply Canadian than usual—pure Ottawa Valley.

"But—"

He turned up the volume on the *Hoarders* show and smiled openly. "No but. No hung boy in your doc—"

"Hanged boy."

"Yeah, well, no hanged boy either." A moment of silence followed. He clearly hoped that she would take the hint and leave. She took the hint—but she didn't leave. Finally he said, "Do you really want to change the title for the second season?"

"Yeah, to *At the Junction.*"

"Good name, but wasn't it *In the Junction?*"

"It was, but now it's *At the Junction.*"

"Did I think that up?"

"No."

"Well be it *In the Junction* or *At the Junction*, there's no hanged boy. Got it?"

This time Trish took the hint and left.

She didn't remember coming down the stairs or hailing a cab, although she did remember how shocked she was when she opened the door to her condo and saw that the newspapers that had somehow occupied every chair, every table, every counter and every available space on her hardwood floors had doubled in size.

She slammed the door and headed to a bar. She needed a drink. She also needed to talk to her other researcher for the show: Decker Roberts.

She tried his number for the third time that day and got his usual message: "Do not leave a message. If I want to get in touch with you, I will."

She took a breath then shouted, "Decker, phone home! Or I'll castrate you and feed your manhood to the Public Broadcaster—it'd be a first for them. Not the castration—the manhood."

She hung up, and the loneliness descended on her yet again as the image of the eight-fingered boy hanging from the lamp post on Annette Street across from the library in the Junction filled her mind.

Then over it the face of the CPBC exec—what was his name?

Andrew Parees. A thought occurred to her: *Is this somehow personal? What does the hanged boy have to do with Andrew Parees?*

Well nothing, since the boy died many, many years before Andrew Parees was born.

—but not before his grandfather was born.

Who exactly was Andrew Parees' grandfather?

And what could he have to do with a gay boy with four painted fingernails on each hand—hanged from a lamp post at the corner of Annette Street and Mavety in the Junction area of Toronto a mere six months before the Junction inexplicably joined the city of Toronto, which then became the only murder that was not transferred to the Toronto Police Service blotter from the Junction? That just disappeared?

Again she swore at Decker. "Fuck, you could help me with this shit!"

34

TRISH—THE GANG MEETS

EDDIE HELD MARINA'S HAND AS THEY ENTERED THEO'S WORLD— thousands of volumes of fiction, nonfiction and porn stacked to the ceiling in every available crevice of his Junction used books shop.

"Thanks for coming," Theo said between coughing fits.

"You should have that looked at," Eddie said.

"Doctors! Blah!" Theo replied. Looking at Marina, he bent forward. "And who is this pretty young lady?"

Marina clutched her father's hand more tightly and tried to bury her head in Eddie's side like a five-year-old.

Theo looked at Eddie, who said, "Marina. Marina's her name, and she's still a little shy."

Theo said, "Sure—that's no problem, young lady. Be as shy as you like. Do you like books?"

"Picture books," Marina said directly into her father's side.

Theo took a quick look at Eddie. "How old are you, Marina?"

"She's fourteen," Eddie said.

Theo suppressed his surprise.

"She's on her own path, Theo—her own path."

Before Theo could question this cryptic statement, Trish strode into the bookshop. At over six feet she often strode rather than walked.

She looked around her at the stacks and stacks of books and had to resist shivering. Her own hoarding instincts had increased exponentially, to the point that there was nowhere to sit anymore in her large three-bedroom condo.

"Something wrong, Trish?" Theo demanded.

"Nope. Love what you've done with the place. It has a definite art dreco vibe. Quite the mess-en-scène." Then she asked without segue, "Where's Leena?"

"I called her, like you asked," Theo said.

"Wanna explain what we're all gathered here for, Trish?" It was Eddie.

"For Decker, I assume." They all turned to the door where Leena was standing, all five foot nothing of her, her once beautiful face now permanently etched with sorrow.

"Hey, Leena, long time."

"Yeah, Eddie, long time. Is this—"

"Marina. Yes, it's Marina."

"Welcome to the Junction, Marina."

"So we're all well met, as the Bard so aptly put it," Theo said just before another coughing fit took him, through which he managed to ask, "What's up?"

"Where's Decker?" Trish demanded.

"He's off the grid, Trish," Eddie said.

"But you know where he is, Eddie. You always know where he is."

"Not this time. No transponder. No cell phone. No contacts."

"For how long?"

"Sixteen days and counting."

"And when's he coming back on the grid like a normal human being?"

"I've got no idea, Trish." Then he added before she could question him further, "None, nada, pas de chose, not a wink."

Marina giggled.

Eddie smiled at her.

"Is he okay?" Trish demanded.

"He's Decker. He's never okay," Eddie said.

In the silence that followed Eddie's undeniable truth, Marina said, "I like Mr. Decker."

"Me too, sweetie, but Mr. Decker is on a path of his own."

"Like me?" she asked, a surprising brightness in her voice.

"Yeah, kiddo, that's right—like you."

35

A BORDER CROSSING

CROSSING THE CANADIAN BORDER AFTER DARK ON A VICIOUSLY cold Manitoba night can have its own special difficulties—especially if the people in the car don't have passports.

A freakishly early storm brought snow that swirled, obscuring the licence plate of their stolen car, which helped a bit, but the young Canadian border guard held out his hand for passports. Viola used her sweetest smile and said, "My dad and I forgot them at home. I'm sorry."

Martin Armistaad raised his shoulders in a "silly-me" gesture as he reached into his coat pocket and felt the sharp point of the would-be architect's compass beside the stupid tooth he'd kept. His fingers moved the tooth aside and opened the instrument—its point ready to do damage if needed.

Then Viola reached out and touched the young border guard's hand. She was surprised to feel the weakness in him. She couldn't name the disease, but his heart was weak—very weak. She looked into his eyes and said, inside his head, *"Don't worry, it will be over soon. You'll never get to the forest, let alone the clearing, but you will sleep dreamless sleep until it all starts again. Your family will miss you, but they will be okay—promise."*

The young border guard withdrew his hand and waved them through.

They crossed from North Dakota into Manitoba then turned east—towards the Junction.

Soon after, Hendrick H. Mallory called the young border guard and assured him that he had done the right thing in allowing the car to pass.

The young border guard was surprised when he found himself saying, "I'm sick."

And I'm sure that meeting number three and number four couldn't but advance your illness, Mallory thought.

"She said something about a clearing and a forest."

"And a glass house?"

"No nothing about a house. What's a glass house?"

"Just a dream some of us have, son, nothing to worry yourself about."

36

LATER IN THE JUNCTION

LATER THAT NIGHT, BACK IN THEO'S CROWDED OFFICE WITH MA-
rina safely asleep amidst a pile of picture books, Trish broached
her concern. She laid out the whole sordid tale of a young gay
man being hung in 1902 outside the library on Annette Street
whose death wasn't even investigated and the Public Broadcaster's
refusal to have it in the documentary that she and Decker and
Theo were working on.

"Okay, so the Public Broadcaster is afraid of controversy, so
what, big surprise," said Leena.

"It's not just that," Trish said.

"Then what is it—and what do you want from us?" Leena asked.

For one of the first times in her life, Trish really didn't know
what she wanted. She'd been propelled forward by a force that
she didn't really understand. That she actually thought didn't exist.

"First off, help me find Decker."

Everyone promised to get in touch with Trish the moment
Decker contacted them. Trish thanked them, then asked Theo,
"What more have we learned about the boy?"

"The one who was hanged?"

"Who else?"

"Besides the fact that his nails were painted black and he
was missing the baby fingers from both hands and that his case

magically disappeared when the Junction joined the big bad city in 1902?"

"Yeah, what else?"

"Working at it."

"And?"

"Well, I may have something."

"From the archive?"

"Yeah."

"What?"

Theo put a photo onto the pitted table that he used as a desk.

"And this is?"

"A wide-angle shot of the Junction's potter's field."

"The Junction had a pauper's graveyard?"

"Well, that poor boy didn't hang on that lamp post until he rotted. Eventually someone cut him down and they threw his body somewhere."

"You mean buried somewhere?"

"Yeah, I guess I do, but paupers are usually just thrown away."

"Usually?"

"Yeah. But look at that photograph."

"Why?"

"There's a gravestone way in the back."

"Paupers don't usually have gravestones."

"But this one did. How did you find this?"

"I know it sounds weird, but I kinda stumbled on it in the Junction archives in the basement of the library. I'd gone over every inch of that damned place time and time again and found nothing. Then yesterday, after we spoke, I found it. Shit, I almost stepped on it. It was there right out in the open—in front of my stupid face."

"When exactly was this?"

"After we met in the archive."

"Yeah, but what time exactly?"

"Around ten thirty in the morning."

Right after I left the CPBC office fighting for the inclusion of the hanging boy, she thought.

"Why does the time matter?"

"Maybe it doesn't. You said paupers don't usually have grave-stones. But this one did?"

"Yeah, look—here's a blowup of the gravestone, best I could do. The first name and dates are obliterated and I'm having trouble making out the last name. Maybe Barees or Harees or—"

"Or Parees? Theo, could that name be Parees?"

"Yeah, I guess."

"Holy shit!"

"What?" Eddie asked.

"The CPBC guy's last name is Parees."

37

OCEANSIDE IS A WORKING-CLASS MARINE TOWN. CAMP PEND-leton is just up the road. It was the kind of place Yslan used to like. Used to feel right at home in. But as she and Emerson made their way to the hospital, she had a strange sense of all this being foreign. Of her being unwelcome here. All those young men with close-cropped haircuts and their already pregnant even younger wives gave her the creeps.

The scene at the hospital was eerily reminiscent of seeing Harrison. How long ago had that been? She was shocked when she realized it was only a few days ago.

The doctors who worked on Dr. Chumley were as baffled as the ones who had treated Harrison.

The prognosis was just as terrifying.

"Why are we here?" Emerson asked as he averted his eyes from Dr. Chumley, who was strapped into a wheelchair.

For a long time Yslan didn't answer, just stared at the catatonic figure. Finally she said, "Due diligence."

Emerson shrugged and said, "Okay. So we've been duly diligent."

As if coming out of a trance, Yslan shook her head, then said, "Let's get back to San Francisco; that's where the trail leads."

"Right."

"Can we get a flight?"

"There's one from the airport off Palomar Airport Road in twenty minutes. I'll make a call."

"Tell Mallory to make the call."

"Okay," Emerson said and turned to his phone, although he knew Mallory had already booked them on that flight.

Yslan took a few steps closer to Dr. Petronius Chumley in his wheelchair and whispered in his ear, "I hope to meet you one day, Doctor." Then the oddest thought shot through her mind: *I'm talking to this man the way I address my father's name carved into the war memorial.* The one who loved bacon.

38

TRISH AT POTTER'S FIELD

TRISH HAD NEVER BEEN IN A PLACE LIKE THIS. GRAVEYARDS CER-tainly—she was at the age when funerals of elderly family members and even the odd acquaintance were a somewhat frequent occurrence—but this was not a cemetery the likes of which she'd ever seen.

To one side were tall concrete towers for sand and other building materials. Across the way were the railway tracks. The place screamed that it was of no commercial value.

She got there by driving up Keele Street, then making a sharp right before she got to the big-box stores on what had been slaughterhouse lands.

She noted in the near distance the remains of the Junction railroad station, where the trunk line from the west used to join the lines going into Toronto. It was also the starting place for the tunnel system that ran under much of the Junction. Now what remained of the old depot was rotting—ignored, like the rest of this forgotten patch of land.

Once out of her car she did a quick three-sixty. To the south she saw the spires of three churches—*Just far enough away not to be infected by this cesspool,* she thought.

She pushed the broken wire gate aside and stepped into the muddy field. To her left was a shed, ahead of her was a rock-strewn field. If there were graves here they were not going to be easy to find.

Then what she had thought was a small boulder in the distance moved, rose and approached her. The boulder proved to be a short stocky man dressed entirely in grey—grey pants, grey shirt, grey shoes, grey hair, almost grey skin, with a wispy grey beard and dancing grey eyes. "Does he know you're here?" he asked.

"Who?"

"The snarler," he said, pointing towards the shed.

"No, I guess not. Does he object to visitors?"

"Hates 'em."

"But he likes you?"

"'Likes' is the wrong word. 'Puts up with' is better."

"And why does he put up with you?"

The little man reached into his pocket and withdrew a handful of herbs. "He makes me split the profit with him."

"You grow them here?"

"Some will only grow in graveyards." He reached into the plastic bag he was carrying and withdrew a long plant with a slender root. He told her the Latin name, then said, "Only grows around the oldest of graves and is worth a small fortune to the Chinese medical practitioners."

"Down on Spadina."

"And up in Richmond Hill, Thornhill, Aurora and points north, east and west."

"Only around old graves, you said?"

Suddenly the man was cautious. Trish held up a hand. "I'm not interested in the plants. I'm interested in the old graves. Will you show them to me?"

"Not the herbs? Just the old graves?"

Trish nodded.

"Promise?"

"On a stack of Bibles."

The man indicated that she should follow him. She did, and around a corner back behind the shed were the graves—if you could call them that. There were only a few gravestones, maybe five or six. The rest was simply unmarked ground. She assumed there were several hundred bodies all told. She checked the photo that Theo had given her and quickly found the headstone. It was, unlike the others, clean and neither chipped nor cracked, though clearly old and weathered to the point that it was very hard to make out the lettering.

She knelt by the headstone and withdrawing some parchment paper from her purse pressed it against the old stone. But as she began to apply pressure against the parchment with a flat stone to get an impression on the paper, she heard a gruff voice shouting at her; "Hey there, missy, what is it that you're on about?"

The boulder man skittered away, mumbling something about his plants—being careful with his plants.

Trish stood and stepped towards the man who had evidently come out of the shed. Shed Man was as wide as he was tall and wore overalls that clearly had not seen the inside of a washing machine in this millennium.

"Eh? I asked yer what yer doin' here?"

Trish was happy to see that she was about seven inches taller than he was. "I'm a film producer," she said, holding out a business card.

The man ignored the proffered card and said, "What are yer doin' here?"

"Looking at a gravestone."

"Why?"

"This was the Junction's potter's field, wasn't it?"

"Come again?"

"Potter's field. Burial ground for the indigent."

"For poor people, aye."

"And criminals?"

"I think yer know the answer ta' that question already."

"Well, yes. I wonder if you could identify the person buried here," she said, pointing at the gravestone.

"Don't it say on the stone itself?"

"It's weathered so it's hard to read."

"Well that happens in Canada. We get some weather in this part of the world. You may have noticed that."

"Do you have records?"

"O' what?"

"Of who's buried here?"

"This ain't no cemetery lady, it's a dumping ground."

"Still . . ."

"Still wha'?"

"There has to be a record of who's here."

"Lady, nobody's here—that's the point of a place like this. Now take your long legs and your tight ass and hie your way out of—What did you call it?"

"Potter's field."

"Yeah, get yourself out of my potter's field. And don't come back. This is private property. Didn't you read the sign? No snooping allowed."

Five minutes later a black rotary phone rang on a rectory desk in the church on Annette beside the Masonic Temple.

The old priest took a long time getting to the thing. The weight of the receiver, as usual, was a comfort to him. He listened to the gruff voice on the other end and was not pleased with what he heard.

He barked a command, then hung up.

He wandered into the sanctuary of the church. His church. It was empty and cold. He sat heavily in the front pew. *So it hasn't gone away. After all these years it rises from cold obstruction and the duty falls to me.*

He'd been warned about what his predecessor had called "the parish debt," but he hadn't thought it would ever come to light, to this.

He got up slowly, heavily, and wondered how long he had before this would literally land on his doorstep.

Then he smiled. He had a role to play, and he'd been trained for just such a role—all his life had led to this. "In harness at last," he said aloud. The vaulted space echoed his words, and it pleased him.

"Ouch, that's my foot!"

"Shhh, Theo!" Eddie said.

"How did we ever let Trish talk us into—"

"No filing cabinets or three by five card files," Eddie said.

"So?"

"So they must have scanned the records."

"Or thrown them out."

Eddie flicked on his flashlight and quickly scanned the interior of the potter's field shed. He found the electronic hookup and swore softly. "No, they scanned them."

"How do—"

"There was an old desktop computer hooked up here."

"But now—"

"Now it's gone."

"Maybe he has a laptop or an iPad or a smart phone," Theo suggested.

"Or maybe he yanked his old desktop out of the wall after he spoke to Trish."

"Why do you—"

Eddie directed the older man's eye from the wall hookup to a tangle of wires. "Remember when we all used to have those coiled snakes beneath our desks?"

"Ten years ago."

Now the wires were there, but no sign of the computer.

"So?" Theo demanded.

"Probably didn't know how to destroy the hard drive, so he took it with him."

"Okay, so now what?"

Crazy Eddie was on his knees scanning the side of the desk with his flashlight. "Something there?"

"Yeah, tape."

"Tape?"

"Well, actually tape residue."

"So?"

"So he may have taped his computer warranty extensions to the side of his desk. I used to do that when I first got suckered into buying them."

"And this helps us why?"

"'Cause, my ancient gay friend," he said as he riffled through a stack of scrap paper in the desk drawer, "if we can find the warranty, then I can identify the computer, and if I can identify the computer I can find it—if it still exists." Then, pulling a torn warranty from the pile he said, "Yes, yes, yes."

At 10:15 a.m. Eddie located the computer and called Trish. "So, what do you want to know?"

"You have full access to his computer?"

"Why else would I be calling? What do you want to know?"

"Get me a printout of everyone who's been buried in that potter's field."

"Hey, I can't hear you—what's that noise?"

"Airplanes. I'm down on Lake Shore Boulevard."

"To see the air show, maybe find a nice pilot to take you for a ride?"

"Eddie!"

"Right. What do you want from this guy's computer?"

She repeated her request for the names of everyone buried in the potter's field.

"Be more exact."

"Okay. Everyone buried there on or around the time the Junction joined the big bad city."

"Year?"

"1902."

There was a pause, and Trish asked, "Okay?"

"Piece of digital pie."

"How long?"

"If it's on his computer, you'll have it on your BlackBerry in ten minutes—tops. I could include several celebrity strippers with that—both male and female if you so wish."

"I don't—just the list of those buried there."

"You mean thrown away there."

After a pause, Trish said, "Yeah—thrown away there."

Eddie suddenly sensed that he was being watched and turned to the door.

Marina was standing there—in her nightgown, sucking her thumb.

"Eddie, you still there?"

Keeping his eyes on Marina, he replied to Trish, "Yeah, we're still here. Gotta go, Trish. You need anything else?" But before she could answer Eddie hung up and walked over to Marina. His foot lift clacked. He gently took her hand from her mouth, but she pulled it away and stuck her thumb back between her lips.

Then she began to cry.

"Why are you crying, sweetie?"

Around her thumb she said, "Because I'll miss being with you."

While Trish waited those ten minutes, her mind wandered to Decker. How Decker had changed her perception of so many things.

39

TRISH AND DECKER

THE SNOWBIRDS ROARED OVERHEAD AND EXECUTED A MIDAIR dive that had the throngs along the Lake Shore roar with approval. Trish pushed her way through the crowd. She checked her Black-Berry—no message yet from Eddie.

A drunk called out to her and pointed at his crotch.

Trish used to forgive Toronto its sins. She'd lived in London and Tokyo and was used to the trials and tribulations of large cities. But in both Tokyo and London, when things got too hairy she'd retreat to the galleries or the theatre—and understand that's why she put up with the big-city nonsense. But of late Toronto was more and more hectic—crazy—and she couldn't find a reason to put up with it. She knew that Toronto was at that uncomfortable stage of growth where the inevitable problems of large cities—violence, inconvenience, rudeness—were on the rise, but it had not yet grown enough to offer the rewards that only a large older city can present to its citizens.

She didn't use to see the problems. Sure, she knew about the shootings in downtown malls—young men with weapons and something to prove—that at times ended with innocent bystanders caught in the crossfire. Even the Mafia-style execution across the road from her favourite coffee shop on College Street hadn't fazed her—but now it did. Since she'd gotten close to Decker they did.

Like the hoarding, she thought.

Decker had a troublingly discerning eye for hypocrisy.

She remembered going with him to Koerner Hall (one of the few truly world-class venues in the city). The concert featured three famous elderly Cuban jazz musicians. At intermission the musicians came on stage for a question and answer session.

Each of them complained bitterly that the communists had destroyed their beautiful country. They were particularly vehement about what had happened to Havana, which they had adored.

It was the reaction of the Toronto audience that drew Decker's ire. As the musicians criticized their communist government, Decker said, "See how this audience is pulling away from these men? Before the intermission they were stars."

Trish had seen it.

"They don't want to hear it, Trish."

"What?"

"That the communist paradise is hardly that."

And Trish looked at the people around her and felt that she was not part of this—whatever this was.

Then there were the times he had been with her in a crowd in Toronto and abruptly asked, "Are these really your people, Trish?" Actually he hadn't asked, he'd demanded an answer to his question.

She'd never answered but instead would ask, "Are these *your* people, Decker?"

"No," he'd answer.

Then she'd ask, "Is that why you're so alone?"

He'd hem and haw about not being alone, about living with Eddie—which he would eventually acknowledge was "sort of being alone." She would then press him by saying, "And is that because you have *no* people?"

He'd always look away, and she'd always say, "Don't do that; just answer the damned question."

To which he'd always say, "What's the damned question?"

To which she'd always reply, "Is that because you have *no* people?"

He'd nod slowly and mutter something about not playing well with others.

It always amazed her that he'd start that conversation, since surely he knew where it led—but over and over again he'd bring it up. And that conversation had changed her, and she knew it.

Before she began to spend a lot of time with Decker, she'd felt part of this city. Now as she walked along the lake shore—with the roar of the air show overhead—she knew in her heart that she didn't feel part of this anymore. As she passed by the Sunnyside swimming pool, which on hot days was crammed with bathers, she remembered that she often used to swim there. Now she couldn't imagine doing that.

The fact that there hadn't been a winning sports team in the city for what seemed like generations often added to the melancholy of her day. Made her buy more and more things and stuff them into more and more nooks and crannies in her condo.

Her BlackBerry buzzed, and she ducked under a Lake Shore overpass so she could see the screen. It was from Eddie. She read it quickly—there it was on Eddie's second page of text: *Seamus Parees, buried potter's field, March 17th, 1902.*

"St. Patrick's Day," she said aloud. "Jeesh!"

She felt her entire world spinning. The air show thundered overhead—but she didn't hear it.

40

MUSICIANS IN SOLITAIRE

LATE ONE AFTERNOON WHILE DECKER WAS BLOWING THE DUST off his hands at the end of another hundred-pie day, he looked up and there—as unlikely as the arrival of the three oriental kings at the manger—were three African Americans getting out of a Range Rover. The largest of the men hopped out first and waved to Linwood.

Linwood passed right by Decker without acknowledging his presence and moved as fast as Decker had ever seen him move, his arms wide as he greeted the three Americans.

Decker watched as the men embraced like long-lost friends, which later that night Decker found was exactly what they were— long-lost friends and jazz musicians, the largest, and the leader, named Marcellus.

For the first time since Decker had arrived in Solitaire, Linwood did not take him on a walk as the night took the day.

That evening Linwood lit a campfire far out in the desert behind the bakery. The three Americans and Linwood sat there staring into the flames and of all things listening to early Duke Ellington records that the Americans had brought and Linwood played on a hand-cranked record player.

The scene was so out of kilter with any reality of Solitaire that Decker knew that he couldn't put it together; like the Brooklyn

Yankees, these images didn't mesh. Then Linwood turned up the volume and indicated to Decker that he could approach the campfire—but not too close.

He got within twenty feet, and Linwood signalled him "no nearer."

The music from the record travelled unimpeded across the vastness of the open desert, seemingly only contained by the brilliant stars overhead.

Decker vaguely recognized the tunes—standards by now—although he couldn't name a single one. The musicians—and Linwood—clearly knew every note.

No one spoke. They all just listened and allowed the music to move them.

When the side ended, Linwood flipped the record over, and as the music picked up again there was movement on the far side of the fire. The eyes of wild dogs reflected the flicker of the flames. Then Decker heard a rustling behind him, but he knew better than to look into the eyes of the wild dogs that would surely be there.

The music played—the dogs' rustling seemed to find the counterpoint to the music's rhythm—then one of the Americans began to scat to the Ellington. A second musician did the same, but this time he was countering both the rhythm of the dogs' rustling and the drone note the dogs' movements created.

The Ellington and scat singers and the rustling grew as one wild but oddly orderly thing until the Ellington came to a wonderful dissonant stop.

Then silence.

A long silence.

Finally Linwood turned to the leader of the musicians, who had not sung a note, and said, "You can't hear the music anymore can you, Marcellus?"

The large black man stood and began to move from the fire.

"You came a long way just to walk away from me now."

Marcellus turned back to Linwood. "I stretched the chords so far apart that I lost it."

"It?"

"The music. I lost the music. It became noise and I couldn't find my way back to the music."

"So what did you do?"

"For a while, nothing."

"Then?"

"I couldn't stand it anymore."

"And?"

Marcellus didn't say anything.

"Then you turned to heroin." It was a statement, not a question, from Linwood.

The black man nodded.

"Did it help?"

"For a while. I could hear it again, Linwood. I could hear it!" The man's voice was hoarse with anguish.

"But now it's gone again?"

"Noise. All I hear is noise."

"You can't even hear the Ellington?"

"Noise. I hear noise."

Linwood approached the man and put a huge arm around his shoulder. He turned to the other men and said, "My people will supply you with a place to sleep and food. Marcellus and I will be back in a day or two—maybe more."

One of the musicians protested: "Where are you going?"

Linwood opened his arm to the expanse of the desert now lit brilliantly by the piercing stars and slender moon—and shrugged. Then he and Marcellus strode off, two large men slowly becoming tiny dots in the vastness of the African desert.

That night Decker was awakened by the sound of music. One of the jazz musicians was working an electric piano, while the other played a soprano sax. They were riffing on a Dylan tune, half mocking, half adulating. Decker got out of his bed, and as he did he heard the old bedsprings produce notes that fit with the music from the players. He pulled the mattress off the springs and plucked one of them. It completed a diminished seventh chord started by the jazz musicians. Then, to his astonishment, he was plucking notes one after another from the springs, and every one fit perfectly with the music coming from the jazz players.

He'd directed musicals but had never played an instrument, never sung, never been able to find harmonies—or rhythms—and here in the Namibian desert in a town called Solitaire after he could not count how many pies he was able to find the harmonies on the bedsprings—and the rhythm on the bedsprings—and music from the taut wires that only minutes ago were nothing more than something to keep his mattress off the floor.

41

AFTER THE MUSICIANS

DECKER ROSE EARLY THE NEXT MORNING, AS HE ALWAYS DID, AND was surprised that the musicians' Range Rover was gone.

He looked back behind the kitchen and walked far out into the desert. He couldn't find any sign of the campfire. He thought that maybe he had gotten disoriented, so he headed out in the opposite direction and once again found no sign of any campfire, let alone record player or Duke Ellington records.

Finally, confused, he gave up and headed back to Solitaire. He was surprised to see Linwood standing outside the kitchen.

"Late. Not good to be late."

"Yes, I guess."

"You guess?"

"Yeah, okay. I'm late. It won't happen again. Where are the musicians? I thought you were going to be gone for a few days with Marcellus."

"With who?"

"Marcellus. The jazz musician. The one who lost the music."

Linwood took a step back.

"Don't look at me like I'm crazy. We were out in the desert, and you were playing Duke Ellington records, and I played along with the two musicians who were left behind when you and Marcellus went for your walk."

"And how was I playing this Mr. Eglinton's music?"

"Ellington, not Eglinton, and on your record player."

"My record player? In the desert? And how did this record player get electricity?"

"You had a hand-crank generator . . . and . . ."

"There's a lot of sugar in those apple preserves. I warned you about eating too much of them."

Linwood turned from him and began to walk away, then turned back, smiled and sang the opening refrain of "Satin Doll"—but he would answer no more of Decker's questions. Although he did say, "Bedsprings are really quite difficult to play well—we should get you a guitar."

The guitar—the music—proved to be the portal that allowed him access to waking dreams on command.

All he had to do was play the opening chords of "Highway 61 Revisited" and he was up in his dreamscape—awaiting Seth's call for help.

42

EDDIE AND MARINA—THE ODDEST DANCE

"YOU THINK I'M STUPID."

"I don't, Marina. I just think you're on a different—"

"Path. Yes, you've said. But you *do* think I'm stupid." She paused, then said, "When you live in so many different worlds it's hard to talk right in just one."

"I don't understand."

"No you don't. Of course you don't."

"Why do you say that?"

Marina turned away. Then, as if to herself, she said, "All your life you look for the glass house. All your life. But you'll be lucky if you even sense the trees—let alone find the clearing. But I'm in all of them at once. Here, the forest, the clearing, the house. I was born in all of them—I'll die in all of them. All of us will."

"All?"

"Do you remember the boy who pooped in the pool?"

It was hard to forget. It was a terribly hot and humid August day, and Eddie had agreed to take Marina and her friends to the large public swimming pool in High Park just south of the Junction. If there was ever a good visual for the phrase "motley crew," they were it. Eddie in his cut-off jeans (as close as he could come to a bathing suit) with his foot-lift contraption in full view. Marina wearing an old, way too large sundress because she refused to allow anyone to see her belly button—what she referred to as her "very centre." And her two friends. One blind and terribly thin, wearing a bathing suit that was too loose so one of his extraordinarily long testicles hung out, and Josh, whose almost three hundred pounds circled his middle and legs in bags of flesh. It was Josh, who bore the cruel facial markings of Down syndrome, who had gleefully defecated in the pool, which drew shrieks from the young bathers around him and angry accusations from their parents: Look what he's done! Why's someone like that allowed in a public pool without supervision? An afternoon ruined by you and your cretin!

Everyone was ushered out of the pool, and the offending fecal matter was removed. Then the entire pool was drained and scoured. Eventually, water began to be put back into the pool, along with excessive amounts of chlorine.

The whole process took several hours—hours of intense summer heat and rising anger from the kids who had been promised by their parents that they would be swimming.

For the first time in his life, Eddie found himself grouped with his daughter and her friends—one of their kind.

Eddie went to defend them but was beaten to it by Marina, who strode forward like a warrior daring anyone to so much as say a word. Suddenly, Josh let out a wail and grabbed his face. Someone had thrown a sharp object that cut him just above his right eye. The huge boy staggered, and Eddie caught him just before he hit the ground. Marina didn't move towards Josh. No. She headed in the opposite direction—towards the boy who had thrown the stone. As the taunts surrounded her, Marina pushed through the mob, grabbed the boy by the ears and began to yell at him.

But words failed her, and gibberish came out of her mouth. In rage and frustration she turned to her father, who quickly ran to her, told the boy to back off and pulled his daughter to his side.

The walk home had been long and silent.

I've never been in a situation like that, Eddie thought.

No you haven't.

Eddie hadn't realized that he'd spoke aloud. Then he looked at Marina.

He hadn't spoken aloud!

Before he could say anything, Marina said, *No, Father, you were not talking. There are many more ways of communicating than simply talking. You think that you and that machine—that computer—are involved in some sort of advanced thinking, some sort of advanced way of communicating. But that's nonsense. A computer is a simple device. Communication is much more complicated than a computer could ever begin to help you understand. For example, look at me, Father. Are my lips moving?*

Eddie shook his head.

And yet you hear me, don't you?

Eddie nodded.

This is our way now. You heard me when I explained about living in different worlds and the clearing and the glass house—not talking, but this way. You are hearing me now the way I've always heard everyone, everywhere. When you live in many worlds like I do, it's sometimes hard to be simple and direct.

Eddie went to speak but Marina had knelt in front of him.

He looked down at her.

She looked up, opened her mouth and pointed to her undone shoelace. "Dada help Marina. Please."

43

SETH AND WJ—KEYS

SETH AWOKE WITH A START. SOMETHING WAS TERRIBLY WRONG—
more wrong than ever before. Yes, he felt the creep of the cancer
in his system, but he'd felt that now for the last ten days.

He shifted on the bed. The handcuff that held him to the gurney rattled. Then it came to him. Last night he'd been sliding out
of control in his dream, a rarity for him. He was a master dreamer,
if there was such a thing. From the moment he'd left his father's
house he'd begun to write about his dreaming. And before he got
so sick he'd completed two full novels about it and left them on
the hard drive of a computer at the University of Victoria library.
He'd made a reference to them in his journal, but that was well
hidden away. However, even in his writing about dreaming he'd
never been yanked from one dream to another as he was last
night.

As he thought about that his entire body began to shake. It
took all of his considerable willpower to control himself and force
himself to concentrate on the here and now—on the inevitable
confrontation ahead with the grey-haired freak. He shallowed his
breathing and allowed a waking dream. For a moment he didn't
see anything—then, turning a corner, there was his father, sitting on a large red rock, a guitar in his hands. He put the guitar
aside and looked at his son. "Explain," he said. And Seth did: the

Wellness Dream Clinic, the grey-haired freak, his kidnapping, and now being handcuffed to a gurney.

"Tell me how I can help you, Seth. I need to help you."

"I need weapons to fight him. I'm here alone, sick as a dog and weaponless."

"You are never weaponless. Never helpless, no matter what the situation, because every personal confrontation plays out like a scene from a script. The choices you make lead either to victory or defeat. Because battles between two people are always intimate, invasive and specific. Human vulnerability, not circumstance, determines the outcome. Find the right weapon to attack your acting partner's vulnerability, and no matter how the scene is written you can win."

"This is not some scene from a stupid play!"

"True—but if you treat it like a scene you may find a way to win."

"So you want me to think of this as if I'm playing a scene? That what is going to happen between myself and the grey-haired freak is a scene, a series of scenes, a play?"

"Unless you have a better suggestion."

Seth turned away.

"Seth, the way to think about it is that both you and your opponent have a key in your respective back pockets. He wants the key you have and you want the key he has. Winning is getting the other guy's key without him getting yours. You already know what key he holds in his back pocket, what you want from him."

"Yeah, my freedom."

"But you don't know what he wants from you—your key. That's the first thing to work on. Find out what he wants from you. Once you know that you can defend your key—and once that key is defended you can begin to attack him to get his key. But start by finding out what he wants from you—your key."

"That's it?"

"No, Seth, that's just a place to begin."

Seth saw his father's image begin to fade. As it did he saw his father pick up the guitar and try to revitalize the waking dream, but he failed and dissipated into the mist.

Seth was amazed at how deeply he understood his father's advice—as if the thoughts were his own, not his father's. He had, as a kid, overheard many of his father's acting lessons when professional actors came to the house in the Junction to prepare for big roles. *So,* he thought, *maybe I'm just remembering.* Then he told himself to stop it. It was time to get ready—to find out what key he had in his back pocket to control the grey-haired freak.

He heard someone throw the door bolt. *Round one—no, scene one,* he thought.

44

HIDING ACTIONS

THEIR FIRST ENCOUNTER HAD BEEN A LENGTHY PROCESS OF FEEL-ing each other out. Neither had scored a serious hit. Seth still didn't know what key he had that the grey-haired freak wanted.

The one thing Seth knew for sure was that when his adversary returned, the war between them would escalate.

He lay back and allowed his mind to roam his memory chambers—not unlike what his father had done while rolling and folding pie dough in Solitaire. And memories came. He had been home from school for some reason. He'd moved into Eddie's room to nap, and much to his surprise there was an air vent there that connected to the living room downstairs, where his father was working with one of his star acting clients. He'd rolled over and moved closer to the vent.

The actor was named Fastman—Steve? Sean? He couldn't recall. But he knew the man's last name was Fastman, that he'd been one of his father's clients for many years and had a terrific career playing leads in Hollywood and Canada.

"Actions have to be hidden," he heard his father say.

"Explain that, Decker," Fastman said.

"If your acting partner knows what you are trying to make him do, then he can always defeat you."

"But I do have to play an action, as in 'If I have the right to write the end of the scene, what would my acting partner do?'"

Seth heard his father laugh. Then Fastman asked, "What?"

"I taught you that in the new students' class. That must have been—"

"At least fifteen years ago."

"Yeah. Well yes, you're right, you have to play actions, and that is exactly the formula that you have to use, but the issue is how openly do you play them. That formula causes the conflict that drama needs because it's our nature—when we see that someone wants something from us, we almost always don't give it to them. You've tended bar, right?"

"What actor hasn't tended bar?"

"When I lived in New York City, I had a high-end pickup bar around the corner from my apartment on the West Side, and they always needed help on the weekends, so they didn't care that I was a really shitty—I mean a really shitty—bartender. But being a bartender taught me a lot about actions. Someone coming into the bar desperate to find someone never, ever did. His desperation made him play his actions too openly. But sometimes around two in the morning a guy would come into the bar happy with his life, happy with his wife and kids—and women would approach from corners of the bar that you didn't even know were there."

"He was hiding his actions?"

"You bet." Then his father had laughed as he added, "Because no one comes into a bar at two in the morning happy with his life, wife and kids."

Seth remembered that most distinctly: "No one comes into a bar at two in the morning happy with his life, wife and kids." Hiding his action.

So he had to make the grey-haired freak show his hand—play his action openly. Show Seth what he wanted from him. Until now, the grey-haired freak played as if it was 2:00 a.m. and he was happy with his life, wife and kids. Seth had to stop him from doing that. "How?" he asked aloud—and his father answered him: "Don't go directly for that. Find chinks in his armour and attack those points. Make his insides move and the whole structure may wobble and fall."

Seth thought about structures falling. About how to make them fall.

He felt a roiling in his intestines—such motion was not a pleasant sensation for anyone with cancer alive in his system. He turned on his side and allowed it to pass. It took longer than before—not good.

But once it did he returned his thoughts to moving the grey-haired freak off his centre, uncentring him, finding a hole in the man's vision of himself.

He rolled onto his back.

Seth thought about his action. *If I had the right to write the end of the scene, what would the grey-haired freak do? Well, fuck, he'd release me. Have I ever played that action before? There was that girlfriend when I was sixteen; that bully in grade school; that damned song that had gotten into my head that I couldn't escape. Leaving my father's house. Well, that was the biggest one, but I hadn't needed anyone's permission—no one was barring my way, except myself. So there was no action to play except against my own fear. Here my fear has a body—the grey-haired freak—although he does not, as yet, have a name.*

His name, Seth thought. *Let's start there.*

He suddenly heard his father's words again. "The choice of the state of being you sit in when you play your action can contribute to a victory in a scene." Then his father's voice was gone. Seth thought about that: "What did I feel while I played that action? What was my state of being? What state of being was I sitting in? Had I forced myself to sit in? I forced myself into I am ascending, I am all powerful, I am alive, I am beautiful. It bolstered me—gave me a running block to push off from. So let's find that now," he thought—although his words were spoken aloud.

He was still a boy chained to a gurney. Nothing overtly seemed to change. But, as he worked, his eyes cleared and a ruddiness came to his face.

If you knew your medieval painting, you would recognize him—Archangel Michael with his flaming sword, ready to do battle.

45

WJ AND SETH—CONFRONTATION, AS WARRIORS CLASH BY NIGHT

THE DAYS THAT FOLLOWED SEEMED TO SETH LIKE IMAGES SEEN through a stroboscope. Flickers of brilliant intensity, then darkness. Then sudden intensity again—miniature, violent plays, all performed in his room, chained to a gurney, for an audience of one: the grey-haired freak.

During one of his lucid pauses, his father talked to him about the power of visualization. "Seth, you have a potent imagination. Project, visualize what you are doing and what you want your adversary to do."

"You mean if I had the right to write the end of the scene what would my acting partner do?"

"You know I mean that."

Seth thought about that, worried about it, since once he visualized something it was not always in his control—it was out there in the world. He assumed that people with the "right" eyes might be able to see what he had visualized—people who sensed the existence of the clearing beyond the forest.

When WJ finally returned to the boy's room, he immediately aimed his remote and the entire space once again became the Duomo. *His projection,* Seth thought.

"Neat trick. Got another one, maybe something in puce?" Seth saw the grey-haired freak break rhythm, so he quickly demanded, "What's this stupid place you keep trying to show me anyways?"

"It's from the synaesthetes' website. Surely you haven't forgotten it already." He paused, then added, "And it's not stupid. Of that, trust me."

Seth instantly knew that was true, but he said, "Really, you skipped the porn sites and landed on—"

"On the synaesthetes' private website."

"Really?"

"Would I lie to you?"

His father's words came to him: "Get him to roll from his centre. Nudge him one way then the other. People are secure when they are on their centres, and you can't get them to reveal anything if they're in their place of confidence. But if you can poke him so that he leaves his centre, get his very being in motion, then he may betray his vulnerability. Once he does, attack that."

Seth smiled and said, "It would be better if you didn't."

"Why's that?" WJ asked.

A bit of motion, Seth thought. *So he doesn't know—good.* What he said was, "Because."

"Not a very enlightening answer."

"If you're looking for enlightenment, you kidnapped the wrong guy."

"No."

"Meaning?"

"Meaning that I didn't kidnap the wrong person—of that you can be sure."

A truth, Seth thought. "How comforting to know that you got the right guy."

"Oh, I got the right guy."

They locked eyes. "Project what you want. See it. Make it real!" His father's voice seemed to be screaming at him.

Seth took a breath and instantly an image from a ludicrous

kung fu movie popped into his head—warriors in full Japanese fighting regalia flying through the air, swords raised. They clashed twenty feet off the ground, sending sparks to the heavens. With a tremendous force of will, Seth caused the image to pause—then he turned the combatants to face him. One was the grey-haired freak—the other was him. The images broke free of his control and flew away from each other only to turn in midair and head back at full speed towards each other. But this time their swords were covered in blood as they clashed, silhouetted against a full moon that had not been there a moment ago.

Seth felt a sharp pain and stared at the grey-haired freak. Had the man cut him? He quickly glanced at his hands and for a moment thought a finger was missing from each.

The grey-haired freak was smiling.

"What?" Seth demanded.

"I saw them, the fighters—I saw into your dream!" He snapped off the lights and left Seth chained to the gurney in total blackness.

"When you use your gift it influences those around you."

"Nice of you to tell me now!"

"Seth, you can only be treated like a child if you permit it. Control the relationship you have with your acting partner and you can win any scene—any scene. Force him to treat you as an equal. First brother to brother, then try to get to older brother or even father. Sometimes calling an actor by his full name establishes a director as a father to a son."

"You mean like those times you called me Seth Roberts?"

"Yeah, like that. As older brother or father you'll be able to move him off his centre."

It was the fourth day, and Seth had been following his father's advice about controlling his relationship with the grey-haired freak for two days. And slowly he was feeling a subtle shift.

The strange man who had kidnapped him was changing their relationship from a bizarre father/son—like a police officer stopping a car that ran a red light—to an older brother/younger brother. Or was it to lover/lover?

The grey-haired freak suddenly stopped mid sentence and stared at Seth.

Seth stared back, then the freak left the room—forgetting to turn off the light.

Both men were weary. Two spent swimmers adrift on an ocean—of what?

Both knew that they couldn't continue this way indefinitely.

It was their eleventh bout—and both doubted there would be a twelfth.

WJ stared at the young man—a boy really—now handcuffed to the chair across a table from him. The boy's cancer was clearly spreading. His cheeks were a jaundiced, ghastly yellow. His breath was raspy and taken in short gulps, his weakness of limb obvious. But the boy sat proudly in his chair, his mind clearly awake and unaffected by the blight in his body, his eyes dark, clear and piercing. A smile creased his face.

More than ten days of brutal interrogation and the boy still smiled. WJ stood—as much to prove that he could and the boy couldn't as any need to change his perspective or stretch his legs. He tried to find the off beat, to speak when the boy exhaled. Once he found it sound burst from his mouth; "Wherever it is you go when you dream, take me with you."

"Why?"

"So that I can feel . . ."

"Feel what?"

"Anything."

He'd said it.

Seth almost couldn't believe it, but there it was—the key that he had in his back pocket that the grey-haired freak was so anxious to get.

He clearly hadn't meant to reveal it, but it had tumbled out of his mouth as surely as his teeth and tongue would have expelled a rotten grape. And there it lay between them, totally changing everything.

"Take me with you!"

"So you can learn how to feel?"

"Yes."

That single word had removed whatever leverage the luring, *The Institution* charade and finally the kidnapping had gained him. "Take me with you," WJ said again. No need now to hold back. "Wherever it is you go in your dreams, take me with you."

Seth heard the echoes from the Old Testament's Book of Ruth— one of the many sections his father had insisted he read, then memorize. But looking at the grey-haired freak he knew that any reverberations from the old book were purely coincidental.

Seth allowed his eyes to roam past the strange man, then he took a deep breath and returned his eyes to him. He centred his voice the way he'd heard his father teach his actors—"Not on the tongue root—that's for scaredy-cats, but on the tip of your tongue so that your lips buzz as you speak and a slight sibilance becomes part of your speech." He knew that metaphorically the ball was in his court, so he thrashed a hard one at the grey-haired freak. "What's your name!" He was pleased to hear that it came out as a command, not a question.

The man hesitated, then said, "WJ."

Seth heard his father shouting, "Once your acting opponent opens a point of weakness, get in there and pry it open."

"That's not a name. I asked you what your name was. So what's your name?"

"As I said, WJ."

Seth hid his smile. The man's centre was in motion—good. Now how to increase that motion till he split apart. "Fine. You ask me to take you along with me and you won't even be honest with me as to what your stupid name is."

"My name's WJ."

Seth received the same mixed signal he had in the previous pronouncements from the man—WJ both was and was not this man's name. "What's your Christian name?"

More hesitation, then, "Bill."

Again a truth and a nontruth. "William, isn't it?"

"Okay. William."

"And the *J*?"

"Why do you need to know this?"

"Why do you need to be able to feel?"

Something heavy and silent sat between the two men. WJ crossed to the table and took his seat. "Enough about my name."

"Why is your name such a fucking secret?" His father's stories about his Russian grandfather popped into his head. Apparently he had two famous sayings: "I don't trust white people" and "never smile long enough that a stranger can count your teeth."

When Seth had first heard these statements he'd asked his father if his grandfather had been an African Canadian. His father had laughed—not a common thing for him. "Why are you laughing, Father?"

"Because your great-grandfather had skin so white it was almost translucent."

"Then why—"

"He meant English people. He didn't trust English people."

Old Torontonians, Seth had thought at the time, then asked, "And the teeth-counting thing?"

"Your guess is as good as mine."

But as Seth stared at the grey-haired freak across the table from him, he guessed that his great-grandfather was talking about identity. The power of hiding one's identity—just like the *J* in WJ. "Is the *J* an initial for your middle or family name?" His demand came out in older brother/younger brother—good.

"Middle."

A truth—but why hide a middle name? "Tell me, then—everyone has a stupid middle name. It's a Caucasian parent's last free kick at the can." Father to son—even better.

"Jennings."

"The *J* stands for Jennings? So you're a William Jennings? As in William Jennings Bryan? William Jennings Bryan the Scopes trial loser, three-time presidential candidate—each time slaughtered at the polls? That kind of William Jennings? And your last name, William Jennings?"

"Connelly. Now take me with you."

"Just like that?"

"Yes just like that—take me with you."

Seth realized how the power had shifted. William Jennings' last statement had clearly been in son/father.

Seth's smile broadened. "Do you dream, William Jennings?" That said father/son. Him the father, WJ the son.

WJ turned away, a wild look on his face.

"Don't even think of lying to me. Do you dream, William Jennings . . . Connelly?"

"No." Younger brother talking to older brother.

Flat truth.

"Is that important?" Son begging a father.

"If you can't dream, you can't learn to feel—simple as that."

"Then teach me how to dream."

"Dream, so you can feel like the monk in the Duomo?" Seth demanded. And before W. J. Connelly nodded, Seth knew he had it, had it all: the syn website, the monk, the look of glory on the boy's face—on *his* face. So that's what he had in his back pocket that William Jennings Connelly was so desperate to get. Desperate enough to create the fake clinic. Desperate enough to kidnap him and keep him cuffed to the gurney all those days.

"Teach me. Please teach me."

Good, Seth thought again; *in very young son/father. Very good—got you!* "You have to dream first."

"You've said as much, so teach me how to dream." Young son/father. For the briefest moment, Seth thought of telling WJ about his two novels, *The Dream Chronicles,* which he'd left on the hard drive at the University of Victoria library, because there was a full explanation there of how to dream—how to waking dream.

"Please, I'll give you anything you want." Lover/lover. "Anything!"

Enough health to see my fiftieth birthday, Seth thought.

Seth looked down. A large red stain was growing at his crotch. The bloodstain didn't surprise him—the fact that he'd peed his pants without knowing it did. Sudden sharp pain in his gut caused him to drop his head to the table.

"Blood," WJ said—Father/son.

"Get me some real medical help if you want me to teach you how to dream." Seth saw WJ hesitate. "A dead man can't teach you anything. Get me some real help!" *Shit,* he thought, I said it in *son/father, shit!*

"And if I do?" Clearly older brother/younger brother.

"I'll teach you."

"When?" Father/son.

"After you take me to the ancient tree, I'll teach you how to dream." A scream of pain came from his mouth.

"The ancient—"

"The tree as old as Africa." And as he said those last words, the pain simply took him. And he retreated to the only world he trusted—the world of dreams—and hoped to hell that it would take him to the clearing and then to the great glass house.

46

BIRDS

SETH FORCED HIS HAND UP INTO HIS DREAMSCAPE, HIS MARKER for knowing that he was awake in his dream. He moved his hand forward and he glided forward. Then, sensing something above him, he stopped. He turned his hand upward and his dreamscape turned skyward. And there it was.

The black speck.

It had been up there for a long time—longer than Seth could remember, at least as far back as the cold day they'd buried his mother. But lately it had stopped being a speck and was becoming a bird. A high-flying bird—circling, patiently.

And as it circled he heard the cracking, like when it was winter and he was a boy walking home from school stepping on the ice-covered puddles. Oozing, frigid water coming up over the top of his boots. He knew where he was. He had left the clearing and was making his way to the glass house. He thought that the cracking came from the glass house. Terrified, he broke into a run. He rounded the last bend in the path and was relieved to see that the great glass house was fully intact. Not a pane cracked or missing, not even a shard of glass on the ground. The figure in the door whose face he'd never seen, clearly waiting—waiting for him?

It was then that he heard the call of the great bird for the first time, no longer a speck but a condor, its wingspan well over ten feet across, floating on the air in lazy circles, the centre of which—the apex—was him. And he understood what the cracking was. His cancer had finally broken through the wall of his bladder and was now alive in his bloodstream. A hungry entity—a searching, gliding thing. A water moccasin, its blunt snout poking into every crevice as its agile body sluiced down the slides of his arteries—looking, always looking, for a weakness to nose its way in.

And when it found one, the great bird would narrow the radius of its circling and slowly descend—for him.

He startled into waking—or was it another dream? Yes, he'd slid from the glass house and found himself on an isolated rocky outcropping surrounded by astoundingly tall leafless trees, every branch of which was occupied by birds. All completely, unworldly silent. They were grouped together by species, and much to Seth's surprise as he looked at them their collective names came to his lips. On the lowest branches were the birds of sympathy: a charm of goldfinches, an exaltation of larks, and a pitying of turtledoves. Above them the birds of judgment: a cast of hawks, a scold of jays, and a parliament of owls. And above them, hunched, the birds of evil: a conspiracy of ravens, a deceit of lapwings, and a murder of crows. And on the tallest tree on its highest branch, the birds of death, the ironically named: flight of condors.

And he knew, beyond knowing, that if he couldn't get back to the glass house and find a way to stay there that this tree-encircled rocky plateau would eventually be his place of ending—his death.

Then he saw them, the swans, and knew that his death was far nearer than he'd ever thought. Hundreds of them slowly, majestically moving towards him—encircling him. What were they called?

Ah yes.

A lamentation—a lamentation of swans.

Then the trees and the birds were gone and the space was empty except for a single Joshua tree—or was it a gas lamp post? Seth couldn't tell because it kept moving back and forth between the two, sliding—worlds forcing themselves to align—but the one thing did remain constant and unvarying: the hanging boy, his fingernails blackened, his hands missing the baby finger on each, desperately trying to loosen the noose around his neck. Screaming.

47

THE CORONADO HOTEL

SETH AWOKE WITH A START.

He went to rise and found himself attached to two IVs and surrounded by bleeping medical monitors. Behind one he saw a woman dressed as a nurse—or maybe she was a nurse. The equipment in the room was certainly the most elaborate medical stuff he'd seen since he came to the San Francisco Wellness Dream Clinic.

He tried to calculate how long ago that was—and couldn't.

"Welcome back."

It was the woman in the nurse's getup.

"Where was I?"

"Pretty far away, but we stabilized you."

"Are you really a nurse?"

The woman looked at him oddly, then said, "Yes, I think so. Are you really a patient?"

Seth ignored her comment. "What's happened to me?"

"Your body almost gave up the fight."

"Fight?"

"That's what cancer is. You went into severe shock, and we almost lost you. That thing in your right hand is a morphine drip. Just press the red button when you're in pain and it should relieve it. If you use the morphine a lot we'll add a Benadryl drip."

"Why?" Seth, despite himself, was warming to this woman.

"Because the morphine causes severe itchiness in most people."

A truth.

She put on a pair of glasses and leaned over him to read the monitor above his head. The pencil in her breast pocket fell to the bed. Seth covered it with his hand. As he did he caught a reflection of himself in her lenses and couldn't believe what he saw. His face was round and puffy. Bags hung beneath his eyes, surrounded by large black circles.

He gingerly moved his hand up to his face and felt the puffiness there. "What's happened . . ."

"To your face? We had to use a lot of steroids. The steroids do that."

"Will it—"

"Go away? Hard to know."

A lie.

"No it's not. Will it go away?"

She sighed, then said, "If we take you off the steroids it will eventually go away."

A truth.

"But if we take you off the steroids your body won't be able to fight."

"Fight what?"

"You've had huge radiation doses. They've killed off almost all of your immune system. So you're vulnerable to almost any bacteria or viral attack."

A truth. A terrifying truth.

"Why so much radiation?"

"Because you were dying."

A quick and accurate ten bars of Handel's Trio Sonata filled the room. "Thank you very much, Nurse. I'll take it from here."

It was the grey-haired freak—William Jennings Connelly playing his old cello.

The nurse packed up quickly and left. Seth allowed his eyes to survey the room. An expensive hotel suite—older, like the spooky old Canadian Pacific hotels.

"Where—"

"Coronado Island, San Diego. The honeymoon suite." He rosined his bow and then put it and his cello onto a large piece of memory foam, which he wrapped around the ancient instrument. As he did he said, "Costs a fortune, but I thought you deserved a treat."

"How long—"

"Since our last encounter? Some time. You fainted—actually gave me quite a scare and no end of trouble. Do you have any idea how hard it is to get a hospital bed and all this equipment into the elevator of an old hotel?"

Seth hit the red button on the morphine pump and mainlined a strong hit of the drug. He felt it numb the place where the snake had entered his liver. Then he felt its glow move through his body. For an instant he thought, *Just pump and pump and all this is over. The swans get to lament and the condor takes me—and it's done.* Finita la musica!

Then he felt the surprising cold of William Jennings' fingers as they pried the morphine drip out of his hand. "No. No, no, no— this will not do. Not do at all. You have much to do before you get to seek oblivion. You owe me, young man—you owe me and you're going to pay me in the only currency that matters."

Seth felt himself floating up from the bottom of a deep pool. "And what currency is that?" he managed to ask.

"Teach me to dream so I can feel the way you feel."

It was coming back to Seth. The key was still in his back pocket. A smile creased his puffy face. "Take me to the ancient tree. Take me there."

"Okay," WJ said as he none too gently pulled the IVs out of Seth's bruised and slack arms.

Seth willed himself to throw the blankets from his bed. When he went to stand he wobbled but quickly found his balance.

"Don't stare. Not nice," he barked. Father/son—good. "Give me a second, I've gotta pee."

WJ looked at him, then nodded.

Seth hobbled to the bathroom and ran the water as he used the nurse's pencil to draw a tiny Joshua tree by the mirror over the sink. He flushed the toilet and came back in the room, reaching for the stand-up lamp by the door to steady himself.

"Hey, maybe we should—" Son/father—even better.

"Now! Let's go now. And take your stupid old cello with us."

48

NIGHT WALK WITH DOGS

LINWOOD DIDN'T KNOCK ON THE DOOR OF DECKER'S TINY BED-room—he simply pushed it open and announced, "You need to understand something."

Decker had no idea what time it was, but it was well after sunset—well after his final pie dish had been washed and dried. "What? What do I need to understand?"

The big man didn't answer, simply turned and left the room.

Decker threw on some clothes and followed him out into the desert.

Neither man spoke for a very long time. Finally Linwood said, "Good."

"What's good?"

"That you've learned not to talk much."

"Thanks. I guess."

"Do you see the eyes?" Linwood asked.

Decker had been aware of dozens of sets of eyes travelling on either side of them for some time. There wasn't enough moonlight to see bodies but enough to catch the flicker of starlight off the dogs' pupils. "Yes."

"Wild dogs. They're here, always here, always watching, always waiting. For a stumble, an arrhythmic step, an off beat to tell them that their time has come."

"Their time?"

"Yes, their time. All things have their time."

Their path, Decker thought—although he knew beyond knowing that it was not his thought. It was Seth's.

"They are the inevitable in every man's life—and I'm not talking about taxes."

And that was it for the conversation. They walked until dawn, and not a word further passed between them. And when they got back to Solitaire, Decker headed into the bakery and began the first of his thousand kowtows of the day.

49

YSLAN IN SETH'S ROOM—THE TREE

THE WAREHOUSE THAT HAD HOUSED THE SAN FRANCISCO WELL-ness Dream Clinic had stood empty for some time before Yslan and Emerson got there. The odd tatter of yellow police tape fluttered in the early morning breeze.

They moved quickly through the faux outer rooms, noting where cameras and microphones must have been. When she pushed on the walls, some of them pivoted away. She quickly made her way down the hall, throwing open doors as she went. All led to the massive emptiness of the warehouse behind them. *Doors to nowhere*, she thought. Then she got to the door at the very end of the hallway. And threw it open.

This was different, no warehouse—a real room with a bed and a closet and a few medical monitors that still bleeped and blopped. She quickly established two things. First, that this had been Seth Roberts' room. Second, that it had been tossed by a pro. Evidently, from the holes in the wall, an angry pro.

She swore softly and took out her BlackBerry. When her call was answered, she didn't wait for the formalities, she just launched right in. "Did you toss the room at the Wellness Dream Clinic?"

"No, of course not," Mr. T protested. "I was there to protect our asset—as you ordered me to do."

"Then who tossed the kid's room?"

"Harrison I suppose."

"Harrison? Leonard Harrison?"

"And nice to hear from you too, Special Agent Hicks."

"Fuck that."

"Fuck what?"

"Didn't it ever occur to you to tell me that Harrison was out at the San Francisco Wellness Dream Clinic?"

"No. Because it never occurred to me that you didn't know he was there. He was your boss, not mine."

"Right."

"And he was on NSA business."

"No, he wasn't."

"Oh."

"Yeah, oh. So tell me what the fuck Harrison did at the clinic."

"Well, I'm not completely sure, cause I was protecting our asset."

"Roberts? Decker Roberts?"

"Yeah, that's how I came across the old Toronto homicide cop."

"And you drugged him and sent him to me rather than telling me to come out there?"

"Harrison said that's what you wanted."

"And you didn't think—Oh, never mind. Tell me exactly what Harrison did at the clinic."

And Mr. T did. Harrison arriving angry, spending a lot of time in the room at the end of the hall, then in the open warehouse.

"And where were you during all this?"

"Where my superior officer told me to be—with the drugged ex–homicide cop who tried to kill Roberts. Our asset."

Yslan thought for a moment, then asked, "Did he say anything?"

"When?"

"Whenever."

"Harrison wasn't very talkative. Told us to drug—"

"Yes, the ex-homicide cop. Then what?"

"Something about had I seen the boy."

"He said that?"

"Yeah, some nonsense about the boy, the boy, number one, the boy. The man was clearly on something. Breathing the ozone with a straw, if you ask me."

"When?"

"When what?"

"When did he say that?"

"At the end."

"After he left the room at the end of the hall?"

"Yeah. Sure."

"Is it yes or no?"

"Yes, after he left the room at the end of the hall."

She hit disconnect, pocketed her phone and looked at Seth's room. Number 1's room.

She looked at the two large holes in the wall—cheap drywall, but it still needed some force to puncture them. She found a tile that had been pulled up—no doubt someone looking for a hiding place in the floor. The small bedside table had been turned over and the drawers emptied. She found the contents scattered in a corner. Two expensive pens, one almost empty, the other full of ink.

"Have you been writing, Seth?" she said aloud.

It was then that she saw the pen drawing on the wall. It was of a large unusually shaped tree—or was it a Victorian-style gaslight?

She righted the bed and saw that the pillows had been slit open—of course, good technique. The bed had been stripped and the mattress T-cut—more good technique.

"The kid's room?" Emerson asked.

She nodded, although she was unsure whether a twenty-something was still considered a kid.

"Nice tree," Emerson said, pointing at the pen drawing on the wall. Then he started into the speech that Mallory had written for him. "You know trees have a mythological significance . . ."

Yslan ignored the rest of what she thought of as Emerson's self-serving exegesis and concentrated on the image on the wall. She remembered Decker's one acting-class lecture on art. There had only been one, so it stood out as anomaly, since he often repeated concepts for his actors, but not this concept. He quoted Gertrude Stein's response to criticism of art: "If you enjoy it, you understand it. In an attempt to understand art we miss the meaning." Then he went on to criticize the Steins themselves, saying, "The Steins surrounded themselves in their Paris salon with Picassos, Matisses, Renoirs, Bonnards, Manguins, Nadelmans, Morgan Russells and Cézannes—paintings, sketches, letters, memorabilia of all sorts—just to get a whiff, a passing tendril of something else. Paintings are reachings—elongated fingers trying to touch that something else." That had engendered a flurry of questions about this something else, but Decker had sidestepped them and gotten on with the class. In fact, Yslan hadn't thought about that lecture until this very moment, staring at Seth's drawing. She adjusted the light in the room and continued to ignore Emerson's endless lecture. In the dimmer light she saw what she thought she'd sensed before. She'd seen something like this tree. Where? Then it hit her. All those months ago when she was in Namibia, grabbing Decker to take him back to help with the bombing investigation at Ancaster College in upper New York State. On their long silent drive to the airport in Windhoek she'd stopped to allow the men to relieve themselves by the side of the road, and there, on the very top of one of the few hills, was a single tree—not so unlike the one on the wall of Seth Roberts' room.

She turned to Emerson, who was still standing in the door frame. His lips had stopped moving. Good. Then she tilted her head to the right.

"Am I out of focus?" Emerson asked.

"No," she said, "but . . ."

"What?"

"Stand still, Emerson."

"Like this?" he said, striking a pose.

"No, just at ease."

"Okay?"

"Yeah. You are perfectly symmetrical, aren't you?"

"What?"

"Nothing. Start in the warehouse, I'll be there in a second."

Emerson turned and left.

Yslan slowly approached the door frame. Emerson was a perfect specimen. Exactly symmetrical—that's why he was so beautiful. But if that was the case, why did it seem that the midsection of the left side of the door frame bulged towards him? She ran her hand slowly along the cheap lumber of the frame and felt it. "Clever, Seth, very clever," she said aloud. She pulled back the wood strip on the left side of the door frame and there it was—a three by five Moleskine notebook.

She glanced at the door, then sat on the upturned bed and opened the small black book.

It was divided into three sections, each carefully titled: "Out of the Forest," "In the Clearing" and "To the Glass House."

She read it carefully, cover to cover. There was a reference to two books he'd written and left on the hard drive of a library computer at the University of Victoria—and a poem on the very last page. She read that twice, then looked at the pen-drawn tree on the wall. "Maybe," she whispered. "He's a resourceful boy, so just maybe this is the way." Then she stopped herself. How long had she been saying what she thought out loud? She didn't know. But it had to stop—now.

50

YSLAN SEARCHES

YSLAN LEFT SETH'S ROOM AND SAW EMERSON READING FROM HIS BlackBerry. "What?" she asked.

He quickly erased the text message from Mallory—*Has she found the tree drawing?*—and turned it to her. She read the ad there calling for actors to play in a new reality show called *The Institution.*

"So? That's what Garreth Laurence told us." She took a quick look at Emerson. He didn't look all that good. She dismissed the notion and turned to the room and thought, *It's why the walls pivot and there are concealed camera ports, hidden microphones—all interesting, but not all that helpful in trying to figure out what happened here.* She knew from Mr. T that Harrison had been there, but where the mysterious WJ was, who the fuck knew. She pushed against the wall behind the receptionist's desk and it pivoted out of the way to reveal the large empty warehouse space. She allowed her feet to lead her. She forced herself not to think, just to follow instinct. She walked into the vast, empty warehouse. Then she stopped and turned back to the set of the fake reality TV show, *The Institution.* She saw Emerson standing by the fake receptionist's desk and a thought hit her. Fake reality? Where's the truth in a fake reality TV show? And how the hell did the words "fake" and "reality" go together? More Brooklyn/Yankees. And more to the point, why were they trying to go together in her mind?

She shook herself free of the thought and walked right to the middle of the huge space. She stopped and allowed herself to turn slowly, taking in every detail, cataloguing them as she turned. Halfway through her turn she saw it: a set of iron stairs leading up to a catwalk. There was something wrong with it; as she approached she saw what it was. The area beneath the stairs had been walled in and painted to look exactly like the wall behind it. Why would someone bother to do that? She banged her hand against the drywall. Hollow. It took her several minutes before she found the hidden latch. She opened the door and was confronted by video monitors on every wall, now unplugged, and what seemed to be a master console in the middle of the room.

Everywhere the most modern of modern electronics—except to one side was a record player, a turntable. She hadn't seen one in years, and she guessed that this one was quite expensive. She hit the power switch and the platter rotated silently. A quick search turned up four albums. All by Yo-Yo Ma.

"Yo-Yo Ma—cello concerts," she said aloud.

There was a simple hard chair to one side—not an office chair at all. Attached to the front left leg was a flat wooden board with holes in it. Beside it were several long strands of hair. As she leaned down to pick one up, Emerson said, "Horsehair, expensive but necessary if you want to get the full sound from a classic cello."

She turned and saw him holding the Yo-Yo Ma records. She wanted to ask him why the hell he kept on sneaking up on her, but her cell phone buzzed—Homeland.

She listened and then began to run.

Emerson caught up to her. "What?"

"They got a positive ID."

"Where?"

"The Coronado Hotel, San Diego."

51

YSLAN AT THE CORONADO HOTEL

THE GUESTS AT THE SWANKY HOTEL, WHICH FEATURED AN OUT-door skating rink despite the eighty-degree temperature, were stunned when they were ordered, "Stay exactly where you are until you are told that you can move."

Forty Homeland Security agents circulated WJ's photo to the annoyed and often annoying guests. Small bits of information began to flow to Yslan's command centre in the front lobby. The man in the photo had arrived two days ago but had left. He'd taken an entire floor of the hotel. Had a hospital bed moved in. A sleeping young man was brought in on a gurney. And a doctor arrived.

"Who was the doctor?"

The hotel manager had no idea.

"Surveillance videos?"

The manager hesitated. Yslan turned to the nearest Homeland Security agent and announced loudly, "Arrest this man."

Before the agent had his cuffs out the manager had "managed" to find the surveillance videos.

While Emerson oversaw the viewing of the tapes, Yslan went up to the room where the boy on the gurney had been kept. The gurney was still there, but of course there was no boy. Rosin dust by one of the chairs suggested that the cello player had been here. And then there was the tiny pencil drawing by the mirror above the sink in the bathroom, so faint it was almost invisible, of the same tree she'd seen drawn in pen in Seth's room at the Wellness Dream Clinic. She leaned down and ran her fingers over the pencil lines. "What does this mean, Seth?"

Her BlackBerry buzzed. "Yeah?"

It was Emerson. "We found the doctor."

There was no doctor in the small desert town. The best that WJ could find was an EMT who came to the motel and administered a huge dose of steroids to Seth. Then he hooked up the boy's morphine drip and gave Seth the button. "You know how to administer this?" he asked.

Seth nodded slowly and injected himself with a long hit of morphine.

At the door the EMT pocketed WJ's money, then said, "This boy needs a real doctor and a real hospital."

WJ held out more money. The EMT took it and left the shabby room.

Moments later, Seth's back arched and he vomited onto the bedspread.

WJ pulled the thing off and threw it out the motel room door, then sat at the foot of the bed and said, "Hold on. The steroids will kick in soon and we'll continue our little journey."

Seth didn't reply—he'd already retreated into sleep.

Viola awoke with a start. She pulled her shawl around her tiny shoulders and stared out the window. "What lake is that?"

"Superior," Martin Armistaad said as he negotiated a tight turn on the two-lane Trans-Canada Highway.

"Cold," she said.

"You're cold?"

"Yes, but that lake is cold—and so deep, so black, so cold."

They both knew it was cold like death, but neither said as much as the deep night of northern Ontario came in quickly and surrounded them.

Without warning or warrant Yslan and Emerson burst into the posh offices of Dr. Henry Kristoff in the Hillcrest district of San Diego. Emerson shoved the receptionist out of the way, and Yslan threw open the door to the good doctor's office. The man was in the midst of a conference call, his speakerphone alive with voices. Yslan strode quickly to the large reclaimed wood desk and hit the disconnect button.

A few moments of bluster and who-do-you-think-you-ares were followed by a surprising contrition and willingness to be of assistance.

"And you didn't think it odd to be called to the Coronado Hotel rather than a hospital for someone that sick?"

"Not actually. I have a very wealthy clientele, and the really rich seem to resent death, as if it were only meant for lesser beings. So I've been summoned to various places on short notice. I was once flown by private plane to an island in the Caribbean to treat a man's dying wife."

Yslan waited.

"And, yes, she died."

"As we all must," Emerson chimed in.

The doctor nodded.

"The Coronado Hotel?" Yslan prompted.

"Two days ago. A very young, very sick man."

"Name?"

"I didn't ask."

"Who called for you?"

"It came through my service." He quickly gave them the service name, and a tech was on it.

"You said the boy was very sick. How sick?"

"Dying. If he had two weeks I'd be surprised."

"Cancer?"

"Badly treated cancer. There is no reason to die from bladder cancer of his sort."

"But he was dying?"

"Most definitely."

"So what did you do for him?"

"Everything possible, then I hooked him up to a strong morphine pump for the pain."

"Was he in much pain?"

"Excruciating, I would think. I filled him up with steroids and a cocktail of supports that might, if he's lucky, extend his life."

Yslan thought about that and finally said, "But not for long?"

The doctor nodded. "The body is a magnificent machine, but just a machine, and it must be treated properly when it malfunctions."

"And it wasn't this time?"

Again the doctor nodded.

Emerson took out the photo of WJ and put it in front of the doctor.

The doctor put on a pair of reading glasses and glanced at the picture. "Yes. That is the boy's father."

Emerson looked at Yslan.

"Did that man say anything to you?"

"Just 'Do what you can for my boy.'"

"That was it?"

"Not another word."

Yslan thought about that, then said, "What about the boy?"

"What about him?"

"Did he say anything to you?"

"At first nothing. He was asleep, which was odd."

"Why odd?"

"Well, as I said, he had to be in tremendous pain. And . . ."

"And what?"

"He was asleep with his eyes open—and his eyes were in constant motion."

"REM cycles?" Emerson asked.

"That would be my guess."

"Fine," Yslan said, "but did he say anything, anything at all?"

"He was in pain and on elaborate medication."

"Yes, but did he say anything?"

"Nothing important—"

"What did he say?"

"The tree, the lamp, the tree, the lamp."

"What?"

"Over and over again he said something about going to the tree, to the lamp, meet me at the tree, meet me at the lamp."

Back in the car, while Emerson was wrapping up, Yslan took out the book she'd found in Seth's room at the Wellness Dream Clinic and read the poem at the end again, slowly:

Story.
With my dad
At the Park.
Hot.
He sat beneath the great Tree.
I wanted to explore.
He said okay.
As I ran down the hill he shouted.
"I'm here beneath the tree."
I looked.
He was sitting on the ground beneath a street lamp.
Old street lamp—gaslight?
He spoke again.

"I'll always be here beneath the tree waiting for you.
"Whatever happens I'll be here—waiting for you."

Yslan looked at the page and saw the tearstains on it and knew that to find the boy she'd have to find the father. And to find the father she'd have to get hold of Crazy Eddie—in the Junction.

52

YSLAN CALLS EDDIE

THE PHONE BURRED ON EDDIE'S DESK AND HE GLANCED AT IT. A phone number he didn't recognize. He quickly punched the number into his ID RECON program and got the message *Federal Restriction*.

Well, he only knew one fed of any sort, so he punched receive and said, "Couldn't stand to be away from me a moment longer, Special Agent Yslan Hicks?"

"Not exactly."

"Too bad," Eddie said, lighting a bomber and hitting disconnect on his phone all in one motion.

His phone buzzed again. "Pizza, Pizza, would you like anchovies on your NSA special or just the usual crap?"

"Eddie, I need to find Decker."

"He's beneath the radar, off the grid, on his own, dross in the wind."

"Eddie!"

"I don't know where he is. And that's the way he wanted it. So unless you have something else on your mind—"

"Seth's in trouble."

Eddie spat the bomber from his lips into the can beside his chair.

"I know you care about the boy."

"Because you've bugged—"

"Yeah. But I know you care about that boy, and I think he cares about you, and I *know* that he's in great danger."

"What does that have to do with finding Decker?"

"I think Seth's been leaving clues about where he's going, but only Decker can decipher them."

"Tell me."

And she did. The tree drawing in the San Francisco Wellness Dream Clinic, the same image in pencil in the Coronado Hotel, the doctor's claim that Seth kept saying "At the tree, at the lamp post." Finally, she read him the poem.

Eddie was on his feet, pacing quickly with his awkward stride, his foot lifter clacking with every step.

"What's wrong?"

Eddie turned and saw Marina in the door of his study, clearly frightened.

"Nothing, honey. Everything's okay."

"It's not!"

"Who's that?" Yslan demanded.

"My daughter. Where did you track Decker last?"

She told him Namibia.

"Okay. He's no genius when it comes to hiding. I'll find him."

"And tell us where he is?"

"I don't know about that." He snapped off the connection and turned the ringer off. She could call as much as she liked, but he wouldn't pick up until he knew what was what with Seth.

He sat heavily back in his desk chair. Much to his surprise, Marina came over, climbed up on his lap and said, without speaking, *You'll find Mr. Decker. You will.*

Fifty-five minutes later he got his first hit. Decker had traded Visa cards, using his old one to get a new one under a false name—one that Eddie had seen before, long ago, when they were kids in school.

He quickly found out that Decker had loaded the card with a seven-thousand-dollar advanced payment. The first charge was a rental car fee from Windhoek's Avis office. He hacked into their site and found the exact vehicle, then he got the vehicle's GPS code and hacked into that. He got its current coordinates, then went to Google Maps and punched those in: Solitaire, Namibia.

His friend—or at least his rental car—was in Solitaire, Namibia, right at the junction of Highways 1 and 6.

He picked up his phone, thought for a moment, then dialed.

"Eddie?"

"Yeah, he's in Namibia."

"I know that, but the country's bigger than France."

"He's at the junction of Highways Six and One."

"Does the place have a name, Eddie?"

"Yeah."

"What?"

"Solitaire—Solitaire, Namibia."

53

YSLAN TO AFRICA

ON THE AIR FORCE JET, EMERSON HAD BEEN ODDLY QUIET FOR some time. Finally, as the jet banked for its descent to Windhoek's military airport, he said, "I thought we were after Harrison's poisoner."

"We are," Yslan replied. "We find Seth, we find WJ."

Emerson nodded.

Yslan stared at him. "You knew that. Why did—"

Before she could finish her question, he turned to her. He didn't look good, which was so pronounced because of his usual beauty. "Yeah, I knew that," he said.

"You okay?" Yslan asked.

But he turned his head away from her and stared out the window at the quickly approaching Namibian desert.

A man lost in thought, Yslan assumed, then she corrected herself: *A lost man.*

He turned to her and said, "You realize you spoke those thoughts out loud?"

She hadn't. She quickly changed the subject. "Are you reporting to Mallory?"

"What do you think?"

"I'm sure you are."

"I am. Who do you think arranged for our current transportation?"

"So he's okay with what we're doing?" Emerson nodded and she continued. "So tell him I'm following a hunch, and before you jump all over me for—"

"I wouldn't. And neither would Mallory. A hunch is just an idea in the pupal form."

She looked at him hard. Was he mocking her? No. The man seemed to be slowly uncoiling, somehow falling apart. *As if he was approaching an ending of some sort,* she thought, then wondered where that thought came from and if she'd spoken it aloud.

"What more do we have in this world than hunches that there are other worlds out there waiting for us?" He turned from her, and his image in the plane's window was somehow buried there—locked in the glass.

The plane banked sharply a second time, and Yslan saw the chopper on the runway, its rotors turning—ready to bring them to Solitaire.

54

CHOPPER

THE DAYS MELDED ONE INTO THE NEXT AS WORLDS SLOWLY aligned, his reality shifting from a memory of Seth as a baby to the burial of his wife to Seth's small hand sliding from his. Decker lost in thought and baking pies—and hearing the music in everything he touched, in every clatter of pan into sink, of every can opener turn, of every whisper of the wind.

He felt light, almost transparent.

Then he heard a sound he couldn't identify and whose music he couldn't find.

The *whop, whop, whop* of a helicopter.

55

TRISH AND COPS

THE KNOCK ON TRISH'S CONDO DOOR LEFT NO DOUBT THAT SHE was required to open it despite the late hour—which, as she knotted the bathrobe around her thin waist, she noted was 3:17 a.m.

More knocking—this time someone shouting her name. Definitely not cool in her high-end building. *Intentionally not cool,* she thought as she opened the door.

Before the younger of the two cops whose badge announced him as Laurence Garreth Jr. (or was it Garreth Laurence Jr.? It was something Junior) could open his mouth she said, "It's late, and unless you have a warrant you're not setting foot in my home."

The other cop, a shorty, had a smirk on his silly little face. A puny thing with a gun and a strut. Trish assumed if this pipsqueak got shot, the police alert would be "Little Asshole down, take your time." He reached into the pocket of his long coat—who wore long coats like that anymore? *More cops copying cops in TV shows,* she thought. He produced a warrant. Trish grabbed it. "I need my reading glasses." She turned her back on them. Over her shoulder she announced, "One step into my home and I'll scream rape."

She found her glasses behind a mound of used wrapping paper, each sheet of which was neatly folded, then stacked on an end table.

She pushed aside the six plastic cutlery trays and eight saucepans so she could sit on the couch. When she reached for the switch of the table lamp she knocked over twenty light bulb packages.

The warrant had her name spelled correctly, the date was right, and her address was accurate. *So much for an easy way out*, she thought. On the top of the second page she saw the purpose of the warrant: "To Investigate a Report of Rodent Infestation."

"At three o'clock in the fucking morning?" she shouted at the cops, who were still standing in the door. She checked the signing judge—the Right Honourable Stephanie Preston. All those details were in order, too. She sighed as she got to her feet, crossed to the door and handed back the warrant.

"Can we come in, Ms. Spence?" Junior.

"Sure. But this is some kind of joke. Who looks for mice at three in the morning?"

"May we come in?" Junior again.

"Yeah. But don't touch anything. My home is a work of modern art—an installation, if you know that term. Every piece has been carefully chosen and placed." As she spoke she allowed her eyes to scan the room—how had it gotten to be this full of junk?

The two cops began their search.

Trish removed a four-foot stack of newspapers from an Eames chair and sat. "Maybe if you tell me what you're really looking for, I'll tell you where to find it," she said.

Junior grunted and went into her bedroom.

Minicop strode into her kitchen like he was Anthony Bourdain or maybe just Guy Fieri.

"Make me some coffee while you're in there," she said. He grunted in reply. What was it with cops and grunting?

Then from her bedroom she heard, "Here." The vertically challenged cop came out of the kitchen and with a grin went into her bedroom. A moment later Junior came out of her bedroom with a mouse dangling by its tail.

Trish howled with laughter.

"What's so funny, Ms. Spence?" Mini cop asked.

"It's frozen, you moron. Look at it, stiff as a board! You brought it in here with you, then claimed you found it."

"That's a serious accusation." Pint-Sized—she'd mentally added a *d* to his name.

"This is a serious farce."

"And this," Junior said, pulling out another official-looking piece of paper, "is a serious citation."

"No doubt already signed by Stephanie whatchamacallit too."

"How do you—"

"You're not talking to the paperboy, whatever the fuck your name is."

"Garreth Laurence."

"Junior. Let's not leave out the best part. I just love it when grown men are juniors, don't you?"

"Well, no doubt you'll love this too, Ms. Spence. Your condo is now officially quarantined. You cannot live here even a minute longer. Get your purse and a change of clothes and you're out of here. A city crew will be in here tomorrow and will remove every item. The cost of which will be appended to your city tax bill. If I were you I'd take this as a warning."

Trish's mouth opened—then shut.

"You're not talking to the paperboy either, Ms. Spence."

She checked into a Lake Shore motel just before dawn. It was the kind of place that didn't ask questions of its patrons and didn't supply toilet paper in the bathroom or sound insulation between the cavalierly named "suites."

She contacted Eddie.

"Trish, it's early—"

"Yeah, I get that. Can you do genealogy searches?"

"Genealogy, astrology, hydroponic gardening—"

"Find me what hive the Right Honourable Stephanie Preston comes from."

She hung up. The couple in the next room finally stopped trying to get into the *Guinness Book of Records*—and she closed her eyes.

When she woke, about two hours later, she noticed that she'd missed a call. She retrieved the message. "It's me. You're not going to like this but the Right Honourable Stephanie Preston is from Clan Parees. She's the wife of that Public Broadcaster guy."

56

TRISH AND ANDREW PAREES

IT WASN'T EASY TO GET A SECOND MEETING WITH ANDREW PA-
rees, CPBC big shot, but Trish had often found her six-foot-plus
frame intimidating enough to get her past any secretary—female
or male, gay or straight.

And that's how she burst into Andrew Parees' office that morning.

"Stephanie Preston is your wife, and the dead boy's name was
Seamus Parees, so what the fuck's going on here?"

To her surprise, Andrew Parees didn't squirm in his chair or
betray in any way that he was perturbed by Trish's unscheduled
entrance or her opening statement.

"Aren't you the persistent one," he finally said.

"Yeah, I guess. Was this some kind of perverse hundred-year-
old homophobic shame?"

Andrew moved slightly in his chair and put his hand on the
thick desktop blotter. For a moment Trish wondered what he
could be blotting that required such a large blotter.

"No," he said softly.

"Then what is it?"

After a long pause, he turned in his large desk chair and stared
out the window at the dozens of new condominiums that were
sprouting like glass mushrooms after a storm on the expensive

downtown streets of Toronto. "It's finally coming to fruition," he said.

"What is?" she demanded.

He indicated all the construction. "It's the result of hundreds of hard decisions, maybe thousands of sacrifices—that's what's building this place into one of the world's great cities."

More of that world-class crap, she thought.

Then without segue he asked, "Have you ever wondered why there are so many churches along Annette Street in the Junction?" Before Trish could say anything, he rose and began to speak. "Ms. Spence, do you recall the mania at the turn of the century, all that Y2K nonsense?" Trish didn't respond. "Do you?" he demanded. She nodded. "Well, that was nothing compared to the fear and anxiety that ran wild when the calendar flipped from the eighteen hundreds to the nineteen hundreds."

"So?"

"Toronto was a very different place back then."

"No doubt."

"But not the way you think. There were no Asians here or very many non-Christians for that matter."

"The good ol' days." Trish tried to be as sarcastic as she could manage—which was pretty damned sarcastic.

"Your cynicism blinds you to the real way of the world, Ms. Spence."

"So . . ."

"So the church—the very foundation upon which this entire city rests—was under attack. Radical ideas from south of the border were taking hold. And darker things, too. Riots in the night, law and order itself was breaking down, and many churches, some along Annette, were burned to the ground as mobs cheered."

"No doubt witches and warlocks were behind all this."

He threw her a hard look. "You are not far from the truth, which once again your cynicism prevents you from seeing. The millennial change had unleashed untold forces. The very fabric of this society, the foundation of all future growth, was coming apart. Rent and torn, it was literally flapping in the wind." Then again without segue he asked, "Have you ever been to China?"

This change of subject completely unsettled her, but she managed to say, "Japan, but not China."

"Completely different idea. Do you never wonder how a small Communist Party can control one point three billion of its citizens?"

"Through threats and extortion—"

Andrew Parees laughed, a big belly laugh, the kind of laugh a father gives to his little girl who has said something infinitely childish. "You read the wrong papers. Sure, there are or were threats and extortion. There are those things here too, by the by. But no, that's not what allows the small Communist Party to control such a huge population."

"Then what is?"

"The fear of chaos. The fear that the deep roots of their society will come up from the ground and all will be thrust skyward into the whirlwind. It has happened in their society several times. And everyone—and I mean everyone—knows that order, no matter how cruelly or arbitrarily applied, is better for the general good than chaos. And chaos, that's what was happening here at the millennial change from 1899 to 1900. The Catholics and Protestants who gave this country solidity—or at least ballast—were being thrown at each other. We were on the brink of giving the anarchist uprising, the fires of chaos, exactly what they wanted—all-out war between the two pillars upon which this city sits, the Catholic and Protestant religions. We were about to cast aside all of the values of this country. All of them. Have you ever lived through a police strike, Ms. Spence?"

Trish knew that during the brief police strike in Montreal in the late sixties more murders took place than in an entire year. But she chose to say nothing.

"I can see from your face that you know of it even if you didn't live through it. Well, a police strike is a minor breakdown in order compared to what was going to happen at the millennial change. So even someone like you can see that it had to be stopped."

Although she felt herself being drawn into a trap, she asked, "And how did they do that?"

Andrew Parees bridged his hands and said simply, "There are only two ways of bringing peace to warring families."

"Marriage and—" The realization struck Trish like a twenty-wheel truck and she collapsed into a chair. When she looked up, Andrew Parees was looking down at her. "No," she said.

"But, yes, Ms. Spence. For the good of us all."

"They sacrificed that boy!"

"Since marriage was out of the question, it was the only way. Surely you see that."

Trish struggled to her feet. "Who else besides you knows?"

"Every sane person—everyone committed to the safety and sanity of this place, to the growth of this city into greatness."

"Every churchman?"

Andrew Parees smiled—a father pleased that his daughter had figured out a simple mathematical equation. "Of course, things didn't go as simply as they should. It seems that my great-grandfather objected. It seems he had feelings for the boy. After his wife, my great-grandmother died, he never remarried—lived alone for over forty years and died at one hundred and two. On his deathbed I heard him say the name Seamus. It was the last thing he ever said, and his will . . ."

"Yes?"

"It insisted that Seamus's grave be attended to—that the whole of his considerable fortune be put to telling Seamus's story."

"But it didn't."

"The law against perpetuities."

"You mean like in that old film *Body Heat*?"

"Yes. You can't control the actions of the living from the grave. The law against perpetuities ensures that."

"So where did his money go?"

Andrew Parees smiled then said, simply, "To the first step towards this city's greatness, to get the Junction to join the big bad city."

"And erase the death of Seamus."

"Yes, and that."

"But why would he be a part of a murder?"

"He wasn't."

"But that boy was hanged from a lamp post."

"Where, Ms. Spence? Where was he hanged? Across the street from what? A lamp post across the street from what?"

"From the library."

"And?"

"And?"

"And what?"

"The old Catholic church. That's it? The church?"

"Ms. Spence. The church and what?"

It slowly came into focus for Trish. "And the Masonic Temple."

Andrew Parees nodded.

"I thought they were mortal enemies."

"Enemies in the public eye—but allies when the need arises."

"Friends of convenience."

"They are side by side on the street, after all. Surely that's no accident. Close enough that when need be they could cooperate. It's how countries are born—and move towards greatness. Enemies joining together and sanctifying the union with—"

"A sacrifice."

Andrew Parees nodded, then his face grew dark. "You have your answer. Now get out of my office—and don't come back."

57

TRISH IN CHURCH

THE DOOR OPENED, AND A DIM LIGHT CAME FROM THE TUNNEL that Trish assumed led to the Masonic Temple next door—a physical link between two supposed enemies. *Like the old cold war hotline between Moscow and Washington*, she thought.

Slowly a crouched figure made his way out of the tunnel. He didn't seem surprised to see her. He closed the tunnel door, locked it and turned to her.

"Ms. Spence, I presume." His voice was pulled back in his throat. The slightest hint of a Scottish accent hid beneath the cigarette-smoke-stained voice.

"Yes," she said. "Andrew Parees called you?"

"Naturally."

His old head seemed to nod, but then again he could just be bobbing his head in the strange rhythm common to a Parkinson's sufferer. "Women aren't allowed in here."

"It's 2013. Women are allowed everywhere."

"Don't be silly," he said, giving a curt laugh. "What a moronic idea, women allowed everywhere." His laugh became a giggly chuckle.

"Not moronic. Modern."

His head shook more violently, and he said, "Foolhardiness. Next you'll suggest women should be ordained."

"They should."

"Why's that?"

"Because women make up more than half of the world's population."

"Illiterates make up more than forty percent of the world; should they not be in charge of forty percent of the world? Wasn't that the rationale people used to vote for Sarah Palin: 'She thinks like us'?"

"That's not the point."

"It's not the point you want to make, but it most certainly *is* the point."

"Not very tolerant of you."

The man drew himself up to a surprising height and with a completely centred voice said, "We're tolerating ourselves all the way to hell, Ms. Spence." His words were simple and unambiguous. He stood completely erect. The shaking had stopped.

"You do know that the Enlightenment happened a long time ago."

"And Galileo."

"Yes, him too."

"Did you ever read the communist's play about him?"

"You mean Brecht?"

"Yes. Have you read it?"

"In college."

"Do you remember the most impressive part of that tainted piece?"

"The pope's ludicrous—"

"No. Don't be ridiculous. What was the most touching part of the play? Come on, even a cynic like you remembers that."

Trish nodded slowly. She did. "The speech of the young monk, Galileo's assistant, pleading with him not to announce his discovery to the world."

"And why didn't the young monk want the heathen to announce his apostasy?"

"Because the young monk had peasant parents who had toiled all their lives, and the only consolation that they had was the belief that they were the very centre of God's concern."

"Yes. That's why the stars and planets—God's creations—circled them. Circled mankind. But your hero, Mr. Galileo, tore down that simple belief."

"Because it was wrong—"

"And the young monk's parents lived their lives in vain because of this supposed truth. They lost their solace. They lost their joy. They lost everything because of what?"

"The truth."

"And has that truth cleared a path to heaven for a heathen like you?" Before she could answer, he shouted, "There are rules that must be followed. Over twenty-five hundred years people have been discovering and distilling those rules. The path. And you and your kind think that you can, in twenty minutes, rewrite those rules? Make them fit your momentary whims? God doesn't care about your whims and fads. He cares about obedience and contrition. You should be down on your knees, begging His forgiveness!"

Trish forced herself to take a deep breath, then said, "That boy was kept in there, then, brought through this tunnel and hung from the lamp post in front of the library."

The old churchman put on a look of childish bewilderment, not meant to fool anyone, and said, "And who exactly would you be talking about, lass?"

Somehow he'd made the word "lass" seem filthy.

"And who is it that you are that you think you can criticize a man of God or the works of the Lord's great church?"

"Just someone committed to reason."

"From the dream of reason comes monsters."

"From the dream of reason comes truth."

The old man gave another harsh, short laugh. "Truth to do what? Truth to what end?"

Trish had no answer to that.

"I repeat, truth to what end? What good is this truth of yours if it doesn't lead you to heaven? Or perhaps you think you'll be the very first to live forever."

"No. I don't think that."

"Then when you die—as we all must—what will become of you? Lie in cold obstruction and rot? Or be picked up by God's breath and shown the path? It's an idiocy to opt for lying in a box and rotting over going to heaven."

Shaking herself free of his assault, she said, "That boy was hung from a lamp post not a hundred yards from here."

"And if that's true, it was done to sanctify this world. To keep the path to heaven clear for those who are wise enough to follow the rules."

58

AT JOSHUA TREE

SETH HAD NO IDEA HOW LONG IT HAD BEEN SINCE THEY LEFT THE Coronado Hotel. He was so weak that he could travel only briefly.

WJ knew that they'd eventually have to walk, so he holed up in another motel, this one just outside the park, and waited until the boy regained some strength.

Finally the boy seemed to have some vigour, and they set out.

Through the windshield Seth watched the moon rise over the desert. Venus had appeared first as if paving the way for the moon. Such a slender slice of a moon. Shortly thereafter Scorpio blinked into existence, its third torso star so red it stood out like a flag. *It was shouting,* he thought. *Shouting for me.*

Seth craned his head to see the western horizon and watched— and shivered—as the Southern Cross rose above the California desert. And he knew in his heart that he was seeing the same sky as his father in far-off Namibia—or was it his father seeing? He simply didn't know.

But he knew he was close. To what, he couldn't exactly say, but he knew he was close.

He glanced to his left, where William Jennings was adjusting the rearview mirror. *He'd finally seen it,* Seth thought. *That car with no licence plate has been behind us for almost an hour, like a wild dog, waiting, just waiting.*

A nasty thought flitted across his mind. *Is that car my death?*

He turned to the side window and saw the shadows of churches. He'd been seeing them for the last half hour, and they were becoming more substantial—less shadows and more corporeal. Then he saw the outline of the library on Annette Street from the Junction, and he knew that all of his realities were slowly coming together at the tree—or was it a gaslight? He nodded as he thought, *At this point, what's the difference?*

He hit the button on the morphine injector two times quickly, and the machine slammed two massive doses into his bloodstream. He arched his back to accept the warmth and thought of it as waves—waves and him on his surfboard, rocking gently, the sun setting over the Pacific and him alive, well. Looking forward to all those years of life ahead of him.

He allowed his eyes to see the undulations of the desert—*Like waves,* he thought. *It's all like waves.* He glanced at his hand wrapped around the morphine injector—*all five fingers remained. So there's still time.*

He guided WJ deeper and deeper into the desert retreat, and the Joshua trees grew in height and number as the churches of Annette Street in the Junction took further shape and substance behind them.

At a crossroads—marked 6 East and 1 South—he instructed the older man to stop the car, then to help him out.

"Take the can we got at the store and the piece of tubing. Now fill the can with gas from the tank."

"How do I—"

"Suction works even in the desert."

It took WJ a few tries and a small mouthful of gas—which momentarily made him stop—but Seth said, "Ever seen a fire breather in a stage show or carnival?"

WJ nodded.

"They swallow a tablespoon of gas every session they do. Four times a day, six days a week, and they're still with us. So swallow-ing a bit of gas won't kill you. Now fill that can."

Another effort and WJ got the suction right—and the small can filled quickly.

"Cap it."

WJ did.

"Now grab your cello and let's go."

The march up the dune took almost all of Seth's remaining strength, but he knew he would make it.

The tree that Seth thought of as *the* Joshua tree was in sight, and it did its odd dance—tree/lamp post/tree/lamp post—and he heard his father's voice: "I'll be here waiting for you. I'll always be here waiting for you."

No matter how much he'd learned to hate his father, he always thought that if things got really bad he'd return to the tree—and his father would be there waiting for him. He knew it made no sense, but did the cancer racing through his system, now attacking at random, make any sense?

Or the old library on Annette now lit by gaslight standing out like a cathedral in the middle of Joshua Tree National Park?

And there, far off, was the tree—on the top of the sand dune. There it was. Then it wasn't—then it was. Then it was a gaslight pole—then a Joshua tree.

Then the pain struck.

Seth's scream stopped WJ cold. He was twenty yards ahead of the boy, part of the way up the dune to the Joshua tree. He turned and shouted, "What?"

Seth ignored him and doubled over. Vomit flew from his mouth and splatted against a flat rock lying on the dune like a sand shark.

He sank to his knees and tears cascaded down his cheeks.

WJ ran towards him, shouting, "Use the morphine, dammit. Use the damned morphine!"

By the time WJ got to him, Seth was holding up the morphine injector and pumping the red button over and over again—to no effect.

"It's empty?"

"Bingo."

Viola shuddered.

"What?" Armistaad demanded.

"So many churches," she said as she stared down the length of Annette Street in the Junction.

"Yeah, fools and their cathedrals," Armistaad said.

Viola didn't respond.

"Do you sense them?"

"Yes," she said.

"Are they near?" Armistaad demanded.

Viola nodded. "Yes—very near."

When Seth and WJ finally got to the top of the dune, the landscape opened, and there was an upland spring. Seth plunged his head into the freezing-cold water—it reminded him of the cold Pacific off Vancouver Island. For just a moment, tears formed at the sides of his eyes.

"Now what?"

Seth had almost forgotten that WJ was with him. He pointed towards the largest of the three Joshua trees, the one his father had sat under and proclaimed, "I'll be here waiting for you. I'll always be here waiting for you," and headed in that direction.

By the time they got there, the slender desert moon was bringing the vista to its ghostly self. Seth pointed at the wisp of a moon.

"What?"

"A moon too thin for stories," Seth said—or was it his father speaking? He remembered when he'd first heard that. He was sitting on a rock in the Maritimes, his father on one side, his mother on the other, and they had told him that there would be no story tonight before bedtime because "it's a moon too thin for stories."

"I've been to the desert before," WJ said.

"Really?"

"To take in Burning Man."

Seth nodded. Naturally that would be his only reason to go to the desert.

"Did you like it?"

"Burning Man?"

"That's what we're talking about, isn't it?"

"Yes."

"Yes you liked it, or yes that's what we're talking about?"

Seth saw WJ hesitate. Finally he said, "I could see that all those around me liked it—were thrilled by it—but I was just there. Just there. Not moved. Just there."

"Like you are here?"

Seth saw him about to say yes then decide against it.

"I don't know."

"What don't you know?"

"Whether I'm just here."

"With your cello."

"And you."

"Yes, in the desert with a dying boy and your cello. How does that make you feel?"

WJ looked away and swept back his long grey hair.

"Don't do that."

"What?"

"Turn away. Don't turn away. And leave your hair alone."

"It's in my face. I don't have a hair band."

"Leave it. Maybe with it across your eyes you'll be able to see better. Don't give me that look. You've spent years looking with your hair out of your eyes and you clearly haven't seen a damned thing, so now let the hair go in front of your eyes and maybe you'll see this place. See how beautiful it is, how otherworldly it is, how of all of us it is. Do you see the library?"

"The what?"

"Look up. Do you see Scorpio? Do you see the third star in its thorax? The red one?"

"No, I don't see any of that."

"You will."

"When?"

"Take out your cello."

"Why?"

"To jerk off with! What do you think you take out your cello for? To play."

"You want me to play?"

"Yeah. I want you to play what you see all around you."

"The sand will—"

"Hurt your cello? Maybe, but it just might improve your music."

"What does this have to do with dreaming?"

"No real musician would ever ask that question."

He began to unwrap the cello from its casing. "But this an Andrea Amati. It was made in Cremona, Italy, in the middle of the sixteenth century. It was gilded to play in the French court of King Charles the Ninth. His mother was Catherine de Médicis. During the French Revolution the instrument was separated from the only other thirty-eight cellos of its kind. It is only one of three that survived. See the letters on the base side?"

Seth looked. PIETATE was engraved there—piety.

"The neck was replaced in 1801, but these are still the original scroll and pegbox. You can see that originally it only had three strings. It has IVSTICIA carved on the treble side."

"Justice," Seth said. "Latin for 'justice.'"

"This cello was exhibited in London in 1872 and 1904 and then in New York City in 1968."

"Is that where you bought it?"

"No. In 1982, after it was featured in an exhibition in Cremona celebrating its three hundredth year."

"Must have cost a pretty penny."

"A fortune. A dragon's haul."

Seth leaned against the Joshua tree—it felt cool, like metal. He felt its strength, its will to endure despite the realities of desert drought and freezing nights. He looked up and knew what he would see—a boy hanging from the lamp post, his fingernails painted black, trying to pull the rope from his neck.

Seth looked down at his hands—his nails were darkening. *It's just the drugs*, he told himself. But he knew it wasn't.

He looked at WJ—the man was still talking. Finally his lips stopped moving. Seth took a breath, then said, "You finished?"

"Excuse me?"

"Are you finished with the lecture about that damned piece of wood?"

After a moment of shock, WJ said, "Yes, I guess I am."

"Does any of that history really mean anything to you? Or is it just the expense and exclusivity of it that you care about? Do you play better music on that cello than you do on any other?"

"Yes."

"Liar. You can't really play music on any cello, can you?"

"Yes I can!"

"Liar! You want me to teach you—stop lying."

"But—"

"So I ask you again, can you really make music?"

After a long pause, WJ whispered, "No."

"Say it out loud," Seth demanded.

"No—never have."

"Fine. Then it's no loss to you if we burn it?"

"Burn it?"

"Are you deaf as well as stupid?"

A stunned silence. The desert wind picked up. The Southern

Cross shone bright over their heads. Scorpio seemed to be chang-ing, the red star now so bright it seemed to pierce the sky.

"Leave the cello here on the ground and go collect some brush. There's lots of dead things here, and they'll all burn."

WJ let the cello fall from his hands and it rocked forward onto the sand. Then he turned and entered the darkness of the gully behind the Joshua tree.

Seth slumped to the ground, his strength almost gone. He touched the wood of the cello and sensed the magic deep within. All the artists who had produced music, great music, on this instru-ment. He allowed his fingers to trace the engraved woman on the back who was missing an arm and had no waist but whose beauty made him for the first time in years think of his mother. He heard his tears hit the cello before he realized that he was crying. "For-give me, please. If there was any other way—forgive me," he whis-pered as he got back up to his feet. He reached down and picked up Andrea Amati's work of genius and moved it several yards west of the Joshua tree and stood it up against a large boulder.

WJ emerged with armfuls of brush and twigs. All suitably dead and desiccated by the dry desert air.

"Good," Seth said. "Now"—indicating the tinder—"put it around the base of your pet cello."

As if in a trance, WJ did as he was told.

"Good. Now open the can of gas."

That seemed to awaken WJ to what was going on here.

"Fine," Seth said. "I'll open it."

Seth quickly opened the can and emptied its contents on the cello and the brush at its base. Then he reached into his pocket and pulled out the other thing they had bought at the desert store—a Zippo lighter.

He tossed it to WJ. The thin moon's rays glinted off its buffed metallic finish, and WJ caught it in his left hand.

"You aren't here to dream, William Jennings Connelly, are you."

WJ slowly shook his head.

"It's to feel that you want—and to get to the glass house!"

Even more slowly, WJ nodded—and flicked the Zippo into flame.

"Toss it on the cello. Kill the thing you think you love to find your way to something you really love."

From where Decker, Yslan and Emerson stood at the bottom of the huge dune, it looked like an ancient petroglyph—two figures and a tiny flame, a slip of a moon overhead, all blessed by the Joshua tree. And the gas lamp post that somehow was alight in the midst of the desert night.

They all saw it—but Hendrick H. Mallory, who had set so much of this in motion, stood even closer than the three at the base of the dune—but saw nothing. And he knew beyond knowing that he would never really see what these others saw, that what had been just beyond the bend in the road all his life would always be just beyond the bend in the road, that he'd only see shadows, as if he were looking through a glass, darkly.

59

MARINA—CRYING

MARINA WAS CRYING.

Eddie leapt out of his chair and ran to her bedroom. She wasn't there.

Where are you, Marina? he screamed in his head.

She cried louder.

He raced through the rest of the house and she wasn't there. *Where are you, Marina?* he screamed in his head again.

He'd been communicating fluently with her for more than two weeks without a word spoken between them. But now he couldn't get her to respond.

Finally Marina shouted through her tears, *By the church!*

Eddie made himself slow his breath and be calm. *Which church, sweetie, which church?*

The awful one!

They're all awful. But which one, Marina? Tell me which one.

The one right beside the other one.

Eddie forced himself to think. *On Annette Street?*

I don't know streets! It was a scream. The girl was getting more and more desperate.

Near the library where we take out picture books?

Yes.

Stay there.

Can't!

Why?

Because the boy is screaming.

What boy?

He's screaming, Daddy. He's hanging from the lamppost and screaming.

60

IN THE GLASS HOUSE

IN THE LIGHT FROM THE BURNING CELLO, SETH LOOSENED THE noose and stepped down from the Joshua tree. "You're here."

"I told you I'd always be here, waiting for you, always."

Yslan clamped handcuffs on WJ.

Seth laughed.

"What?" she demanded.

"That's so unnecessary now," Seth said. He looked down at his hands—his nails were black. He held up his hands and wiggled his fingers—all five. A crack of lightning and it began to rain, thick heavy drops. *Rain in the desert,* he thought. *Of course there'd be rain in the desert—and the Junction.*

Trish stumbled out of the church. The cold rain greeted her. She put up the collar of her coat but the rain quickly soaked her to the bone. She strode forcefully into the storm.

She almost knocked over Marina, who was standing beneath the lamp post across from the library—sobbing.

"Marina?"

The girl turned and cowered back, slipping on the wet sidewalk and falling to the ground.

"Don't be frightened. Remember me? I'm Trish, one of your dad's friends."

No flicker of recognition from the girl.

"Does your dad know you're out here by yourself at night?"

The girl shook her head, oblivious to the rain. She began to cry again.

"What's frightening you, Marina?"

The girl pointed at the lamp post and shouted, "Don't you hear him? Don't you hear him screaming?"

"I hear him—and I see him," a southern-accented woman's voice said.

Marina and Trish turned to see Yslan standing beside a very handsome man. Both were looking up at the lamp post, which was almost invisible—seemingly lost in the rain.

The thick rain opened something deep in Yslan, and she found herself falling. When she reached out to stop her fall, her hand landed on polished granite and in the slash of lightning she saw her father's name and his dates on the memorial wall. Then she heard gunfire and saw him, crouched in the deep undergrowth of the Mekong Delta, ten years younger than she was now and frightened—so terribly frightened.

Another flash of lightning brought to terrifying light other men in dark pajamas, moving through the tall grass, coming closer and closer.

She tried to move, but her foot was stuck in something. She looked down and saw she was wearing army boots, and her left one was stuck in the sucking mud. She turned and felt the weight of the M16 in her hand—and knew—beyond knowing—that she was going to witness the death of her father.

She felt herself yank her foot free and then she heard herself whisper a prayer—to her, his unborn daughter—for a long life, for joy, for meaning. Then she felt the bullet enter her chest just to the right of her arm—then another and another and another.

Then she felt strong hands pulling on her shoulder. She opened her eyes, and Emerson was there in the rain, and his lips were moving but she couldn't hear his words. Then she did—but his lips had stopped moving. She heard his words in her head.

Eddie rushed to his daughter, but she pushed him aside and moved towards the handsome man.

"You see him, don't you?"

Emerson nodded.

"And you?" she asked Yslan.

"I do, Marina. Yes, I see him."

The rain began to pelt down in sheets.

"His screaming is stopping," Marina said.

"The portal is closing," Emerson said, "We don't have much time now. I can't follow you, Yslan. I'm in the forest but not in the clearing."

Yslan looked around, and she was standing in a beautiful clearing in the midst of a seemingly impenetrable forest. And silence—unearthly silence.

Then out of the undergrowth stepped Martin Armistaad and Viola Tripping. The man had a sneering smile on his lips. The girl/woman's face was stained with tears.

"Good," Martin said, grabbing Viola by the soft part of her upper arm. She winced.

"Let her go," Yslan demanded.

He shook his head and said, "You have no idea where you are."

"Let her go," Yslan repeated.

Viola said simply, "He needs to be here—we all need to be here."

"But he's—"

"A nightmare," Viola said. Her voice was steady. "Without nightmares there are no dreams."

"Sure," Martin said and smiled. "Let's go."

"We're not all here," Viola said.

"They'll be waiting for us, won't they, Ms. Tripping. They'll be waiting for us in the glass house."

Viola nodded and turned to her left. A path through the forest that had not been there before was now . . . there.

She smiled and led the way. As they moved along the path, the forest closed in behind them. They followed the turn in the path and saw the great glass house in the distance. Someone was in the doorway and waving them on.

"Come on," Martin said and started to run.

"What's he going to find, Viola?"

"Nothing unless you're there."

"What?"

"Aren't you that which allows this all to happen?"

The catalyst, Yslan thought. She looked at the figure in the doorway, waving them on, and she knew it was her—had always been her.

Then without taking a step they were at the door, and Yslan was indicating that they should enter.

They did and were immediately blinded by an intense surgical light.

They shielded their eyes—then they heard it. The high, whistly voice: "Where do you want this killing done?"

And slowly the image of a boy—Seth, naked on a metal table, his hands tied together in front of him as if in prayer, his finger-nails black—came into being.

Then appearing from the light they saw Decker approach his son.

Then Seth was screaming: "I never agreed to this. Let me up. I'm here against my will."

There was a sigh from the darkness, then a high thin voice, almost a whistle, said, "Not against Mine, though."

Somehow that voice seemed to be coming from every direction.

Seth twisted to see who had spoken. He was surprised to see that he wasn't in a room at all but at the crossroads of two highways. What he thought was a surgical light was an intense desert sun.

"Where do you want this killing done?"

His father! Fuck, his father.

Seth pulled at his restraints again, which had somehow changed from metal to something soft—like lambskin. Then he sensed the blood. He felt its stickiness—and he knew where he was: The portal at the dream temple at Epidaurus. He was wrapped in a sheepskin—the pelt of a recently sacrificed animal still thick with fresh blood.

For a moment the word "sacrificed" reverberated in his head, growing louder and louder until he heard, "Down on Highway Sixty-one." That thin, whistly voice again: "Yes, down on Highway Sixty-one."

"Father! Father!" Seth shouted.

Someone stepped forward and momentarily blotted out the sun.

"Seth."

Seth took a breath and tried to stop the rising terror. "Father, what are you doing?"

"Doing?"

"Yes, doing! What are you doing?"

"That which must be done."

The sun glinted off the blue edge of the surgical scalpel in his father's hand.

"Don't do this, Father. Don't!"

The scalpel scythed through the air. Seth yanked his hands, still bound as if in prayer, high enough to deflect the blade but not before it cut both his hands—cleanly removing the baby finger from each.

He felt pressure on his chest. His father's right hand was there, pressing down hard. The scalpel in his left hand was in motion again.

A gush of blood fountained up from Seth's belly and bathed his face.

He swallowed blood—his blood.

He gagged. His body convulsed.

His two fingers fell to the floor.

Blood fountained up on Decker—and he smiled.

Decker looked at his hands—he was missing the baby finger from each. Seth stood over him with the scalpel in his hand.

"Seth. Seth!"

The boy seemed to come back from a great distance.

"Seth?"

"Father?"

"Use the scalpel, Seth. The last duty of a father is to show a son how to die. Use the scalpel. Put your hand on my chest."

The boy did.

Decker put his hand on top of his son's and the boy wrapped his fingers around his father's.

"Now, Seth, now, and we can put this nasty old world behind us."

The boy stepped back and shouted, "No!"

"Please, Seth, please."

Then there was a blur—Martin Armistaad held out the would-be architect's compass, its sharp point aimed directly at Seth. He was running towards the table and shouting, "Don't. Don't! We all have to be here!"

And then Yslan raced forward and threw herself at Martin. The man's body flipped forward under the force of her tackle. The two of them smashed into Seth as the point of the compass cut deep into his side.

The boy cried out as he stumbled and grasped for balance against the slab.

But he was off by a foot, and he'd forgotten the scalpel was still in his hand, now in his father's heart. They all stood back as Decker's life flew from him like a wild beast finally unleashed.

AFTER

HE FELT SOMETHING SOFT IN HIS HAND AND LOOKED DOWN. fingers slid across his palm, then held on tight.

He looked up—Seth.

Six-year-old Seth dressed in a new black suit. They had just come home from the funeral, and he was holding Decker's hand.

The doorbell rang.

"It's open," Decker called. Eddie came in with his daughter Marina, her face alive, her eyes bright. "Hi," she said. "I thought Seth might like some company, but if you think it's not appropriate—"

"No," Decker said. "No, it's completely appropriate. Please come in."

She moved past Decker and ran into the kitchen and embraced Seth.

Eddie held out his hand. Decker took it. It was then that Decker realized that he was missing the little finger from each hand.

Without a word, Eddie turned and walked back to his car. Decker noticed that he wasn't limping—no clack when he moved. Decker called out, "She loved you, you know that, don't you?"

Eddie turned back and nodded. Then slowly he said, "Yeah, I know that."

• • •

Yslan awoke with a start. There was someone cooking in her kitchen. Bacon. She threw on a robe and moved slowly towards the kitchen. It was a man. An older man, maybe in his sixties. In good shape with a Marine tattoo on his left arm. He turned and smiled. "Hey kiddo, I cooked you some bacon, good at any hour."

Trish opened the door to her condo and called out, "Can I help you guys? Maybe some coffee?"

"Yeah, coffee would be great," came back from up the stairs—followed shortly by two men carrying an overlarge chair. At the door one of the men asked, "Should we take off our shoes?"

"Yeah, if you wouldn't mind."

They did, then entered the completely empty condo and asked, "So where do you want this chair, ma'am?"

From Seth's room, Decker heard the sounds of early Bob Dylan. He knocked on the door. "Can I come in?"

"Sure."

Decker entered the room.

"Do you miss her, Dad?"

"You bet."

Seth gave a small smile.

"You gonna be okay, Seth?"

"Yeah. You?"

Decker smiled and held out his arms to Seth. The boy hugged his father, then they walked out onto the second-floor balcony. Over the boy's shoulder Decker saw the night's star display. The Southern Cross was low on the horizon.

"What do you see, Seth?"

The boy turned to the window and said, "Scorpio rising, as always."

Decker nodded, then looked more closely at Scorpio rising—the third star in its torso blood red but pulsing erratically.

Decker shivered.

"What, Dad?"

Decker pointed, and as he did, the red star blinked out. For a moment there was a hole in the body of the scorpion. Then a crystalline white star blinked into existence. "Scorpio," he said.

Seth smiled and said, "Yeah, Scorpio."

They stood there for a long time, sensing the coming of autumn to the Junction, the trees clinging to their leaves but knowing they would lose the battle, that winter was on its way.

But Decker wasn't worried by that.

He held out his hand—and Seth took it.

Then father and son stood side by side as the world changed, and Decker thought that the crescent moon was all there would ever be. No more waxing and waning—just a slip of a moon, too thin for stories.

But Decker was wrong.

In far-off Afghanistan, it was beginning again as an Afghani dancing boy stepped forward with a ludicrous smile on his painted face, feeling the huge dose of opium coursing through his system. His mascara-covered lashes made him even prettier than he usually was when he danced for the tribal leaders. He'd painted his fingernails black—he thought they were so pretty.

He drank more of the milky drink and seemed to float.

The two holy men, each the leader of a warring sect, came into the tent. The boy smiled at them lasciviously.

The men nodded to their respective bodyguards, who grabbed the boy and held him down.

Each holy man took out a pair of garden shears, and after eyeing each other quickly snipped off the dancing boy's little fingers.

The boy was so drugged that when the bodyguards released him he held up his bloody hands and laughed at the stumps.

His laughter stopped when they tightened the noose around his neck. And, as they yanked him skyward, the two leaders of the warring sects signed the truce, and the moon—for the first time in human memory—began to grow again.

ACKNOWLEDGMENTS

I'd like to thank the literally thousands of actors I've had the privilege of working with over the past twenty years. Although they thought me to be their teacher, often they were the teacher and I the student. I owe them a profound thanks. To name but a few by their first names: David, James, Tatiana, Scott, Gord, Noam, Jonas, Patrick, Melee, Saad, Megan, Alexandra, Joris, Trenna, Anthony, Peter, Taylor, Neil, Paula, Jimmy, Stephanie, Tee, Ryan, Jordan, Maurizio, Kas, Jeremy, Jeff, Glen, Rae, Bruce, Marvin—and so many more. My thanks.

And one last—the composer and collaborator on my Broadway show, *The News*, Paul Schierhorn, who had music itself in his being and is no longer with us.

ABOUT THE AUTHOR

David Rotenberg has directed on Broadway, in major regional theatres and for television. He directed the first Canadian play in the People's Republic of China—in Mandarin.

His bestselling historical fiction novel *Shanghai* has been optioned by Darius Films, and the Junction Chronicles series has been optioned by Don Kurt, who produces the Emmy award–winning series *Justified*.

David has been a master acting teacher for more than twenty-five years. He is the artistic director of the internationally renowned actor training studio the Professional Actors Lab that now has branches in Vancouver, Stratford and Los Angeles. His unique techniques draw students from as far afield as Turkey, South Africa, Mexico, China, the UK and, of course, across Canada and the United States.

He lives in Toronto with his wife, Susan Santiago.